To Ann
Jean E. Hudson
2014
Jeremiah 29:11

THE FRUIT OF THE
SPIRIT SERIES

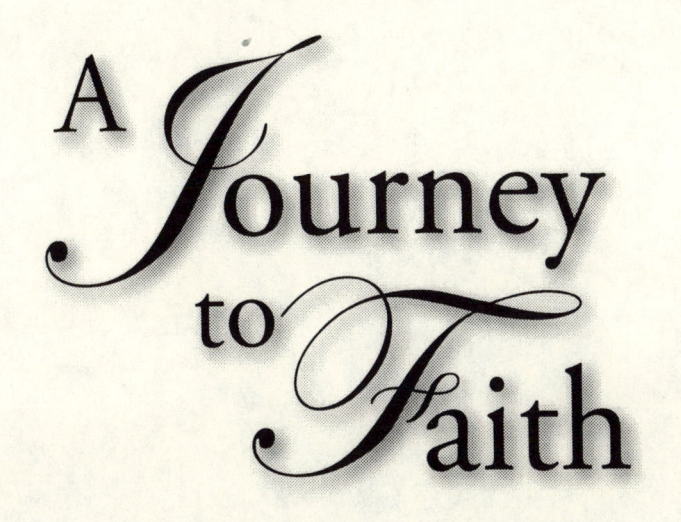

A Journey to Faith

Jean Ellis Hudson

Order this book online at www.trafford.com
or email orders@trafford.com

Most Trafford titles are also available at major online book retailers.

© Copyright 2013 Jean Ellis Hudson.

All rights reserved. No part of this publication may be reproduced, stored in a retrieval system, or transmitted, in any form or by any means, electronic, mechanical, photocopying, recording, or otherwise, without the written prior permission of the author.

Printed in the United States of America.

ISBN: 978-1-4907-0843-0 (sc)
ISBN: 978-1-4907-0833-1 (hc)
ISBN: 978-1-4907-0844-7 (e)

Library of Congress Control Number: 2013912813

Trafford rev. 07/18/2013

Trafford
PUBLISHING   www.trafford.com

North America & international
toll-free: 1 888 232 4444 (USA & Canada)
fax: 812 355 4082

Dedicated to
my husband Jimmy
and
my sister Penny,
two of the greatest supporters ever.
I love you both so much.

CHAPTER 1

It looks like it might snow, Moriah thought, looking up into the heavy clouds. *They're just full of snow. I gotta get this wood split and get it in the house. I am no good at this. I wish . . . .* She didn't finish her thought but picked up the piece of wood for the third time to try to split it with the axe.

Moriah was a slender, small-boned woman with long, dark hair and lovely green eyes. Jeff had always loved her eyes. *Ah, Jeff, where are you? How are you? Are you still alive? Are you ever comin' home? The war's been over for almost eight months. I can't last here much longer by myself.* A big tear rolled down her cheek, followed by several more as she thought about her husband Jeff. He had been gone for three years fighting with the Virginia Infantry in the war between the states. She had seen him only once during that time when he had managed to come home on leave for a week and that had been over a year ago. It had been a wonderful week but far too short. The only news she had received was that he had been wounded several months ago, but she didn't know if he was still alive or dead. She couldn't face the possibility that he might be dead. She had held on here at their farm but just barely with the help of good neighbors. One day soon she would have to move to Georgia to live with her parents.

She had paused in trying to split wood while she was thinking, and now she glanced up at the sky again as the first big flake drifted slowly down to the brown, lifeless ground. *Well, at least, maybe it'll be a white Christmas*, she sighed. *Christmas is only five days away and, oh, wouldn't it be wonderful if . . . .* Her thoughts trailed off as her eyes swept the woods around their farm and caught movement in the long path up to the house. She squinted her eyes trying to see who it might be. *Probably just Sam from the next farm over. He's been so good to see after things on the farm while Jeff's been gone, but, no, that doesn't look like Sam. This one is walking and, in fact, limpin' . . . . Limpin'! Could it be . . . ? No, it can't be. But he walks like . . . Jeff!*

Moriah dropped the axe and started slowly walking toward the figure coming up the path. Softly she said, "Jeff? Is that you?" Then louder, "Jeff, is that you? It is." She began to run toward him and he began to limp faster toward her. "Moriah, I'm home! At last, I'm home!"

They ran into each other's arms, crying and laughing, hugging and looking. "Oh, Jeff, I've missed you so much. I didn't know if you were alive or—not. I love you, Jeff! Please don't ever leave me again."

"I won't, Moriah. I'm home to stay. I've missed you, too, and I love you. I'll tell you all about what's happened to me, but let's go inside out of the cold. I need to rest bad."

Moriah took her newly returned husband by the arm and together they went into the house and sat down by the fire where Jeff could thaw out. She began to prepare food for him while he began to relax. He didn't talk for a while but finally started to open up and tell her about the horrible things he had experienced in the war.

"Moriah, I don't want to scare you, but it was awful. The whole war. Everythin'. All the dyin' and killin'. I don't ever want to see what I saw again."

"I'm so sorry, Jeff. I know it must have been terrible. But what happened to you? How were you wounded?"

"I was hit in the stomach with grapeshot shrapnel. I was unconscious for about a week, they said. All I remember is pain and fadin' in and out a few times. They said I kept callin' out for you. I've been in the hospital for some months. Don't really know how long exactly. They finally said I was strong enough to leave, but there was no way to get home but walkin' and hitchin' a ride. It's took me, I guess, a month to get home. Ah, it's good to see you, Moriah. I didn't know if I'd ever see your beautiful face again. But, thanks be to God, here I am lookin' at you! You look thin and pale, girl."

"Jeff, you're the one who's thin and pale. Just let me get my hands on you and I'll fatten you up. Oh, Jeff, I'm so glad you're finally here." Moriah began to cry. "I didn't think I could hold on much longer. I didn't know if I would ever feel your arms around me again. Thank you, Lord!" Wiping the tears from her eyes, she dished up some of her homemade stew and bread and set it out for Jeff, feeling so proud to be able to do that simple thing again for her husband.

Jeff ate heartily, and then they sat together before the fire in their favorite place, Jeff in the rocking chair and Moriah sitting on the floor with her head in his lap. She just couldn't take her eyes off him! Jeff began to grow sleepy and finally dozed off. She let him sleep awhile and then woke him up enough to get him undressed and into bed. She stood looking at him for some time as he slept. *Oh, how good it is to have him home, but he looks so pale and thin. I hope he's alright. I'll nurse him and feed him and he'll be well before long. He's still as handsome as ever to me with his dark hair and eyes.* She reached to push back a lock of brown hair from his forehead. "Oh, my love for you is so great, it's almost overwhelmin', Jeff!"

Moriah knelt before the rocking chair near the fireplace. She prayed aloud, "Oh, Heavenly Father, thank You for bringin' Jeff home to me alive. Thank You for him and the love we share. You gave us to each other a few years ago and I thank You for that. Thank You for sparin' his life and mine in this awful war and bringin' us together again. We love You, Lord, and we'll praise You for the rest of our days for all the good things You've done for us. In Jesus' Name, Amen. And, oh, Lord, heal Jeff and help him be as good as new soon. Thank You, Amen."

❖ ❖ ❖

As the days passed, Moriah realized how lacking in strength Jeff really was. He was going to need a lot of nursing to regain his strength, but she was eager to do all she could to help him get back to normal. Their days fell into a pattern of sleeping late, eating as much breakfast as she could coax down him, talking for a while by the fire, followed by Jeff resting while she did the necessary chores. Since it was winter, chores were not too strenuous, except that splitting wood! The war had taken most of their livestock; the horses and chickens were gone as well as all the cows but one. Somehow Old Maude had missed being stolen. Moriah had found her wandering down by the creek after a Union raid one day. Maybe Old Maude knew how to hide! Moriah was very grateful to have even one cow left. Times were hard. All the food she had canned or dried last summer would have to see them through the winter. Maybe when Jeff was stronger he could go hunting for some meat. They could sure use some.

After about three weeks of Moriah's good cooking and loving care, Jeff did regain some strength and began to take long walks with Moriah every day down to the creek and back, walking a little further every day. These were good days for Jeff and Moriah. They had each other and shared many dreams and hopes for the future as they walked and talked together. In the years ahead, Moriah would look back on these days with a warm heart as some of the best they ever had because they had each other. If she had known how short they would be, she would've filled them even fuller with making memories with Jeff.

❖ ❖ ❖

It was about the middle of March, 1866, and Moriah was now sure that she was expecting a baby. She had suspected it for a few weeks but wanted to wait and be sure before she told Jeff.

On one rather mild March morning, Jeff was out in the barn milking Old Maude when Moriah decided it was time to tell him about the baby. As she opened the squeaky barn door, Jeff looked up and said, "Good mornin', darlin'! You're up early. Come, give me a kiss from the prettiest girl I know anywhere."

"Oh, Jeff. You're too good to me." She leaned over and kissed him as he sat on the stool. Suddenly, she was shy in trying to tell him he was going to be a father. She wandered around the barn some, and, of course, he knew she had something she wanted to say.

"What are you wantin' to say, lass?"

"What do you mean, Jeff?"

"You look like the cat that ate the canary. What is it?"

"Jeff—how would you like to be a father?" This was followed by silence for a short time. Jeff jumped up and cried, "You mean—we're goin' to have a baby!"

Moriah nodded.

"Whoopee!" He grabbed her and hugged hard. "Oh, I better be careful with you." Moriah only laughed.

What a glorious time they shared that day! They talked and planned, tried to think of names for boys and girls, talked about building a cradle, tried to decide what "he" would do when he grew up! Moriah reminded him it could be a girl.

As the day drew to a close and the sun was going down, they knelt together and prayed for this new life God was blessing them with. Jeff prayed first, "Father, thank You for lovin' us, dyin' for us, and livin' for us. Thank You for Moriah, and, oh, Lord, thank You especially for blessin' us with this little life inside my wife's body right now. Help everythin' to go well and help us to be the parents You want us to be." Before he could finish, Jeff was crying openly and freely for the blessings of the Lord. Moriah took up the prayer, "Lord, thank You for Jeff and his love and for this new life we're bringin' into the world. Help us to be fit parents and to give this baby all the love we can. Help him, or her, to be strong and to serve You all his days. In Jesus' Name, Amen."

❖ ❖ ❖

Moriah began to notice small changes in Jeff as the next few days passed. He moved slower, had to stop often to rest or catch his breath, and sweated a lot. He still had not gained much weight. She began to worry and pray. She couldn't lose Jeff now. Not now!

Jeff also was aware of the changes but said nothing to Moriah. He was afraid too and prayed often. He knew he was growing weaker but didn't understand why. He thought he had been getting stronger for a while but now—he knew he was wasn't.

One lovely spring morning with a touch of green beginning to show in the trees and woods, Jeff was out splitting wood, Moriah's favorite job she always reminded him! Moriah stepped out on the porch and began, "Jeff, did you know it's March 26? It's only four days till your birthday! What special—." She stopped short as she watched Jeff wipe sweat from his face with his sleeve, slump against the old stump they used to split wood on, and then roll to the ground. "Jeff!" she screamed, running to him. He was conscious but very weak. "Oh, Jeff, we've got to get you in the house. Can you help me?" He tried to nod, but his head just lolled to one side. Somehow Moriah managed to get him in the house and into bed. She never knew where the strength came from.

For the next twenty-four hours Moriah never left Jeff's side except to bring him broth or a cold cloth for his head. He ate little and slept a lot. Around noon the next day he was more alert than he had been and began to talk.

"Moriah—I love you. I always have. Ever since we was kids."

"Don't try to talk, darlin'. Save your strength."

"No, I need to talk. I need to tell you—. Moriah, I'm not goin' to make it."

"No, Jeff! Don't say that! I can't go on without you." Tears were streaming down her face.

"Yes, you can, Moriah. You have to—for the little one," placing his hand on her abdomen. Jeff was crying now too. "You gotta be strong, girl, for the child. I wish I could've seen him. He'll prob'ly look like you, dark hair and green eyes. I hope so. Give him twice as much love since I won't be here to give him mine."

"Jeff, please—stop. I can't stand to think about this."

Jeff looked off in the distance and knew it wouldn't be long. "Moriah, I gotta say some things. Teach the boy to love God, to be a Christian, to have faith. He can make it if he has faith in God and you can too. Will you name him Clemmons after my father?"

"Yes, Jeff. Whatever you say. I love you so much."

Moriah was on her knees by the bed, holding him as close as she could. Her tears dripped off her chin onto his face and chest. "How can I make it without you Jeff?"

"Faith. You know—'the substance of things hoped for and the evidence of things not seen'—." His body went limp and Moriah knew he was gone.

"No, no, no! Jeff, come back to me. How can I make it?"

CHAPTER 2

Moriah stayed on her knees beside Jeff holding his hand for several hours—crying and trying to pray. She couldn't seem to find the words to pray—not yet. She felt so numb. As the day drew to a close, she realized upon waking that she had dozed off out of exhaustion. When she first awoke, she had trouble remembering why she was on her knees beside the bed. Then she remembered and hoped it was a nightmare, but she cast her eyes up and saw Jeff still and cold. Tears welled up again and spilled over. *What am I goin' to do? Jeff had said—what was it—faith. I've got to have faith for myself and the little one.* Slowly she dragged herself up feeling stiff and chilly and knew what she had to do. The last thing she could do for Jeff. She removed his clothes and began to wash his body to prepare it for burial. As she slowly worked, all she felt was numbness. None of this was real somehow. It felt like a dream, but she knew that she had to do this. When she had completed her task, she dressed Jeff in his best homespun shirt and pants and the only boots he owned—the ones he had worn to war. *He had been so proud of those black boots when he bought them before the war. Now they're just old and worn thin. I wish I had somethin' better to bury him in.*

She wandered into the kitchen but wasn't hungry. She sat at the table and wearily laid her head on her arms. *Somehow I'll have to get word to Sam and Bess. They'll help me bury him.* Tears began to flow again and with them came a prayer, "Oh, Lord, You're goin' to have to help me. I can't make it on my own anymore. Help me to have faith like Jeff talked about. Lord, help me know what to do." She grew quiet and soon drifted off to sleep out of sheer emotional exhaustion.

❖   ❖   ❖

Moriah awoke the next morning with the sun streaming in the window in her face. Out of emotional and physical exhaustion, she had slept until ten o'clock. She lifted her head and looked around. Once again, she had to recall why she was sleeping at the table. When realization came, she slowly pulled herself up as if the weight of the world were on her and forced herself to return to the bedroom to be sure Jeff's death was real. It was. Her heart had never felt so heavy—or so broken.

"Hallo, in the house!" came a call from outside. It was Sam Jones, their neighbor who had been so helpful while Jeff was gone to war. Moriah was glad she wouldn't have to ride over to their farm to tell them. Wrapping her shawl around her in the cool of the spring morning, she walked to the door.

"Hello, Sam."

Sam knew something was wrong immediately by the weary, beaten look on Moriah's face. "What is it, child? Has somethin' happened to Jeff?"

"He's gone, Sam. Jeff's dead."

"Whadda you mean? What happened?"

"He collapsed day before yesterday while he was splittin' wood and died yesterday." Her shoulders began to shake with sobs and she began trembling all over. She leaned against the door frame for support.

Although Sam was sixty years old, he came quickly to her side and helped her into the house to a chair in the kitchen. "Don't fret, child, I'll go get Bess and she'll come over and be with you. Don't worry about a thing. We'll take care of things for you." Sam left quickly to get Bess.

After Sam left, Moriah sat for a while at the table without really thinking anything. She walked to the window and looked out at the trees beginning to put on a few leaf buds and the crocuses pushing up through the ground. It wouldn't be long until the jonquils and daffodils would be up and blooming. *Jeff loved this time of year. He always said the early spring reminded him of a revival of life after the deadness of winter. Dead—yes, Jeff is dead and will never see the springtime again. New life—yes, I have new life growin' inside me right now, but Jeff will never see it either. What did the preacher say a few weeks ago about death? Oh, yes, "When a child of God, a believer in Jesus as Savior in a personal way, dies, he will go to heaven—a place where there is no more sufferin', pain, heartache. A place filled with happiness, joy, and love forevermore." Jeff will see the crocuses in bloom all the time and more wonders than I could ever imagine. He will see the little one—someday. I'll see Jeff again one day. We'll all three be together.* Moriah's heart lifted at the thought of that reunion. *But until then, I have to be without him. Help me, Lord, to handle the lonely days ahead.*

About half an hour after Sam left, Moriah heard the sound of horses pulling a wagon, moving fast up to the house carrying Bess Jones, her neighbor and friend for the five years she and Jeff had lived here. Bess was a good woman, more like a mother and a friend.

Bess burst into the door and flew to Moriah's side in the kitchen. She didn't say a word but engulfed Moriah into her ample arms and bosom. Moriah laid her head on Bess' shoulder, holding herself tight, afraid to let go. Bess rubbed her back and made soothing noises softly in her ear as she held her tight. "It's alright, baby, you can let go. Relax. Bess is here. We'll take care of everythin'." Slowly Moriah began to relax, and as she did the tears began to flow, softly at first and then in great, racking sobs. She was tired of being strong and having to handle things. She was so glad Bess was here.

The two neighbors and friends stood, embracing and crying, for some time. Finally, Moriah pulled back and wiped her face. "Bess, what am I goin' to do without him? I've been without him enough already because of the war. And now he's gone forever! What will I do? Where will I go? He'll never get to see his son now. He so wanted a boy. I hope it is a boy and I hope he looks like Jeff and acts like Jeff and loves like—."

"Child, slow down. Come, sit down and let me make you some coffee." She began to work as she talked. "You can only take one thing at a time. Right now let's get some food in you and then we'll see what needs to be done." Bess had not known that Moriah was expecting. *Oh, my, she thought, this poor child. How is she goin' to handle things all alone? And with a baby on the way.* Bess clucked her tongue in sympathy and sadness, as she put the coffee on. She scrambled some eggs and sliced some bread and made Moriah eat.

After cleaning the neat kitchen, Bess sat down at the table with Moriah. "Moriah, you know how sorry I be. I wish I could make it all go away, but I can't. But I know God will take care of you and the little one. In the Good Book, it says He will never leave you or forsake you. God loves you, and Jeff, as much as ever. Trials come in this life, child. They come to ever'body at some time or other. The Good Book says that these hard times make us stronger and teach us things. Don't give up, Moriah. Let God build strong faith in you through this."

Moriah didn't say anything, and Bess could only hope she had listened. Moriah went to the bedroom with Bess following close behind. Moriah was once again startled by the cold paleness of Jeff's face which made it more real that he was actually gone. Tears began to flow from both women who loved Jeff as they stood together.

After spending the afternoon with her, Bess asked Moriah to come home with her or to let her stay with her, but Moriah insisted she'd be alright by herself. Bess hated to leave her but promised she'd be back the next morning.

When Moriah was alone, she went into the bedroom again as darkness came and lay on the bed beside her husband and held his hand as the tears softly came again. "I love you, Jeff. I always will. And I'll teach our son to know you and to love you and God. I promise." She lay still for a long time before sleep finally stilled her thoughts.

❖ ❖ ❖

The next few days were a blur for Moriah as neighboring families and church folks came by with food and kind words. She knew they meant well and and she supposed it helped some, but the time would come when they all went home and she would be alone. What then?

The day of the funeral dawned clear and bright with a sky so blue it looked painted. A gentle breeze blew making it seem cooler than it was. Moriah had decided to bury her Jeff in the grove of evergreen trees a short distance from their house because she knew he loved the green of spring. There were so many people at the funeral she couldn't begin to count them. The preacher read the Twenty-Third Psalm, and then folks sang "Sweet Hour of Prayer" and "Amazing Grace."

> "Amazing grace! how sweet the sound, that saved a wretch like me!
> I once was lost, but now am found, was blind, but now I see.
> Through many dangers, toils, and snares, I have already come;
> 'Tis grace hath brought me safe thus far, and grace will lead me home.
> When we've been there ten thousand years, bright shining as the sun,
> We've no less days to sing God's praise than when we first begun."

Preacher John had many kind words to say about Jeff that made Moriah feel proud, about Jeff fighting in the war and being wounded, having to get home the best way he could, and how he loved his wife and then his unborn child.

Moriah still felt that none of this was real. Surely she would wake up and find it was all a bad dream, but, no, the preacher was almost through.

"Ashes to ashes, dust to dust," intoned the preacher as he dropped a clod of dirt on the casket. Bess looked at Moriah who was supposed to go next and hoped she wouldn't fall apart, but Moriah surprised her by reaching for a handful of dirt and slowly letting it fall through her fingers onto the casket. She also threw a flower onto the casket after kissing it. "Goodbye, Jeff. I love you and always will. I'll take good care of little Clem till we all see each other again."

Moriah and Bess walked arm and arm away from the grave back to the house. People would stay a while after the funeral to eat and visit some more. Just more custom, but Moriah was ready to have some time to herself.

"Bess, I want to thank you and Sam for all you've done for us. You've been so good to help with everythin'. I can never repay you for all you've both done."

"Don't be silly, child. You're just like one o' my own. I love you and Jeff like you was both my children."

"Thank you, Bess. I have one more thing to ask of you. When my time comes, will you be here to help bring little Clem into the world?"

"Course, I will. I'd be proud to help bring little Clem, or little Sarah, into the world. You know, it could be a girl, Moriah."

"No, it'll be a boy. I know it will. His name will be Clemmons Jefferson Brown after Jeff and his father."

❖ ❖ ❖

Sam Jones and other neighbor folks helped look after the farm that spring and summer as Moriah's pregnancy advanced. They milked and fed Old Maude, planted and tended the garden, preserved vegetables and fruits for the winter, split wood for the winter, brought meat occasionally, and provided a shoulder to cry on when it was needed. Moriah was sick in the beginning of the pregnancy, but this soon passed after about four months. Moriah was able to keep the household chores going after that, and she spent a lot of time hand sewing baby clothes, blankets, and booties, all the things little Clem would need. As she sewed and knitted, she began a habit that would last for years to come. She began talking to little Clem out loud about his father—what he was like, what he looked like, how much he loved Clem and wanted to be with him but couldn't, how one day they would all be together again in heaven. She wanted him to know his father. And she talked to him about God, his heavenly Father, and about Jesus, His Son. More than anything she wanted little Clem to know Jesus, so he could see his father one day in heaven.

❖ ❖ ❖

"Push, Moriah! Push! It won't be long now."

"I can't push anymore, Bess. I just can't!"

This had been going on for several hours. Sam had stopped over early that morning to take care of Old Maude and discovered that Moriah was in labor. He got home as fast as he could and sent Bess back to be with her. Bess had helped birth about half the babies of their neighbors. She knew as much as anybody about birthing babies.

It was August 15 and a very hot day. Moriah was bathed in sweat and thoroughly exhausted. She had been in labor since early morning, and it was now the middle of the afternoon. Bess was tired too, but seeing new life come into the world had always renewed Bess and made her praise her God. She didn't want to be anywhere else at this moment. The pains were coming closer together now. It wouldn't be much longer.

"I can't take anymore! Stop it! Stop it!" screamed Moriah. Each pain made her scream and arch her back in pain.

"Child, there ain't no stoppin' it now!" laughed Bess. "It's alright, Moriah, everythin' is goin' fine. I've helped bring many babies, and everythin' is fine. Just try to relax. Breathe deep. Rest between pains if you can. It won't be long now."

Moriah tried to do what Bess said, but the pain never left her now and it hurt so bad. Finally, Bess said, "Alright, child, give a good hard push now. It's time."

Moriah pushed as hard as she could and then heard Bess say, "Here he is, Moriah! And it is a boy! Hello, little Clem." *Praise the Lord! He looks healthy*, she thought to herself. She cleaned the baby and gave him to his mother.

Moriah gently took Jeff's and her little baby boy into her arms for the first time, and soft tears fell from her eyes at how precious a blessing he was. At last, she had him to hold in her arms and next to her bosom. Thank You, Lord, for this fine boy You've given us and that he is healthy!

"Bess, he does look like Jeff! Oh, I'm so glad! The oval shape of his face and the strong chin is just like Jeff's and the brown hair. I can't tell what color his eyes are. Oh, little Clemmons Jefferson Brown, I love you, and your daddy loves you too. He would be so proud if he was here, but, you know, somehow I think he does know about you." She cuddled him close and wept in joy, relief, and sadness.

Bess interrupted Moriah's time with little Clem, "Moriah, I think he weighs a good eight pounds or more. He's a good size boy, and he seems healthy. He does look like Jeff," peering over at the baby. "And you did fine, too, Moriah. These things are never easy, but they shor' are wonderful when they're over."

"Yes, Bess," responded Moriah. "He is wonderful." Bess wasn't sure if she meant God, Jeff or the baby, but no matter. They were all wonderful.

CHAPTER 3

September 1, 1866
Landis, Virginia

Dear Ma and Pa,

I know it's been a long time since I've written you, and I'm sorry. I've been so busy. Our baby has finally been born! Little Clem is two weeks old and he's beautiful! He looks just like Jeff with his oval face and strong chin. Bess, our neighbor who helped deliver him, says his eyes are turnin' green like mine. Jeff wanted little Clem to have my eyes, so I'm glad they're changin'. When he was first born, he did look awfully red and wrinkled, but Bess says that's normal. He changes every day. And he's growin' so fast! I can't wait for you to see him. He keeps me very busy and I love every minute of it. Bein' a mother is all I ever hoped it would be. I think he smiled at me the other day. Bess says he prob'ly had gas or somethin'.

I really wish Jeff was here to see his son. He would be so proud! He would teach him all kinds of things—walkin', talkin', milkin' Old Maude, splittin' wood, huntin', fishin', ridin'. I know I'm ramblin' on. I still miss Jeff so much, and I still cry sometimes. It's so hard at night. I get so lonely. I guess I never realized how much we shared. For the first 3 months or so I walked up to his grave every day and sat and talked with Jeff. Gradually, I have discovered that I don't need to do that as often now. I take little Clem and we walk up whenever I'm feelin' lonely for Jeff. I'm just pourin' myself into little Clem.

Our good neighbors, Sam and Bess Jones, have helped us so much. I couldn't have made it without them. Sam arranged for a tombstone for Jeff's grave and paid for it himself. I am forever in debt to them for all they've done. And they've been like grandparents to little Clem. One of the reasons for writin' is to tell you that I would like to take you up on your offer to come and live with you now that little Clem has been born. I hate to leave this place and our home where Jeff and I shared so many memories for the 5 years we had together, but I see now more clearly that I can't keep up a farm alone. I can't keep askin' Sam and Bess to do so much for us. They're gettin' older. It will be very hard leavin' here, but I look forward to seein' both of you again. I haven't seen you since Jeff and I left over 5 years ago. You must have changed a lot, and I know I have. And I especially can't wait for you to see your grandson, little Clem!

We should arrive there sometime late this month or perhaps early October. I love you both.

Your lovin' daughter,
Moriah

Moriah reached into the desk and drew out an envelope. On the front she wrote:

Jeremiah and Ruth Jakes
Hooperville, Georgia

It will be good to go home again to south Georgia and see my parents after so long! I want little Clem to know them, and I want them to teach him the things I can't. I really do need their help now.

❖ ❖ ❖

"Bess, how am I ever goin' to be able to leave our home and—?" Moriah broke off. She looked around the front room with boxes and piles of this and stacks of that, and then her gaze followed the path up to Jeff's grave. That was going to be the hardest part. Leaving Jeff.

"Well, Moriah—. First off, come sit down and rest a spell. You've been workin' too hard." Moriah obeyed.

"Child, I know leavin' is hard. I've done my share o' leavin' in my life. I left four graves up in Pennsylvania when we come here. Both my parents, not very old either, my brother who died of a fever, and a small grave for my first born child—a boy, he was. A fine little fellow. He was trampled by a horse when he was two and before anybody could get to him he was hurt too bad to live. He died two days later. It near 'bout broke my heart in two. And Sam's. He always blamed himself. Thought he coulda and shoulda stopped it somehow, but he couldn't have."

With big tears tracing down her cheeks, Moriah reached over and hugged Bess. "I never knew. You must have suffered somethin' awful."

"Sam and me both did. But we learned a few things too. We live in hard times. Bad things happen to ever'body. The important thing is not to lose faith—faith in God mostly but also in yourself and other people too. Sam and me didn't get bitter. We know now God knows what's best for all of us. Trust in God, that's what faith is. When He took little Brewster, He knew what He was doin'. He knows best. We couldn't see it, and we still don't understand.

But I'll tell you one thing—we're stronger people than we were before 'cause we let God take the pain and sufferin' and turn it into love and comfort for other people. That's how I know how you feel and what you need, Moriah, even though I haven't lost Sam. I can help you in ways I couldn't have before. There's always hurtin' people, Moriah. Let all this make you into somebody who can help them when they hurt."

They sat quiet for a few minutes. "Mercy, me, I never meant to give a speech!"

"I'm glad you did, Bess. I needed to hear what you said. You pray that I can be that kind of carin' person for other folks."

"I'll say one more thing. Prob'ly the most important job you got now is to teach little Clem how to have faith and trust in God and to live it in ever' circumstance in his life."

"I'll try, Bess. I've already been prayin' that God will show me how to do that. Jeff asked me to do that just before he died."

Bess pulled her large frame off the chair and pronounced, "Well, this ain't gittin' the job done. We need to get this sortin' finished before the auction and sale tomorrow. I hope you can get a good bit of money for your household goods. It shor' will help you and the little one out."

"Again, I'm so grateful for all you and Sam have done. He's arranged everythin' about auctionin' off the furniture and farm tools and sellin' the farm. It should be enough to see us back to Georgia and have a little nest egg, too. It's goin' to be hard watchin' our things be sold off, but I can't move all these things to Georgia. Jeff would be the first to say it's the thing to do. Let's see if we can finish up sortin' out the personal things I want to keep."

They worked on for a while as they sorted and decided what to leave and what to keep, stopping every now and then to reminisce about something they saw or remembered. Suddenly Sam knocked on the door and came in.

"You two still at that! My, my, are you takin' more'n you're leavin'?"

"No, Sam, not really. It's just hard decidin' on some things—like Jeff's clothes. What do you think I should do with them?" Moriah asked.

"Well, I tell you. Why don't you let me take 'em? There's a man I just happened to think of who's down on his luck. He could prob'ly use 'em. I run into him just the other day."

"Oh, that's a good idea. Jeff would like that. Sam, I want to tell you, too, that I—we appreciate all you've done for us. I'm especially grateful for you arrangin' for us to travel to Georgia with the Mutter family as they move there. We'll feel a lot safer bein' with another family, since it's just little Clem and me."

Sam was a man who was uncomfortable with praise and thanks, so he just said, "The Lord just worked it out His way. That's all."

❖ ❖ ❖

The day came when the auction was over and the farm was sold with all the papers duly signed. Sam had bought a wagon for Moriah and little Clem to travel in which was large enough to carry what they were taking, mostly small, personal items. The wagon was loaded, and the time had come to depart. Sam and Bess were on hand to help with last minute details and to drive Moriah and little Clem to meet the Mutter family a few miles south.

Sam and Bess held back as Moriah and little Clem walked for the last time up to Jeff's grave. It was late September, and the leaves were turning their beautiful red, yellow, and orange colors and falling to the ground. Moriah's long skirt brushed through the leaves as they climbed. The air was cool and crisp even though the sun was brightly shining. It was a perfect fall day, except for saying good-bye. This was the moment Moriah had dreaded.

When they reached the grave, she knelt beside it and placed a bouquet of late fall flowers she had picked near the headstone which read:

Jefferson Andrew Brown
1843-1866
Beloved Husband and Father

She began to speak quietly, "Jeff, we're leavin' now. I love you and always will, no matter what. I'll never forget our days together and the love we shared. I know you remember, too. Little Clem is with me now and he looks so like you, except for my green eyes, that my heart races when I look at him sometimes, rememberin' you." Tears began to run down her cheeks and drip on little Clem's head. She brushed them away. "I'm goin' home to my parents, Jeff, because I can't make it here alone anymore. I know you understand. This is hard, Jeff. But I have to think of little Clem and do what's best for him. I know you'd want me to. I promised you before you died that I'd teach little Clem to love and have faith in God and to have the same myself. You said then that faith is 'the substance of things hoped for and the evidence of things not seen.' Bess put it very simple—trust God to do what's best. I promise you again that I'll do my best to learn it and teach little Clem too. Goodbye, Jeff. You're always in my heart." She knelt there a few more moments, placing her hand on the grave, before looking around at the land and woods that Jeff had loved—the evergreens that shaded his grave. She would remember it always. She rose and went to the waiting wagon, looking as bravely as she could to the new life that awaited little Clem and her.

CHAPTER 4

The Mutters have been really helpful to us, lettin' us travel with them to south Georgia, Moriah thought, *but I really would like to hurry and get home. They want to stop too often. I just want to get home to see my parents and take a nice, long bath and sleep on one of my mother's feather mattresses. I am so tired, hungry, and sore. And little Clem is so fussy and tired. He needs a good rest, too.* Moriah paused in her ruminating for a moment and suddenly realized where her thoughts had taken her. *Oh, Lord, I'm sorry. My attitude is terrible. I should be more grateful for this way You've provided for us to get home. This is one *of those "tribulations that worketh patience" I was readin' about last night in the Bible. Everythin' we experience in life can be used by You to teach us and grow us. Oh, Lord, help me to trust You in ALL things.*

Moriah glanced back at little Clem who was asleep for the moment. She had rigged a bed for him in the back of the wagon with a blanket suspended over him and held down with boxes to protect him from the sun. She turned back around and spoke to her driver, "Thomas, it surely is wonderful of your Pa to let you and your brother, Nathaniel, take turns drivin' my wagon for me. And it's really nice of the two of you to be so willin' and faithful to do a good job. We've been on the road two weeks now. Does it seem longer to you?" she spoke this while wiping her face with a cloth.

"Yes, ma'am, it does. And you're welcome." Thomas, the tall, skinny, fair-haired fifteen-year-old, was the one who didn't talk much. Nathaniel, his short, stocky brother, talked her head off.

"How long do you think it will be before we get to Albany?"

"Don't really know. Pa said last night it might be another week. Depends."

"Yes, I guess it partly depends on the weather and if we have any problems. I suppose I'm just anxious to get home. I haven't seen my parents in over five years! I surely have missed them. And I'm anxious for them to see their new grandson!"

"He's a fine boy, ma'am."

"Yes, he is. He's very special. I grew up near Albany in a little town called Hooperville. It's about forty miles south of Albany. Ever hear of it?"

"Yes, ma'am." She wished he'd talk a little more. It would make conversation more interesting and make time pass faster.

"Where are you folks headed?" Moriah thought perhaps he'd talk more about himself and his family.

"We're headin' to Bainbridge, ma'am."

Well, he's polite anyway, she thought. "Why, that's only down the road from us. We're practically neighbors. Why was your family in Virginia?"

"We was visitin' my grandparents."

Moriah decided she'd talk and just let him listen. "Well, my husband, Jeff, and I moved there when we got married a little over five years ago. My husband just recently died, and now I'm returnin' home to my parents because I can't keep runnin' the farm by myself. My parents are Jeremiah and Ruth Jakes. They've lived in Hooperville all their lives and their parents before them. The Jakes go back a long way. They've always farmed and raised cotton. Pa owned two slaves before the war who helped him on the farm. He worked right alongside them. Pa always worked hard and treated his slaves fair, more like hired hands. Ma always took care of them when they were sick. I guess they're gone now. Pa must be killin' himself workin' so hard, but as little Clem grows up he can help and I'll do all I can." Moriah glanced back at little Clem to see if he was still asleep. He was and Moriah was glad. Her arms had grown weary holding him so much these two weeks.

I wonder what changes I'll see when I get home. What has the war done to my parents and the farm and their lives, she wondered to herself. *I've seen plenty of changes in Virginia and all the way we've traveled south so far. What will home be like?*

"You know, Thomas, I heard that Atlanta was burned in the war. I wonder what it'll look like now and if they've started to rebuild it. We came to Atlanta once when I was a child. It sure seemed like a big city to me then. And, of course, Jeff and I passed through on our way to Virginia after we married. So much has changed. I just don't know . . . ." Thomas glanced over at Moriah, but she didn't notice it.

"Yes, ma'am, I've seen a lot of changes myself," Thomas spoke forcefully. Moriah quickly looked at him. "My family lost everythin' in the war. Our home. Our land was taken. We have nothin' but what's in these wagons. We're goin' to try to start over. Don't know how, but we gotta try. We thought about stayin' in Virginia, but it just didn't work out. Yes, ma'am, there's been a lot of changes."

Moriah was quiet a moment taking all this in and finally she responded, "Thomas, I am genuinely sorry. I had no idea. You've all had it very hard. I will pray for you all. I mean that. God will provide. Trust him and keep faith and He'll take care of you."

"Trust God? Humph, where was God when we lost everythin'? Why'd He let it happen? Huh? Why?" Big tears formed in Thomas' eyes and he brushed them away with the back of his hand.

"God still loves you. We live in hard times. Bad things happen to ever'body." *Thank you, Bess, for teachin' me*, she quickly thought. "My husband died because of the war, and it changed my whole life, but I still believe God knows best and is takin' care of little Clem and me. Just trust, Thomas, and don't be bitter. Bitterness will destroy you inside. Are your parents bitter?"

"My parents? No, they still believe in God and the Bible, but where has it got us? We still don't have no place to live—nothin'!" He choked up and couldn't go on.

"You don't have to talk anymore, Thomas, but I promise to pray for you and your family. God will provide. I don't know how but He will. Promise me you'll try to pray, too."

"Humph! Maybe," was his only reply.

❖ ❖ ❖

As the miles slowly moved by, Moriah found much to pray about. She discovered she could pray sitting, walking, standing or even eating. First, she prayed for little Clem to grow in faith and trust Jesus someday, then she prayed for herself and her parents, for Sam and Bess Jones, and then for Thomas and his family, "Oh, Father, be with Thomas' family. They've lost so much. Help them to know they can still depend on and trust You. Provide them a place and a way to live. Most of all, Lord, reach out to Thomas, soften his heart and the hard shell he's buildin' around himself. Help him be open to You again. Thank You, Lord. In Jesus' Name, Amen."

❖ ❖ ❖

At times Moriah would walk beside the wagon to get exercise and sometimes carry little Clem if he was awake. The time seemed to go so slowly. As something to fill the time, she began to notice her surroundings more as they traveled farther south. She was always awed by the Appalachian Mountains, and she recognized the end of those mountains in north Georgia, what most folks called the Blue Ridge Mountains because they looked so blue. She remembered the red clay soil of north Georgia from visiting there as a child. It was so different from the soil in south Georgia which was mostly sandy. How did people grow anything in north Georgia?

❖ ❖ ❖

As the days passed, Moriah began to recognize towns as they moved into middle and south Georgia, like Griffin and Thomaston. Macon should be right over there, and Columbus just to her right. When they neared Americus, Moriah's heart leaped. *It won't be long now. Albany is the next town and then Hooperville! Ma and Pa, I'll be there soon! It's October 8, maybe in two more days! Oh, I can't wait!* The leaves had turned their beautiful fall colors and there was a crispness in the air. She bundled little Clem ever tighter and herself.

The night before they would reach Hooperville, Thomas approached her after their evening meal around the camp fire when the others had begun to head to their wagons to sleep.

"Ma'am? Could I talk to you?"

"Of course, Thomas. What is it?"

"I just wanted to tell you. I prayed like you said, and I feel a lot better. I think God will take care of us. He seems a lot closer now."

Moriah impulsively hugged Thomas while his face turned several shades of red. "I am so glad, Thomas. I have really prayed for you and your family. Don't give up. Don't ever give up on God. He's workin' even when it doesn't seem like He is."

"Thank you, ma'am. I just wanted to tell you that." And with that, Thomas went to his wagon. Moriah stood for a few moments looking up to the stars, thanking God for His power, love and grace that could get through to Thomas. She felt assurance in her heart that he'd be alright with God's help.

❖ ❖ ❖

October 10! We're here! At last, we're here! Just another mile to the farm! Oh, Ma and Pa, I have longed to see you for so long and to be held in your arms ever since Jeff died. Please be home!

As the wagons neared the farm, she began searching for signs of life and for how things looked. So much to see at one time! The house, which was not a large one even though it had two stories, looked a little run down and the barn needed repairing. The fences could use some repair. A little whitewash would help. Her parents had about 100 acres here with good, rich soil and a creek that ran through it as a tiny tributary of the Flint River. But where were her parents? Her eyes kept moving, hoping to see some movement. The wagons came to a stop before the white picket fence she played on as a child. So many memories! The lump in her throat was so large she could barely swallow. Tears threatened to spill over. She jumped down from the wagon and ran toward the house just as her mother opened the door and came out. They met in a strong embrace and many tears flowed from both. They couldn't speak for a while.

"Ma, it's so good to see you. You look fine. I've missed you so much."

"Oh, Moriah." Her mother completely broke down and used her apron to cry into. Ruth Jakes was not a tall woman, and her coloring was dark like Moriah's. The difference was the gray streaks now running through her hair and the wrinkles beginning to show around her eyes. She walked a little slower than the last time Moriah had seen her.

"Moriah!" She turned to see her Pa come around the corner of the house and be swept up into his embrace. Jeremiah Jakes was a tall man, over six feet, with reddish-blonde hair and beard, now speckled with some gray, and gray-green eyes. His big arms engulfed his daughter and hugged her hard.

"Pa! I've missed you so much. It's so good to see you." She wanted to stay here forever in their embrace. "Ma, Pa, you've got to see little Clem!" They walked over to the wagon, and Moriah picked up little Clem to show him to his grandparents. They were all crying so that it was hard to see.

"Ma, meet your grandson, Clemmons Jefferson Brown. Little Clem, here is your grandma," reaching over to put him in Ruth Jakes' arms for the first time. They were all speechless for a few moments.

"He's beautiful, Moriah! Just like I knew he'd be," Ma crooned. "Look, Jeremiah, he looks like Jeff, and he's got Moriah's green eyes."

"He's a charmer, little'un. He's already got my heart!" Pa spoke up, trying to swallow his tears.

"I'm not the little'un anymore, Pa. Here's the little 'un now. Oh, Pa, Ma, I want you to meet the Mutter family who have let us travel with them from Virginia. They've been so good to us."

Following introductions, the Mutters helped unload Moriah's things and take them into the house. They were invited to stay for the night, but they wanted to go on. They had family in Bainbridge who would let them stay there. Ruth and Jeremiah gave them a sackful of food and many thanks. As they started to leave, Moriah approached Thomas quietly and shook his hand, leaving a little money from her nest egg in his hand. "God bless you and your family, Thomas. Thank you for all you've done."

❖ ❖ ❖

Moriah and little Clem did a lot of visiting with Ma and Pa that afternoon. All three of them wanted to talk at the same time to catch up on everything.

"Moriah, we were heartbroken to hear about Jeff dyin'. We know how much you loved each other. It just seems more than a body can bear, don't it?" This came from Ma who was crying again into her apron.

"Yes, sometimes it does seem more than I can bear, but God has provided and is slowly fillin' the hole in my life. Little Clem is what held me together at first, and I guess he still is. He's my life now, and I want to teach him, with your help, all the things he needs to know about livin' and growin', hurtin' and hopin', most of all about faith and trust in God. That was the last thing Jeff asked me to do—to teach little Clem how to have faith in God. I aim to do it the best I can with His help and yours. Will you help me, Ma and Pa?"

"Little'un, you know we will. Jeff was a smart man. First, for marryin' my daughter, and second, for knowin' Who to trust."

"Pa, call me Moriah. You're holdin' the little'un now. Do you mind?"

"No, I don't mind. Just give me some time to get used to it. I've called you little'un since you were born. Give me a few days!"

Ma had been quiet for a while and then finally spoke, "Moriah, you've grown up. You seem so much older than when you left. I like it. It makes us seem more like friends. I'm so glad you're here."

"So am I, Ma. I've missed you both so much." She hugged both of her parents once again. "Pa, how are things now after the war?"

Jeremiah glanced up and then stared down at his grandson. "Bad. Couldn't be much worse. I really hate to see the world he'll grow up in here in the south," nodding at little Clem. "The bottom fell out of the cotton market some time ago, and the docks are full of rottin' cotton that nobody wants to buy. We've got a ton of it we can't get rid of anywhere. I always meant to 'diversify', as they call it—plant some other money-making crops, like peanuts. I just never got around to the trouble of doin' it. I never thought we'd see the end of cotton. If it wasn't for the food we grow and preserve, we wouldn't be makin' it."

"Pa, is it too late to plant some other crops?"

"No, in fact, I've already started plannin' for that. But the real problem now is the taxes. I've heard tell that they're goin' to be higher this year, and they're not givin' any extra time to pay. We got some bad government now, Moriah. They're corrupt and they don't care what happens to the southerners now. All they want is their big money. The carpetbaggers and scalawags are the scum. Do you remember Jonas Williams that lived down by the bottom land?" Moriah nodded, with green eyes wide full of concern and fear. "He's now our tax collector! Not a more shiftless man ever lived! And he goes around lordin' it over the rest of us while he drives his fine carriage and wears his fine clothes!"

"Now, Jeremiah."

"I know, Ruth. But you know what I'm sayin' is true. Times are hard, Moriah, and they're goin' to get harder I fear. I even looked into sellin' our place—."

"No, Pa!"

"Child, we may have to. But you know what those carpetbaggers offered us for the place—practically nothin'! Not even enough to start over on. We've worked so hard on our farm. Our life's blood has gone into every square inch of land. Our life is here—has always been here. My father and his father before him. What are we supposed to do? Just walk off and leave it?"

Moriah thought about the Mutter family and wondered what they would do.

"We have family buried here. Moriah, you even have a brother and a sister buried here." Moriah's mind went back to her baby sister Lydia who had died when she was two days old with scarlet fever. And William her brother who was killed in the war. He was only seventeen.

"It makes my blood boil to think about lettin' some rich Yankee come in and take our land. No, sir! It won't happen!"

Ruth reached over for Jeremiah's hand to calm him, but he shook her hand away because he didn't want to be calmed. This went too deep.

"Wait, Pa, I have somethin' for you. Just a minute." Moriah left the room and was back quickly. "Pa, Ma, I want you to have this." She laid a small bundle tied up in a handkerchief in her Pa's hand. "The Lord provided this for us, and now I know why. You can use this to pay the taxes and get started on some new crops. Ma and me, and one day little Clem, will work together to keep food on the table, and we can sell butter and eggs and who knows what else."

"Wait, Moriah, I can't take your nest egg. You may need it."

"Pa, we all need it. We're in this together now. We have to help each other."

Jeremiah's eyes filled with tears as he looked over at his wife of nearly thirty years who was again crying into her apron. "Our little girl has grown up, Ruthie. I don't know how to say thank you."

"You don't have to, Pa. You've said it a million times in all the things you've done for us all our lives. Just teach little Clem. Alright, Pa?"

"Yes, Moriah, I can do that."

❖ ❖ ❖

Moriah helped Ma in the kitchen fixing supper on her wonderful cook stove Pa had bought her before the war while Pa played with little Clem. Moriah watched them from the kitchen and commented to her mother, "I'm glad Pa is here for little Clem. He needs a man to help him learn to be one and to teach him all the things I can't. And I know Pa will teach him faith in God."

"Yes, he will, Moriah. The best he knows how. Look at the two of them. They're just made for each other." No one of them knew how true this would be one day.

As they sat down to a supper of ham, chicken, homemade soda biscuits, vegetables, and Ma's wonderful bread pudding, they joined hands and Pa returned thanks, "Thank you, our Father, for this food and the hands that prepared it." He squeezed Ruth's hand. "And thank you, Lord, for bringin' our daughter Moriah home to us and for the extra blessin' of the little'un. Grow him strong in faith for You and help him always walk close to You. For Jesus' sake, Amen."

CHAPTER 5

The first night they were home Moriah was tired but restless. There had been so much travel and excitement that it was hard to sleep. She got out of bed, put on her warm robe, checked on little Clem who was sleeping soundly, and decided to go downstairs. For some reason she felt melancholy and couldn't really explain why. Maybe it was coming home again and seeing all the things from her childhood and growing up years that caused a flood of memories to come to her mind. It might be good to wander through the house and reminisce a little. Maybe that would put things to rest in her mind.

Moriah took up an oil lamp as she descended the old, oak stairs. Memories began to flow. She remembered sliding down this banister enough times that it became very smooth. It still was, running her hand down it. She also remembered falling down the stairs once and almost knocking herself unconscious! Her mother had almost gone to pieces! Moriah had always been a tomboy. There wasn't much she wouldn't try.

Suddenly a memory filled her mind. She had been walking down these stairs when Jeff had first come to the house to court her. They had been so young—only 17! How handsome he had looked that first night! She had felt weak as she descended the stairs. *If I had known how really kind and lovin' Jeff was, I wouldn't have been nervous at all.* Another memory came to her. She had walked down these same stairs on her wedding day in her beautiful white, satin gown with all of the little pearl buttons down the back and sleeves that her mother had sewn for her. *Oh, Jeff had been very handsome that day! And they were both so nervous!*

Moriah walked on into the dining room where she was drawn to the oak sideboard that her mother had always treasured because it had come from her mother and had originally been built in Pennsylvania. It just seemed natural to look for sugar cookies or even those wonderful hand-twisted doughnuts in the tin her mother had always kept in the sideboard. There were some cookies there! She nibbled one as she went. When she was a child, it was difficult to keep the tin filled with two active youngsters around—she and her brother William. *Oh, how I miss William right now*, she thought. *I wish he was here so we could argue again about who got the most cookies. I probably need to go out to the cemetery tomorrow.* She idly opened the two drawers where her mother kept the silverware and tablecloths. They were still there. These were precious articles too because they came from Grandmother Gundersen. *What was this?* Moriah picked up several folded papers in the drawer that had "Butterick Pattern" printed on the front. She slowly unfolded them to find different shapes drawn on paper. She unfolded a large one and stood back to see the shape of part of a woman's dress. *My, my,* thought Moriah, *I've got to ask Ma about this. I've never seen such a thing!*

Moriah's eyes surveyed the rest of the room. The large oak dining table with eight chairs was still there with a big bouquet of fall flowers in the center. Ma loved flowers. The whatnot shelf was still in the corner. She went over to it and handled several items. On the shelves were things she and William made or found and brought home to Ma, like the Indian arrowhead William had found when they had visited north Georgia. They were not worth much, except the love they represented, but Ma had kept them all. There was the butterfly she had caught and mounted on a board for Ma to keep. And there was the first embroidered picture she had done—"God Bless Our Home"—and it was such a poor job, but Ma had loved it. *Oh, my, look, there's the wooden button that came from my grandfather's coat!* Ma was certainly sentimental. Moriah realized that she was becoming sadder by the minute.

She pulled herself away and wandered into the parlor, as Ma liked to call it. This was where the family lived, talked, laughed, cried, read and prayed. So many memories here! Moriah looked around at the furniture which was mostly oak and very sturdy but comfortable. Pa insisted it be comfortable! There were the horsehair chairs and sofa for company, the hickory rocker over by the window for reading, and the maple desk she had loved to play on when she was a child. She couldn't resist looking at it again. There she found several daguerreotypes—one of Pa and Ma together, one of William, and one of Jeff and her on their wedding day. As she stood looking at the last one, she smiled, felt a tear slide down her cheek, and then felt her heart squeeze in sadness. She glanced up and noticed the maple quilt stand her father had made, with her grandmother's handmade quilt stitched in the "Saint Anne's Robe" pattern, thrown across it. Her mother certainly treasured these things.

Moriah walked over to the two maple "settin'" chairs before the fireplace. This had to be her favorite place in the house because it was here that Pa would read to the family from the Bible at night and pray aloud for each one of them. She had always known that Pa had faith in God because he showed it and lived it every day. This was where she rode on his bouncing foot while he held her by the hands as a tiny child. This was where she had found the Lord at the age of ten with the help of her Pa.

Suddenly Moriah fell to her knees before one of the chairs and began to weep and sob aloud. "Oh, Jeff, this is where you asked me to marry you six years ago! Oh, Jeff, I miss you so much. Why did you have to go away so soon and leave me? I need you. I miss you. I want us both to see little Clem grow up. He needs his father! Oh, God, why did you take Jeff so soon? Why? Why? Why?" She pounded the chair seat with a clenched hand, and the sobs came almost uncontrolled. "How can I go on? How can I live?"

"Moriah," Pa spoke softly. He crossed the room to her, knelt down beside her, and took her into his arms to offer comfort as best he could. This was his child hurting so deeply!

They sat together on the floor for some time while Moriah continued to sob and moan. Jeremiah's legs grew numb and cold, but he wouldn't have moved for the world because Moriah needed him. *My poor baby! You've needed this for so long. Cry it all out. It's alright*, thought Pa. Jeremiah was weeping openly also because he knew how deep the hurt went with Moriah, but he also hurt himself. He had loved Jeff like a son and had hoped one day to see them move back to south Georgia to be close to family. He wanted his daughter's happiness more than anything. What could he do? How could he help? *Heavenly Father, give me the wisdom to know what to say and when to say it. Give us all strength and courage and faith to get through this trial. You know what's best. Help us trust You.* Jeremiah prayed in his heart.

As he stroked her hair, he spoke her name softly, "Moriah." Her crying only slowed a little. "Moriah, your Ma would be tellin' you that you're goin' to make yourself sick. I know you need to do this and it's alright. You cry as long as you need to. I'll stay right here with you." Several minutes later Moriah's crying grew less and slowed to a stop finally. She felt spent, empty, used up, and so tired. She lifted her head and looked up at Pa. "Oh, Pa." With that she grabbed him around the neck, and he thought she was going to start over again, but she didn't. She lay her head on his shoulder and rested.

"Pa, God must think I'm a terrible person."

Pa leaned back so he could look her in the eyes. "Why, child, God loves you so much that His heart breaks in two at your sufferin'! He's probably cryin' too. I am." She reached up and brushed his tears from his face and then from her own.

"I thought I was bein' so strong. I thought it was goin' to be alright, but the memories started comin'. I couldn't stop the tears, Pa. It hurts so much to lose Jeff. How can I ever make it without him?"

"Moriah, let's get up and sit a while. My legs ain't what they used to be."

"I'm sorry, Pa. Let me help you."

They took a seat, and Pa took her hands in his large, rough ones. "Right now, it's so hard you don't see a way to make it, but God will provide a way. Ever' day, ever' month, ever' year will get a little easier. You'll never stop bein' sad or missin' Jeff, but it will get easier. I can promise you that. Life will come back into those beautiful eyes and face."

"I thought I had so much faith that it would be better already, but I got to thinkin' about our weddin' and so many other things. It all just overwhelmed me, I guess."

"Moriah, trials come into our lives to teach us faith and how to trust God. He allows it for a reason. No, I don't understand it. I never will either. But the important thing, now listen, is to keep trustin' a faithful, lovin' God to do what's best even though we can't understand it. Trust God, Moriah, trust Him." He pointed upward to emphasize his point. "But don't try to do it all at one time. Take one day at a time. Trust Him just for that day. Faith is somethin' that grows a little at a time, like a plant. You start out with a little seed and with water and sunshine it grows to a full-grown plant, if it survives the winds that come against it. That's the way we are. God puts His seed of love and salvation in our hearts, and then He nourishes it and protects it against the trials and sufferin' that are bound to come to all of us. But we have to let Him help us. And let us help you. If you feel like talkin' about Jeff, then do it. If you feel like cryin', then do it. It's all part of what will take you where God wants you to be. Does that make sense, child?"

"I think so, Pa. It's goin' to take a long time. Will you always be here for me?"

"You know I will. Any time you need me."

"I'm so tired. I hope I can sleep now." Moriah yawned.

"I have a sure cure for that. Let's go in the kitchen and drink some warm milk. That'll work ever' time."

They rose to go into the kitchen when Moriah put her hand on his arm. "Pa, thank you. Thank you for listenin' and carin'."

Pa put his arm around her shoulders and hugged her close as they walked. "I'll always be here, Moriah. And so will God."

❖ ❖ ❖

Pa walked her back to her room upstairs after the warm milk and saw her into bed. "Sleep well, child." Moriah snuggled down under Ma's brightly colored patchwork quilt and deeper into the feather mattress. It felt so soft and comfortable. She soon dozed off to sleep. Jeremiah had watched her from the door until she fell asleep. *She's exhausted, not just from cryin' but from tryin' to be strong. Poor child, why does she have to go through this?* He paused a moment as if listening. *I know, Lord, You have a reason for everythin'. Help my unbelief too, Lord.*

Jeremiah slowly, tiredly walked down the hall to their room. He quietly opened the door trying not to awaken Ruth.

"Jeremiah, is Moriah alright?" He jumped when she called his name. He thought she was asleep. Somehow that woman knew everything!

"I thought you was asleep, Ruth. How'd you know I was talkin' to Moriah?"

"I heard noises a while back and got up to see about it when I saw you was gone. When I heard the two of you in the parlor, I came back to bed and started prayin'. I thought you might need it."

"I did, Ruth. It is so hard to watch your own daughter suffer like she is and not be able to make it all better."

"I know, Jeremiah, I know. I feel the same way. We can pray, we can talk to her, we can listen, and we can just be here for her. That's all I know to do."

"Ruth, pray that I have the faith in God I was talkin' to her about. It's hard sometimes."

"I will and I have. God's given you a lot of faith, Jeremiah. Maybe He knew you'd need it. Moriah's goin' to be alright because she comes from good stock. The two of us will have plenty of time to talk as time goes by."

Jeremiah got into bed beside his lovely bride of nearly thirty years, and they snuggled close. "I love you, Ruth. God gave me you, too. I'm forever grateful."

"As I am, Jeremiah."

CHAPTER 6

September 2, 1867
Hooperville, Georgia

Dear Bess and Sam,

I know it's been several months since I've written. It's just that this past summer has been very difficult, and it's taken all of us to keep things goin'. Fortunately, my nest egg, that you both helped me get, paid our taxes for this past year, but they are soon due again. I don't know what we're goin' to do this year. We're thankful the cotton-pickin' is almost done for this year. We hope to make some profit off it. It won't be much, but we can use any amount. Pa heard some talk the other day that some people are workin' on developin' a way to use cotton seeds for different things, like maybe fertilizer. Pa says that could be a real boon to the cotton farmers. Pa is gettin' started raisin' peanuts and growin' corn as well as cotton, but it's goin' to take some time to see any profit, he says. He was also able to trade off for two hogs. When the time comes, we'll either eat them or sell them, whichever we need the worst. Ma and me have canned, dried, or preserved all the vegetables and fruits we can for the winter. Our root cellar is almost full for which we are thankful. God is providin' through the work of our hands. Ma still trades butter and eggs at the general store for salt, pepper, and coffee. If nothin' else, we won't starve. Pa still has his honeybees, so we're able to sell what we don't use ourselves. He's started makin' sorghum syrup too which we can sell. Well, enough of that, God is providin'.

Little Clem is now a little over a year old! It's hard to believe that much time has gone by. I wish you could see him. He looks so much like Jeff. My heart skips a beat when I look at him sometimes. I want to ask you and Sam to pray for little Clem. He doesn't seem to be learnin' to do things as fast as other babies his age. Ma and I have talked about it. He's not walkin' yet, and he hasn't even tried to pull up on things. He doesn't seem to have an interest in toys and things like that too much. He may look at them and then his eyes just wander off. He doesn't cry much, but then he doesn't laugh much either. He can sit quietly playing with somethin' or chewin' on somethin' for a long time. Just pray for him, Bess, that he'll grow like he's supposed to. I know the Lord is in control, but I don't know if I can take it if somethin' is wrong with little Clem! I love him so much!

I still miss the two of you and think about you often. I still pray for you. Please keep prayin' for all of us. God bless and keep you.

Your lovin' friend,
Moriah

❖ ❖ ❖

"Where are you headed, Pa?" queried Moriah.

"Just headed down to the spring house with the milk. Walk with me?"

"Of course. When I was a little girl, I used to try to take big steps like you, but I could never quite reach it. Remember?"

"Oh, yes. I remember a few times you tripped and fell tryin' to keep up."

Moriah stepped up to open the spring house since Pa's hands were full.

"Thank you, Moriah." Jeremiah lowered the jars of milk he was carrying into the pool of cold water inside the house. The pool was formed by a spring which ran through the spring house. He had built the house some years ago to have a place to keep milk, butter, and other perishable foods. It was built under a huge, old elm tree for shade, had double walls stuffed with moss, and even had a double roof. Milk and butter kept well here even in the summer. It was a wonderful treat in the summer to keep watermelons and muskmelons here because they were kept so cool. Sometimes they'd have a "watermelon cuttin'" and invite neighbors in. Moriah and William loved to spend time in the spring house in the summer, wading in the pool to cool hot feet. Those were good times before the war. It seemed as if all they did now was work.

Pa spoke as they left the spring house, "You look worried, Moriah. Is somethin' on your mind?"

"I—I guess there is. I'm worried about little Clem. Pa, he just doesn't seem to be growin' and learnin' like he ought to. He's over a year old and he hasn't walked yet or talked. He just seems to sit and stare a lot. What do you suppose is wrong with him?"

"Oh, Moriah, I don't think anythin' is wrong with him! Some children just don't pick up on things as fast as others do."

"Well—maybe you're right. But still—."

❖ ❖ ❖

One night a few weeks later Jeremiah and Ruth were sitting before the fire in the parlor, enjoying a few, rare moments of rest. Jeremiah was simply sitting there with his long legs stretched out before him on a hassock staring into the fire while Ruth's hands were busy, as always, with handwork. This time she was doing the fingerwork on a small section of a quilt she was making. She spoke first, "Where are your thoughts, Jeremiah?"

"Oh, nowhere much. Just restin'. Very rare these days. Actually, I was just thinkin' that I was glad somebody came up with the idea of matches to start a fire. It sure beats the old flint rock. Somebody's always inventin' somethin' to make things better. I'd like to have an idea like that and make some money off it."

"Seems like we think about money an awful lot these days," put in Ruth.

"It's sure become more important than it ought to be. Seems like it takes bushels of it to get by anymore. That reminds me. We're still short on the taxes this year. How are we goin' to make it, Ruth? We've worked ourselves slap silly, and we're still short. It makes a man mad, Ruth. I want to provide better for my family, and I'm givin' it all I got and it ain't enough."

"Jeremiah Jakes! Shame on you! Look around at all you've provided for your family. We have more than we need. We're rich compared to some folks. Don't ever think I'm sittin' around thinkin' I wish we was rich. I've never thought that. I love our house and farm and everythin' we've been provided. Did you notice that I said 'been provided'? God is the Provider. All things come from Him. Don't ever forget that!"

"Don't have a hissy fit, Ruth. I'm chastised. Say no more. God has provided greatly for us."

"Besides, Moriah and me are always lookin' for ways we can help to make the tax money too. I'm makin' this quilt right now for a lady whose family has just moved down south. She's goin' to pay me five dollars for it! That'll help. And she wants me to weave her some linen cloth for tablecloths, napkins, curtains, and towels. She'll pay well. And Moriah has taken in some sewin' to do. People have always bragged on her handstitchin'. That'll brin' in some money too. I reckon God will provide other ways, too."

"Why haven't you told me about this sooner, Ruth?"

"I—didn't know if you'd approve or not."

"Well—I don't really like it, but it seems we have no choice. Maybe between us we can make that tax money."

They were quiet for a while, each thinking their own thoughts. Ruth broke the silence.

"Jeremiah, I need to talk to you about little Clem."

"What about him, Ruth? He seems fine to me."

"He's not comin' along like he ought to be by now. He oughta be walkin' by now or at least pullin' up like he's fixin' to walk. And he hasn't talked yet, not a word. It just ain't right, Jeremiah. Somethin's wrong. I just feel it in my bones. I—I'm afraid he's goin' to be slow in his mind. I don't know how to tell Moriah."

"Are you sure, Ruth?" Jeremiah's eyes were wide with concern. "Moriah tried to talk to me not long ago about somethin' like that, but I didn't really listen like I should've. I've got to watch the boy closer."

"Moriah's playin' with him right now. Let's go and watch." They pulled themselves to their feet and went upstairs.

Moriah had little Clem sitting on a blanket on the floor of their bedroom playing with him or at least trying to. Ruth and Jeremiah quietly stood at the door watching. Moriah's back was to them. Little Clem was a cute little fellow. He was plump but short with brown, unruly hair and a cowlick that always stood up in the crown of his head. He looked a lot like his father with a rather oval-shaped face with a few freckles across his nose and a strong chin, and he had Moriah's green eyes.

Moriah was trying to get him to take a hand-carved, wooden toy horse from her to play with, but he just continued holding a toy boat in both chubby little hands while chewing on it. He didn't seem to be aware that his grandparents were there. He had never been one to reach out in eagerness for someone, even his grandparents, although he would reach for his mother.

"Little Clem, take the toy from Mama. I love you, little Clem. You can trust me. Look at me, little Clem. Look at me." *Oh, Lord, please don't let little Clem be deaf. Help me know what to do.* Moriah slapped her hands together sharply, and little Clem, as well as Jeremiah and Ruth, jumped. *Thank you, Lord, he's not deaf!* Moriah swept little Clem into her arms and hugged him hard. "I love you, little fella. You will always be special to me, even if you never walk and talk. But I'm goin' to believe you will and I pray and pray and pray for you, little Clem. God loves you even more than I do, so that must be an awful lot because I love you so much my heart almost stops. Your daddy loves you too and he wishes he could be here, but he's in heaven waitin' for us. Come on, little Clem, let's try to walk again."

Moriah stood and took little Clem by the hands and pulled him to his feet to try to help him walk. His chubby legs just folded underneath him while his chubby bottom sat with a plunk on the floor. Moriah tried several more times, but he just couldn't do it. She tried to get him to crawl to her by holding both toys several feet in front of him, but he just sat there sucking his fingers not even looking in her direction. She went over and sat beside him pulling him unto her lap. A thought occurred to her, and she pinched him on the leg. He whimpered. *Well, he's not paralyzed, thank God. He can feel.* She hugged him to her and began to cry softly as she rocked back and forth, praying aloud, "Oh, Lord, help little Clem to walk and talk. Please, Lord. Help my faith, Lord."

Jeremiah and Ruth quietly turned and walked downstairs, arm in arm. When they were again seated in the parlor, Ruth spoke first, "Oh, Jeremiah, can you see what I'm sayin' now? It breaks my heart." She began to cry, reaching for the corner of her apron.

Taking Ruth's hand, Jeremiah agreed softly, "Yes, Ruth, I see. What can we do?"

"I don't know, Jeremiah. I don't know if Moriah can take it after all she's been through."

"Moriah's strong. She's shown that. God won't put more on her than she can take, or us either. He's growin' faith here—in all of us. That takes time and usually sufferin' to accomplish. He loves us so much that He's willin' for His children to suffer to accomplish in us what He knows is best. We have to wait on Him, rest in Him, and, above all, trust Him with all we've got. He's in control."

"I know, Jeremiah." Ruth sat staring at the fire for a few moments. "We have to help her. We'll all work on teachin' little Clem everythin' we can. We won't give up! And we'll pray! Oh, how we will pray!"

❖ ❖ ❖

The next morning before sunup Ruth and Moriah were making cornmeal mush, scrambled eggs, thick slices of homemade bread with plenty of butter, blackberry jelly, fresh milk, and coffee for breakfast. Growing most of their own food guaranteed they would not go hungry. As they worked, Ruth was thinking of some way to talk to Moriah about little Clem and what they had witnessed the night before. *Lord, help me have the right words.* "Little Clem sure is growin'. Won't be long before we have to make him some more britches."

"Ma, I need to talk to you about little Clem. You know, he really isn't growin' that fast. And it worries me that he still can't walk or talk. He doesn't even show much interest in toys or people. What do you think is wrong with him, Ma?"

"Moriah, I have to tell you somethin'. Your Pa and me—well, we was watchin' you and little Clem last night when you was tryin' to play with him. We both see now what you're sayin'. Little Clem—oh, Moriah, I don't really know how to say this! Little Clem is goin' to be—slow."

"What do you mean—slow?"

"His mind and his body just aren't goin' to be what other folks' minds and bodies are. He's goin' to be slow in his mind, Moriah."

"No, no, no! It can't be true." Moriah began to cry. Ruth put her arms around Moriah and pulled her close. Mother and daughter stood, crying together over a common bond as only women can. "I'll be alright, Ma." Moriah pulled back. "I really have known for some time that what you're sayin' is true. I just didn't want to admit it or believe it. There must be somethin' we can do!"

"We can all work together to teach little Clem everythin' he can possibly learn. And we can pray hard for him, Moriah. Harder than we've ever prayed for anythin'. God will hear and answer our prayers. I believe that."

"Thank you, Ma. What would I do without you and Pa?"

There was much prayer going up for little Clem that night. Jeremiah and Ruth were on their knees by the bed in their room, praying fervently. Moriah was doing the same in her room.

"Heavenly Father, You know my heart is torn and hurtin' for little Clem. I know You love him even more than I do, and I love him with all my heart. I know there must be a reason why You let him be born—like he is. I don't understand it, and my heart wants to cry out—Why? Lord, grant me the faith to trust You for the whys. Help me remember that You know best, even when we don't understand it." Tears were flowing freely now. "Please, Lord, help little Clem to learn everythin' he can. Help us to teach him the right way and the right things. Oh, God, if he never learns to walk or talk—." Moriah choked up so that she couldn't go on. Finally, she continued, "If he never learns to walk or talk, help me accept it. I won't love him less if his mind is—slow. I'll probably love him more. I want what's best for him. Jeff would want that too. So, Lord, guide us in everythin' we do for little Clem. I feel so helpless, Lord. I don't know what I should do. Show us the way. Give us wisdom. Take little Clem in the palm of Your great hand and protect him throughout his life. Help him to grow up and accept Jesus into his heart one day. Oh, God, make him a man of faith, like his Pa and my Pa. Thank you, Lord, for what you have done for us already and what You're goin' to do. In Jesus' Name, Amen."

Moriah was exhausted as if she had fought a battle, which indeed she had in her spirit, to give little Clem to the Lord. This was the first of many such prayers for little Clem through the months and years ahead, at least the years that she would have with him.

CHAPTER 7

"As soon as we finish these baskets, Moriah, I need to get started on weavin' those things for Mrs. Morgan. She wants the linen next week." Ruth was working feverishly to complete all her work to get the money before tax time. Moriah felt her mother had been working too hard, but then they all had. There was just no time for anything else.

"Ma, how did you learn to make baskets?" Moriah asked.

"Oh, my, that goes back a ways. My parents were from the mountains up toward Pennsylvania, you know, and basket-makin' is one of the skills they grew up learnin'. My

Ma passed it down to me. They used to make them out of most any kind of wood, like white oak, hickory, pine, honeysuckle, willow, hazel, cornstalks, whatever they could find. Then sometimes they would dye them different colors using walnut, butternut or hickory nut hulls. Sometimes just time and use colored 'em."

"What did they use them for, Ma?"

"Oh, sometimes for siftin' flour or winnowin' wheat, rye, oats or other grains. Course, we used 'em to bring back goods from the general store. A woman, especially back in those days, couldn't get by without an assortment of baskets. Not as much true now. In fact, these baskets will probably just decorate somebody's house, but that's alright as long as we can sell them. Mr. Pike at the general store said he'd take all the baskets and brooms we could make. So, while I start the weavin', you start tyin' the brooms. Moriah, did you—. Look!"

Moriah and Ruth both stopped to look at little Clem who had been sitting near the side of the porch where they were working. Little Clem was standing up while holding unto the porch railing! Standing up!

"Ma, Ma, look! He's pulled himself up and he's standin'!" She hugged Ruth and ran to little Clem who simply looked up at her with no expression. She grabbed him up and danced around the porch. "This is what we've been prayin' for! Thank you, Lord, thank you! Ma, he may be two years old but better late than never. He's goin' to walk now! I know he will! All our work has paid off. I have worked with him for hours to try to get him to walk. You know what else—I believe he's not as slow as we feared. I think he can learn. It may take him longer than other children, but he can learn. Yes, you can, you sweet little fella!"

Ruth was standing with the corner of her apron dabbing the tears that came in a rush. "Oh, Moriah, I believe he will! I truly believe he will! Thank you, Lord."

Later that day at supper Moriah had a surprise for Jeremiah. After they had finished eating and were savoring Ma's special plum cake, Moriah quietly got up and set little Clem on the floor beside Pa's chair. Then she resumed eating. After a few minutes Jeremiah felt something on his leg. He looked down and there was little Clem hanging onto his pants leg, standing on his own two feet!

"Moriah, little Clem is standin'! He's standin'! Praise God, he's standin'!" He looked at his two loved ones at the table who were wearing big smiles and tear streaks on their cheeks. "You two already knew this, didn't you?" Both of them nodded. "When? How? Why didn't you tell me?"

Ruth spoke first, "He just did it for the first time this mornin'. We wanted to surprise you tonight. Isn't it wonderful, Jeremiah? He will walk. We just believe he will walk!"

Jeremiah threw his arms out to his sides and hollered loud enough for the neighbors to hear! "Hallelujah! Thank you, God!"

❖ ❖ ❖

Jean Ellis Hudson

November 4, 1868
Hooperville, Georgia

Dear Bess and Sam,

It was so good to hear from you again. I hope you are both recoverin' from your sickness and feelin' much better. We (Ma and Pa too) pray for you both all the time. You are very special people to little Clem and me. We want to keep you healthy as long as we can.

The best news I can give you is that little Clem can stand and walk on his own! Yes, can you believe it? We've all prayed so hard, and God has answered with yes. I wish you could see him, Bess. He's three now, short and chubby. He may be slow developing, but he's going to get there. I just know that one day he's goin' to overcome all this and be a very special young man. God has told me in my heart that this will happen. My faith seems stronger now than ever, not just because of this answered prayer but also because of the hard things we've been through—losin' Jeff, sellin' our farm and movin' back home, lack of money, little Clem's slowness. It seems to me it takes the bad with the good to make us have more faith.

And, Bess, little Clem spoke his first word just two days ago! He said, "Ma-ma," clear as anythin'.

It won't be long before he's talkin' up a storm. I'm so happy I could burst! Thank you and Sam for prayin' for little Clem. All of our prayers have made a difference.

Write as soon as you can. I can't wait to hear from you!

Your friend,
Moriah

❖ ❖ ❖

"Look, little Clem, see what I found," Jeremiah encouraged.

"G'amps! G'amps!" Little Clem waddled over to his grandfather. Little Clem was four years old and almost as wide as he was tall, which was only about two to two and a half feet. He had added words to his vocabulary but only a few, and he had trouble pronouncing some of them. He often had a blank look on his face as if trying to understand but not quite making it. He had developed the habit of passing the back of his hand across his forehead when he was puzzled and was trying to think, forming a habit that would last for many years. When he was asked a question, he would stop walking, pass his hand across his forehead, think a while, and then give an answer. The answer didn't always go with the question, but he was getting better all along. Moriah, Jeremiah and Ruth were so proud of him. "Look, little Clem, it's a doodle bug. See that tiny hole in the ground." Little Clem squatted down to see the tiny hole. "Right there, see. That's where he lives. Let's get him to come out so we can see him. Okay?"

Little Clem thought a minute, passed his hand across his forehead, and said, "K."

"We have to sing him a song, little Clem." Jeremiah took a stick and began to turn it around and around in the tiny hole while he said,

> Doodle bug, doodle bug, fly away home.
> Your house is on fire, and your children are alone.

Up from the tiny hole came the doodle bug! Little Clem looked and then he turned his plump little face toward his grandfather with a big grin. He passed his hand across his forehead and repeated, "Dooda. Dooda bug."

Ruth had been watching from a distance as they played their game. She adored both of the men in her life and loved watching them together. She approached them. "Ruth, I've been showin' little Clem the doodle bugs. Come join us."

"G'amma. Ook. Dooda."

"Yes, my darlin'. I see the doodle bug. Come and give G'amma a big hug." Little Clem dutifully went to his grandmother and hugged her around the neck with all his little strength. Ruth's heart always swelled with love for this little one sent from God. They had learned so much from him and for him and certainly about faith and trust in God.

❖ ❖ ❖

"Is everybody ready to go yet?" shouted Jeremiah from the wagon in front of the house. "Come on. We're goin' to be late for church!"

"We're comin', Jeremiah." This came from Ruth as she hurried her brood out to the wagon. First came little Clem, now seven, who had lost much of his baby fat and was beginning to grow a little taller. He was still short for his age, but he was growing. His unruly brown hair with the perpetual cowlick now had some reddish highlights like his grandfather. On Sundays he was always dressed in his best linsey-woolsey pants and coat, which his grandmother had weaved and sewed for him. Everyone who met him thought he was a handsome little fellow. He followed his G'amps everywhere he went and was learning how to do many jobs on the farm with some help. He was becoming tanned from being outdoors so much. Moriah and Ruth were both excited about the way he was developing. Moriah spent a great deal of time teaching him all he was able to learn, telling him about his earthly father and his heavenly Father. Moriah spent much time in prayer for her little Clem, too, as did the rest of the family.

Moriah came out last and pulled the door shut. She was dressed in her best Sunday linsey-woolsey dress which was a nutmeg brown. She and her mother made all their clothes, even to the weaving of the cloth. Times were hard, and they were grateful that Ruth had learned these skills growing up. It had certainly kept the family in clothes.

The latecomers got into the wagon and they were off to church. They all looked forward to church on Sundays. Their community church was about two miles away, and on cold mornings like today it was a brisk ride. On cold days Jeremiah always fixed foot-warmers for each of them for the ride. Since little Clem's feet didn't reach the floor when sitting, Jeremiah had only fixed three metal boxes with holes in the lids which were filled with red-hot coals in ashes to rest their feet on in the wagon. Most folks carried them on into the church because the church building was not heated very well. It usually got warmer as the morning wore on. They didn't have many really cold days in south Georgia, but there were a few.

They usually started with singing, then Sunday School, followed by preaching and more singing. In warm weather, they would bring overflowing picnic baskets and have lunch under the trees in the churchyard, but in cold weather they usually headed home to the fire. Today they would go home after church.

The service this morning started with a favorite hymn of Jeremiah's, "The Gospel Ship":

> The gospel ship is a good old ship,
> She is both safe and sound.
> Oh, who wouldn't sail on the gospel ship?
> For the glory land she's bound.
>
> Our fathers walked in the good old way,
> The way is easy found.
> Oh, who wouldn't sail on the gospel ship?
> For the glory land she's bound.

For the sermon this morning Pastor Finch chose I Kings 19:11-12:

> "And he said, Go forth, and stand upon the mount before the Lord. And, behold, the Lord passed by, and a great and strong wind rent the mountains, and brake in pieces the rocks before the Lord; but the Lord was not in the wind: and after the wind an earthquake; but the Lord was not in the earthquake: And after the earthquake a fire; but the Lord was not in the fire: and after the fire a still small voice."

As the pastor preached on the subject of hearing the still small voice of God, Jeremiah sat back with arms folded and listened intently with one leg crossing the other at the knee. Little Clem sat exactly the same way with one small leg hiked up on the other with his arms crossed. He simply adored his grandfather and imitated him in every way he could. At home little Clem would put an old, empty pipe in his mouth and sit by Jeremiah in front of the fire after supper.

As they were leaving church, the Jakes stopped often and talked with folks they knew and welcomed one new family to the congregation. The Jakes were a well-liked family.

The Justice family in the church was just getting into their wagon when their young son, Timothy, spoke up, "Look at that boy Clem. He's dumb, ain't he?"

"Timothy Justice, don't ever let me hear you say that again! Do you hear me? That's one of the kindest, most lovin' and givin' families in our church. Little Clem is a little slower than some other people, but he's not dumb! He's learned how to love people which is more than I can say about you!" Mrs. Justice responded. "Wait till I get you home! Straight to the barn without dinner."

❖ ❖ ❖

"That's the way, Clem. Throw it outta your hand like this?" Jeremiah demonstrated to little Clem again how to feed the chickens. He had shown him many times before, but he usually caught on slower than others would. But he almost always learned to do whatever the task was. He could feed the chickens and two horses they had, slop the hogs, milk the cow, and help clean the barn—with some help. They were all so proud of him for learning what he had. Jeremiah was very patient with little Clem, for which Moriah and Ruth were grateful.

"Alright, Clem. Come on and let me show you how to whitewash a fence. You'll love this. And your Ma will, too, when she sees you covered in white! Just for fun, let's ride Jackrabbit out to the fence. Want to?"

"Yeah!" was little Clem's response. They went over to the barn where Jeremiah set little Clem up on Jackrabbit's back. Jeremiah led the horse by his reins while little Clem jumped up and down like a "real cowbo'," as he usually said. They rode out to the picket fence around the house which was only about a hundred feet, but Jeremiah wanted to get little Clem used to sitting on the back of a horse as soon as he could.

Jeremiah helped him down, then asked, "Are you ready to learn to paint, my little friend?"

"Gonna paint me?" queried little Clem.

Jeremiah had to fight the urge to laugh. Instead, he answered, "No, Clem. We're gonna paint the fence." All the while he was thinking that little Clem would probably look painted by the time they were through.

About two hours later, Ruth and Moriah were hanging linens on the clothesline and happened to see what their menfolk were doing. They were so caught up in it that they completely stopped their work and began to watch the painting. Jeremiah had a big brush and little Clem had a small one, and everything Jeremiah did, little Clem copied, or at least he tried. He would stick his brush in the bucket of whitewash and leave a trail on the ground to the fence where he slopped it around on the boards. Jeremiah was letting him do it his way. Ruth and Moriah hid their laughing behind their hands, as little Clem missed the board and came down on the top of his head with the brush full of paint. Little Clem looked like he was going to cry; that is, until Jeremiah took a brush full of paint and dabbed on top of his own head! Little Clem and Jeremiah both rolled on the ground laughing. This was the joy life was made of.

"Well, Moriah, it looks like some folks are goin' to have a bath tonight whether they want to or not."

When Moriah didn't respond, Ruth looked closely at her. Tears were running down her cheeks. "What's wrong, Moriah?"

"Oh, I'm happy but sad too. I was just thinkin' of Jeff and how he would've loved doin' these things with little Clem. But I'm so glad, so very glad, that he has Pa to teach him how to be a man."

"So am I. Like I said before, they were meant for each other."

CHAPTER 8

"Moriah, since Clem has just turned eight, I think it's time to drop the 'little' and just call him Clem. What do you think?" Jeremiah asked.

"Well-ll, I hadn't thought of it before. I suppose it'd be alright."

"Well, I just think since he's older now, it would be better not to call him little, especially in front of his friends at church. He's startin' to grow up now." Clem had never gone to formal school. Moriah and Ruth had taught him at home.

"Alright, Pa, I understand. We'll call him Clem from now on."

Clem came out of the barn at that moment, leading Jackrabbit. Moriah watched her son as he came toward her. He had grown so much although he was still not too tall, but his skin was tanned, his hair lightened by the sun with the ever-present cowlick, the freckles standing out on his nose, his slimness evident, his walking with more confidence, his leading Jackrabbit with assurance. None of these things escaped his mother's notice as he came toward her. He still had difficulty thinking and speaking at times. He was quiet a great deal and soft-spoken when he did speak, but her boy was doing well. *He's goin' to be alright, Lord. You've taken care of him well. Jeff would be so proud and I am, too.*

"Thank you, Clem. You're a wonderful son and I love you very much." Moriah hugged him and he hugged her back.

"I love you, Ma." He had never been embarrassed about hugging her and expressing love, even in front of other people.

"I'm goin' for a ride on Jackrabbit. He needs a run."

Jeremiah answered for Clem and himself. "We're goin' to finish pickin' that cotton, so we can get it to market. That alright with you, Clem?"

"Sure, G'amps. I like to work with you." Jeremiah smiled and put his arm around Clem's shoulder as they started to walk off. "Guess you'll have to go by yourself, Moriah. We men have things to do."

Clem stretched around Jeremiah's arm and waved goodbye to his Ma.

❖ ❖ ❖

Moriah chose one of the hottest days of the year in south Georgia to go for a ride. It was hazy, hot, and humid as summer often is in the deep South. For some reason she felt the need to get out of the house and away from work for a while, to ride Jackrabbit as hard as she could across the pastureland to the creek, and to feel the wind rushing into her face and blowing her hair. She had done this many times growing up and loved the feeling it gave her, so she felt no qualms today as she set out.

As she and Jackrabbit reached the edge of the pasture, she dug into his sides as a signal to ride hard. They raced across the pasture as the grass rushed by underneath them. As a child, she had always felt riding like this was almost like flying—moving with no effort. It was exhilarating and cleansing because it cleared the cobwebs out of her mind. Oh, how she loved it! She truly hoped one day Clem would ride like this, and somehow she knew he would. As they approached the grove of poplar trees by the creek bank, she slowed up and began to walk Jackrabbit who was breathing hard. The horse picked his way along the creek bank among the ferns that grew there. This was one of her favorite spots to visit when she needed to think or pray. It was quiet and peaceful and a little cooler.

Suddenly, a water moccasin slithered in front of Jackrabbit, startling him, making him rear up on his back legs and whinny loudly! Moriah was thrown backward off the horse and landed hard in the creek where the back of her head hit a rock! She lay unconscious in the creek with blood beginning to seep from a head wound with no one within hearing distance.

❖ ❖ ❖

Picking cotton was one of those hot late August jobs that had to be done. It was exceptionally hot this day. Jeremiah and Clem were drenched in sweat. Jeremiah was proud of how Clem held his own and stayed with it until the job was done.

"Clem, have I ever told you about some of the cotton-pickin' superstitions I've heard of?" Pa asked.

"No. What's a super—?"

"Superstition. It's something people make up that's not real, but a whole lot of people start believin' it and it seems real. Like, there's one that says if you pick cotton out of the boll and let it fall on the ground, you will not have a successful cotton-pickin' season."

"Really, G'amps?"

"No, Clem, remember a superstition is not true, but a lot of people think it's true. You have to learn to tell the difference between what's real and what's not. There's another one that says if cotton is seen blowin' across a field, a snow storm will follow shortly. Look, Clem, what do you see over yonder?"

"A cotton boll the wind is blowin' around." Clem stopped and looked up at the sky and back at Jeremiah, passing his hand across his forehead. "I don't think it's gonna snow."

"Exactly, Clem. You caught on real quick. Let's head to the house. I'm about wore out and wet as a new puppy. I'd say it's pretty close to suppertime, wouldn't you?"

"Yessir!"

As Jeremiah and Clem were coming from the barn after storing the cotton they'd picked and cleaning up a little, Ruth met them on the way.

"Jeremiah, I'm beginnin' to get worried. Moriah went on her ride about two hours ago and still hasn't come back. I'm afraid somethin' has happened to her."

"I'll go look for her, Ruth. That's longer than she usually rides. Clem, go on in with your G'amma, and I'll take Bitteroot. It'll be faster that way."

"I wanna go, too." Clem responded.

"No, stay with your grandmother. I'll be back soon." Jeremiah swung up on the back of Bitteroot and headed off. He looked at Ruth and mouthed the word, "Pray."

"Come on, Clem. Let's you and me go inside. We'll pray for your Ma and G'amps."

❖ ❖ ❖

Jeremiah rode hard across the pasture. He knew where to look because from childhood Moriah had always loved that grove of poplar trees at the creek. It was her playhouse and sanctuary. As he approached the grove, he spied Jackrabbit grazing off to the west but riderless. His level of concern grew. Fear caught in his throat when he first saw Moriah lying motionless in the creek. *Oh, God, no, please let her be alright! Please, Lord, please!* Jeremiah was off the horse before it stopped, running to her side. He splashed through the creek and fell to his knees in the water beside Moriah. He looked her over, and at first, didn't see anything wrong, but then he noticed the streaks of red in the water around her head. "Oh, God, no, no, no!" he cried aloud. He tried to tell if she was breathing but couldn't. Finally, he felt her heart beating faintly. "She's alive! Thank God!" With trembling arms, he gently scooped her up and carried her to his horse and draped her across. This wasn't too comfortable, but it was the best he could do. He wished he had the wagon. Jeremiah whistled for Jackrabbit and he came running. He mounted Jackrabbit, and as quickly as he felt would be safe, they made tracks toward home.

Every step of the way home, which seemed an eternity to Jeremiah, he breathed the same prayer, "Heavenly Father, please let her be alright. Please let her live and be alright."

At long last, he came in sight of the house and saw Ruth and Clem on the porch anxiously watching and waiting. They both began to run to meet Jeremiah long before he reached the picket fence. Ruth didn't waste time. She ran to Moriah to see her condition. She willed herself not to cry or waste precious time carrying on. "Jeremiah, get her in the house right now. Lay her on the bed in her room. I'll get what I need. Hurry!"

Jeremiah obeyed without hesitation. As he carried Moriah inside, he told Clem over his shoulder, "Put the horses up, Clem."

Clem stood for a moment watching until G'amps and his Ma were inside and then slowly turned to the horses. After putting them away, he slowly walked back to the house. Anyone who had known Clem for long would recognize that he was trying to process everything that had happened to understand it and know how to react. As he entered the house, Jeremiah called him aside into the parlor.

"Clem, your Ma has been hurt pretty bad. She hit her head when she fell from her horse, probably on a rock in the creek. It was probably a snake that caused Jackrabbit to bolt and she was thrown. She's lost a lot of blood and is unconscious."

"What does that mean? Unconscious."

"It means she's not awake. We must pray for her, Clem."

Clem turned to walk out of the room when Jeremiah said, "Clem, why don't you stay here with me and we'll pray? We might just get in the way up there." He indicated the stairs with a nod of his head.

"No, I want to be with Ma." Clem continued slowly walking, dragging himself up the stairs like an old man. He quietly went into his mother's room and stood inside the door when he saw her in bed, pale from loss of blood and still unconscious.

"Clem, why don't you wait downstairs with G'amps? There's nothin' you can do here," Ruth suggested.

Clem approached the bed. "No, I want to stay with Ma. How is she?"

"She's lost a lot of blood and she's unconscious. The bleedin' has stopped, but I—I just don't know. We'll have to wait and see."

Clem drew a chair up beside the bed. "Can I sit here and wait?"

Ruth glanced at Jeremiah who had followed Clem upstairs. Jeremiah spoke first, "Sure you can, Clem. It's where you belong. Let's all pray together for your Ma."

No one spoke a word, but they all fell to their knees by the bed. Jeremiah reached out and took one of Moriah's hands. They all joined hands then.

Jeremiah prayed, "Lord, we come to You now on behalf of our daughter, Moriah. Lord, You already know that she's hurt and how it happened. We believe You are still in control and that You love her even more than we do. You don't want harm to come to any of Your children. So, we have to believe that there is somethin' for us to learn here and for her." Jeremiah's voice choked up at that point and he faltered. In a few moments he continued, "Lord, spare Moriah's life, please." He was now speaking from a father's heart. "We love her so and we need her. Clem needs her. Oh, God, we cry out to You to touch Moriah's body, heal her, restore her to us. Give us courage and strength to help her as much as we can, but we know You can do far more. Speak to her heart and let her know that we love her and want her back. Help her to wake up and be alright. We pray all this in Jesus' Name, Amen.

❖ ❖ ❖

The next morning found Clem asleep with his head cradled in one arm which was propped on the bed beside his mother and his other hand holding one of hers. He had stayed all night with her. His grandparents couldn't get him to go to bed at all. Ruth had also stayed all night while Jeremiah rode the several miles into Hooperville to bring the doctor back. They were all haggard and tired, and Moriah's condition had not changed.

Jeremiah and Dr. Malcolm finally arrived about dawn. He shooed them all out of the room while he examined her, even Clem. When he finished, he called them back in. "Folks, I don't know of anything I can really do for her beyond what I've done. It was good the bleeding had stopped, and I've stitched the cut on the back of her head. Besides that, we can only wait and see. I'll stay as long as I can and watch her to see if she regains consciousness. The rest is up to the good Lord."

Clem resumed his spot by the bed with his hand in Moriah's. Jeremiah and Ruth stepped out in the hall with the doctor. "Jeremiah, I wish there was more I could do, but I can't. Some things are beyond medical science."

"I know, Dr. Malcolm. But God is still in control. He's bigger than medical science. Ruth, why don't you fix the doctor some coffee and maybe a little something to eat? And while you're there, eat something yourself. I'll stay with Clem." When he kissed Ruth on the cheek, he noticed how pale and worn out she was and the hollow look in her eyes. *Oh, God, please spare Moriah for all of us.*

❖ ❖ ❖

The next day in late morning Clem was sitting in his place by the bed holding Moriah's hand when he felt her move. He looked up and she was stirring in the bed.

"Ma!" Clem cried.

Ruth was beside him in an instant. "Moriah, can you hear me? Are you alright? Squeeze my hand if you can hear me." She felt a gentle squeeze. "Praise God! He's answerin' our prayers!" She went to the door and called for Jeremiah to come up. He took the stairs two at a time and fell on his knees by the bed.

They all watched as Moriah's eyelids fluttered a few times and then gradually opened. She squinted from the light and then opened them, looking around as if trying to understand. Her gaze came around to Clem.

"Clem." Clem threw his arms around her as best he could and burst into tears.

"Ma, you're alright. I missed you. I love you."

"I love you too, son." Suddenly she began to cough deeply and with difficulty which really hurt her chest.

"Don't say a word, Ruth. I'm goin' for the doctor." Jeremiah left hurriedly.

❖ ❖ ❖

After Dr. Malcom examined her, he stepped into the hall outside the bedroom. "She has pneumonia. In both lungs. This has probably developed because of being in the cool water for a few hours and then lying in bed for two days. I've given her some medicine, but there is really nothing else I can do. It's still up to the good Lord. I'm sorry, Jeremiah, Ruth." The doctor left.

As the day wore on, Moriah coughed more and more and grew weaker. About mid-afternoon, she weakly spoke to Ruth for the first time that day. "Ma. Clem. I want to see Clem."

Ruth bent over the bed, holding Moriah's hand. "He's right here, darlin'. He hasn't left your side."

"Clem, I need to talk to you. Can you hear me?" Moriah whispered.

"Yes, Ma. I'm listenin'."

Jeremiah and Ruth stood holding onto each other with tears streaking their faces as Moriah talked to her son.

"Clem, you know I love you with all my heart. Your Pa loved you that way, too." She stopped to cough and try to breathe. Then she continued, "There are some things I need to say to you all. Ma and Pa, I love you and thank you for all you've always done for me and for Clem. We couldn't have made it without you." She paused again.

Jeremiah and Ruth had moved closer to the bed. "We love you, too, precious Moriah. Why not just rest and try to sleep? You don't have to talk now."

"Oh, I do, Ma. So many things I haven't said yet." Tears ran from her eyes onto the pillow. "I feel the Lord so near." She smiled. "It won't be long, Jeff."

The heads of her three loved ones jerked up, and Clem shouted, "No!"

"It's alright, Clem. The Lord has told me He's goin' to take care of you all just like He always has. Clem, what I want to say is for you to keep faith in God, trust Him with all your heart, soul, mind, and strength. Give Him your whole heart and life. Live for Him. Do what's right. Be honest and lovin' always like you are now." Her speaking was interrupted by a fit of coughing. When it passed, she continued, "Clem, I've tried all my life to trust God. And He's never failed me yet. He's always right, just, faithful, true, lovin', givin'. I've let Him down so many times, but He's always been there for me—to forgive me, pick me up when I failed. He'll do the same for you. He already has, you know. His hand is on you, Clem. He'll guide you if you'll let Him. Pa and Ma will be there for you, too, Clem, won't you?"

"Of course, we will, Moriah, always," choked out Jeremiah. Ruth was weeping uncontrollably as she watched her last living child pass from life. She turned to Jeremiah and threw herself into his arms so he could hold her.

Moriah continued, "Clem, I want to pray for you now. Heavenly Father, thank You for the life You've given me. Thank You for my parents and their love." She choked up but calmed herself. "Thank You for my husband and for my son, Clem. My special, special little Clem. Take him in Your lovin' care, Father. Protect him, help him grow into faith and trust You with his whole heart. In Jesus' Name, Amen."

Moriah lay quiet for a few moments. Clem was watching her face and said, "I love you, Mama. Please don't leave me."

"I have to, darlin', but it's alright. God is with you." To Clem, it looked like her face was shining when she said, "Jesus—Jeff—."

And then she was gone.

CHAPTER 9

Jeremiah and Ruth clung to each other, weeping openly. The depth of grief and sorrow they felt was beyond expressing to anyone but God. He understood because He had given His only Son.

Clem put his head down on the bed beside his mother and cried, still holding her hand. He stayed that way for some time and then slowly picked himself up from the chair and stood looking at his mother. Then he slowly turned and left the bedroom. He was confused and hurt and didn't know what to do. It was the first time in his eight years of life that he didn't have his mother to turn to and depend on. He paused outside the bedroom for a moment and then headed outside. The heat assaulted him as he went outside, but he didn't feel it. He slowly dragged his heavy feet with the old, worn-out brown clodhoppers on in the direction of the barn. He stepped into the relative coolness and dimness of the barn and closed the big double doors.

Clem stood inside the doors and felt like he had never felt in his life. The first thing he noticed was his legs trembling, then his arms and hands, and finally his shoulders. The sobs tore through his throat and out of his mouth like cannonballs! He didn't understand exactly what was happening. He ran to the hay pile and threw himself bodily into it where he laid sobbing and weeping so loudly that the cow and horses became restless. "Mama, Mama! Come back! Come back! Don't leave me! Please, God, bring her back!"

Ruth and Jeremiah wept by their daughter's bedside for some time, too. They were aware that Clem had left, but they had to deal with their own grief first and they knew he'd be safe. Ruth leaned against Jeremiah's large chest while his arms encircled her. There were no words because none were needed. They had experienced this twice before with their other two children. The grief and hurt seemed to go deeper this time, maybe because she was the last of their children or perhaps because they had had her for a longer time. They each knew what the other was feeling and thinking because they had been "one" for many years.

Some time had passed when Ruth sat up and began to wipe her face with her apron. She was coming to life again and knew she had to handle things. "Sometimes that keeps a body goin'," she used to say, "just knowin' what you gotta do."

"Jeremiah, go see about Clem. He needs us more than ever now."

Jeremiah's grief was deep also, but he knew what he needed to do and that was to help Clem as best he could. "He's probably in the barn. I'll go see to him while you take care of Moriah. What do I say to him, Ruth? I don't understand myself." A sob caught in his throat.

"I know, Jeremiah. Neither do I. But God does and He has a reason for this. We just gotta trust Him. Somehow. And we gotta teach Clem to trust Him. That's what Moriah wanted more than anythin'."

As Jeremiah turned to go, he glanced back to see Ruth begin to wash Moriah's body and prepare her for burial. Another sob caught in his throat. *Why, God? I don't understand. Why did You have to take her? Clem needs his Ma so much, and we all love her so much. God, help me trust You even when I can't understand. This is goin' to be mighty hard, Lord. Give me the words to say to Clem. Help him somehow not to be bitter toward You. Help him, God, help him, and us, to go on.*

As Jeremiah left the house, thunder began to rumble and the crackle of lightening was overhead. A sudden thunderstorm had popped up as was common in the South as the summer days heated up. Before Jeremiah got to the barn, the rain began to come in a sudden but brief downpour, wetting him to the skin. He seemed not to notice. His steps were slow and measured, and his feet felt like lead weights were attached to them. This was probably the hardest thing he'd ever had to do. Jeremiah let himself in the barn quietly, and when his eyes adjusted to the dimness he spotted Clem in the hay. He slowly walked over and sat down next to Clem, propped his arms on his bent knees and hung his head. He listened to Clem's sobs for a few minutes, with the thunder and lightning so vibrant outside, and then he offered, "Clem, I'm here when you're ready."

Several minutes passed before Clem rose up from the hay. His unruly hair was disheveled and bits of hay stuck to his hair and clothes. As soon as he saw Jeremiah's long face and sad eyes, he threw himself into his grandfather's arms. "Oh, G'amps, why do people have to die? I don't understand. I want my Ma back."

Jeremiah's strong, muscular arms surrounded Clem's small frame, and he simply held him and sat quietly. He was waiting for God to give him the right words.

When Clem's tears had abated somewhat, Jeremiah spoke, "Clem, can we talk now? There's some things I need to tell you, but I want you to listen real close. If you don't understand, tell me and I'll try again. Alright?"

"Yessir," replied Clem as he sat up.

"Did I ever tell you about my Pa? I don't think I have. He was a strong, good man, a believer in God. He and my Ma both. Anyway, my Pa and me had a special relationship, kind of like what you and me have. We could talk about anythin', and we did a lot of things together. I learned a lot from him about farmin', raisin' cotton and children, and, most of all, about God, especially havin' faith in God. Trustin' Him. Do you understand, Clem?"

"Yessir, I think so. Like you trust me to do what you tell me and I do it. Is that it?" he asked while passing his hand across his forehead.

"Good, Clem. My Pa trusted me like that, too, and I always tried to keep his trust by doin' what he told me to. It's the same with God. We need to trust Him because He will always do what He says He will do. He also trusts us to do what He tells us to. Well, my Pa had such faith that he really believed the scripture in Job that says, 'Though He slay me, yet will I trust in Him, He also shall be my salvation.' That sounds hard, but it means that even if God took his life or let his life be taken from him, he would still trust God and believe that God was doin' what was best. Are you with me, Clem?"

"I think so, G'amps."

"Let me go on. I had heard my Pa quote that scripture many times and explain it. He sure lived by it. He always believed that God knew what was best. I didn't know that we would have to go through a situation when I'd have to learn the real meanin' of it for myself. One day Pa was in town to pick up supplies, and as he was comin' out of the general store a drunk man came out of the saloon with a gun shootin' wild. He shot and killed my Pa." Tears sprang to Jeremiah's eyes as he remembered. "I was only about fifteen when it happened. I was hurt so bad I didn't think I'd be able to handle it. I cried for weeks and wouldn't talk to anybody, even my Ma. I was angry, most of all at God for takin' him. My Ma talked to me finally when she realized what was causin' the problem. She set me straight, but I still had to struggle and fight inside myself to accept what had happened. I went off by myself traipsin' in the woods and fell on my face under an oak tree. I prayed so hard and cried and prayed and cried till finally God spoke to my heart. He told me how much He loved me and my Pa and how I needed to trust Him. That was a special time. It still took me a long time, but I can say now, 'Though He slay me, yet will I trust in Him.' I believe this now as strong as my Pa did then. You see, Clem, God is good and His love is so big. He promises He'll always take care of us and do what's best for us even if we don't always understand it. We don't understand why He took your Ma right now, but one day we will. I believe that. Until then, we have to keep faith in God. Clem, don't be angry at God or me or yourself. Just trust God. Alright?"

Clem's wet, tired, small face looked up at Jeremiah. "I don't understand it all, G'amps. But I'll try to trust. I promise." Jeremiah couldn't help but notice the trust already showing on Clem's upturned face. Such innocence and childlike faith! *That I should have that kind of faith toward You, God*, were Jeremiah's thoughts. *He trusts me. Never let me fail him, God.*

"But, G'amps, why do bad things have to happen?"

"Son, you've asked a hard question. Christians live in a world where bad things happen. God doesn't keep us from all bad things because it helps us to grow stronger in our faith and makes us more like Him. Sometimes it's so we can comfort other people who have hard times. Sometimes hard things happen to test us to see what we're really made of, but remember He knows how much we can stand and He won't put on us more than we can handle. Even losin' your Ma. You see, He knows that you can handle this and be stronger one day because of it. He's tryin' to help you grow into a strong man of faith, Clem. You know, your Ma told you that God had His hand on you and I believe that too. You've been through some hard things, Clem, losin' your Pa without ever knowin' him, hard times here without much money, and now losin' your Ma. God's gettin' you ready to be a special man someday. I want to be around to see it. So right now, suffer for 'a season', that means for a while, and then God will do mighty things in you. Can't wait to see it myself!"

Passing his hand across his forehead, Clem replied, "That's a lot to think about."

"Yes, it is. Will you promise me you'll try to have faith?"

"I'll try to have faith. But I'm so little. How can I have a lot of faith?"

"The Bible says you only have to have faith the size of a mustard seed. You remember when we planted those mustard seeds. Remember how small they were. The Good Book says if you have that much faith, you can move mountains. It doesn't take a lot of faith, just faith in the right One."

"God, I know. I'll try, G'amps, but I'm gonna miss Ma so much. What will we do without her?"

"Well, we've got each other and a great big God who loves all of us. Are you ready to go in the house now?"

"Yessir."

They rose together, left the barn, and headed toward the house. "Well, it looks like it's quit rainin'. We sure needed some rain. Look, Clem, at the clouds around the sun where it's settin'. Pretty, ain't it? Remember that rhyme I taught you.

> Pink in the mornin', sailors take warnin'.
> Pink at night, sailors' delight, no more rain in sight.

When they reached the house, Ruth met them at the door with dry clothes and hugs. After she fed Clem, she tucked him in for the night, but not before he could ask, "G'amma, where is Ma right now?"

"She's in heaven, Clem. Right there with Jesus and your Pa. She's happy and isn't sick anymore and never will be again. One day we'll see her again. Goodnight, Clem. I love you."

"I love you, too, G'amma." When Ruth had left, the tears began to silently run down his cheeks. "God, help me have faith, like G'amps said." His hand passed across his forehead. "Help me understand." And then more softly, "I love you, Mama. I'm gonna miss you. Tell Pa hello for me."

❖ ❖ ❖

For the next two days, neighbors and church friends came to the house to bring food and whatever help they could offer. Clem's unruly hair was worse than usual because it seemed that everybody patted him on the head or ruffled his hair when they said to him, "I shor' am sorry about your Ma, boy. Terrible thing to happen." Then they'd move on to speak to his grandparents. Clem grew tired and wished all that part was over with.

The funeral was on the third day which dawned bright, hot and humid. Moriah's body was taken to the church in a wagon for the service and then back to their homeplace for burial in the family cemetery. Two neighbor men had dug the grave next to the other graves of the Jakes' children. Preacher Holloway made some comforting remarks, read Scripture, and prayed, and, as was customary, he threw a handful of earth on the casket and repeated, "The Lord giveth and the Lord taketh away. Blessed be the name of the Lord." When he concluded the service, he spoke to each family member, hugging Ruth and shaking hands with Jeremiah and Clem.

Many friends left then, but others returned to the house with Jeremiah and Ruth to talk and eat some more. Ruth had to make Clem go into the house, so he wouldn't watch the men fill the dirt in the grave.

After some time had passed and all the neighbors were gone, the family went back to the graveside. Clem went directly to the grave and sat down beside it and laid there his small bouquet of late summer flowers he had picked for his Ma. He wanted to stay there at the grave, so he could be close to his Ma, or so he thought. He didn't fully understand, and it would take a few years for him to get a perspective on losing her. But he would get there.

Ruth busied herself for a few moments plucking a weed or two from the graves of her other children and brushing the accumulated dust and dirt from their tombstones. She had always taken special care of the graves, not because she thought they were still there, but out of respect for the dead. She knew where her children were. They were all in the hands of God now. Home. Safe at last from all harm. That gave Ruth comfort and hope because she'd see them all again. What a reunion that will be! She brushed a tear away and spoke. "Jeremiah, you need to make a tombstone for Moriah like the others."

"Yes, Ruth, I will. I'll take care of it as soon as I can. Why don't we go back to the house? Are you ready, Clem?"

"No, sir. I want to stay here with Ma." Jeremiah and Ruth exchanged looks.

"Ruth, why don't you go on back? Clem and me will be along in a minute." When Ruth had left, Jeremiah spoke to Clem as he sat on the ground beside him, "You know, Clem, God has prepared a place for us in heaven that is so beautiful we can't picture it. Streets of gold. No nighttime. The river of life flowin' through it. The best part is—Jesus is the first one we'll see. He's waitin' on us. There won't be any sufferin' or heartache or tears anymore. That's where your Ma is, and now she's with your Pa. They are so happy! They look forward to seein' you and all of us one day. So, Clem, your Ma's not in that grave. Oh, her body is, but her spirit is in heaven. You don't have to stay by the grave to be close to her. She'll always be in your heart wherever you are and wherever you go. Do you understand, Clem, what I'm tryin' to say?"

Clem hesitated for a few minutes while he passed his hand across his forehead. "Not all of it. Would it be alright if you go back to the house and I stay for a little while?"

"Of course, Clem. You want to say goodbye. That's good, son. Just come on home when you're done."

"Yessir."

Clem had a lot to think about and he couldn't do it all at once. It would take some time. Right now he leaned over and laid across the grave as if trying to hug it. "Ma, I love you always. And I love Pa. Tell him for me. G'amps says one day I'll get to be with you again if I love Jesus in my heart. I do love Jesus. Tell Him for me. But right now, Ma, I miss you so bad!" Big tears began to roll like drops of rain. He cried for a short time and then slowly rose and walked toward the house occasionally looking back.

CHAPTER 10

Jeremiah had a surprise for Clem and he couldn't wait to get home to show him. He could feel it squirming around inside his shirt. His neighbor, Abe Fortham, had told him sometime back that his cocker spaniel Frankie was going to have pups, and he'd asked Jeremiah if he wanted one. Of course, Jeremiah's first thought was of Clem. A perfect companion for him! So, here he was, trying to keep the auburn-colored, long-eared, silky-haired pup inside his shirt until he got home.

As he rode into the yard, he called out, "Clem, come see what I've got for you!" Clem came from the barn to see what Jeremiah was talking about.

"What is it, G'amps?"

"Got a surprise for you," spoken as he climbed down from Jackrabbit. He unbuttoned his shirt and out popped the furry head. "Here, Clem, he's all yours!"

"A puppy! Thanks, G'amps!" He took the puppy and it immediately began to wash his face with his tongue. Jeremiah and Clem both began to laugh. Clem sat down in the grass and let the puppy crawl over him and try to lick him. Clem began to roll over and over in the grass while the puppy ran around him and tripped over him. Clem and Jeremiah laughed so hard they cried. Ruth came from the house to see what all the noise was about. When she saw, she stopped and put her hands on her hips. She looked cross and had, in fact, been cross a lot lately. "Jeremiah, where'd you get that thing?"

"Abe Fortham's dog had pups, and he gave me one for Clem." He walked over to Ruth and whispered, "I thought it'd make a good companion for him since he lost his Ma."

"Jeremiah, it's another mouth to feed. And that's one thing we don't need around here. Who's gonna look after him? I have more to do than I can handle now."

Jeremiah looked at Ruth for a moment and realized how much pressure she was under. His heart went out to her. "Ruth, Clem will take care of the pup and he sure won't eat much. He's only six weeks old."

"Well, I don't know. It sure is the boniest dog I ever saw. It'll probably eat us out of house and home!" Ruth continued to watch the antics of Clem and the pup until finally she softened and even laughed. Jeremiah made a note in his mind to talk to Ruth later.

"Well, you two, come wash up for supper. And the dog stays outside!" Ruth went back in the house.

"Better do what she says, Clem. Put the pup in the barn for now until he's a little bigger. You need to think of a name for him."

"I have already. Boney!" They both laughed.

Later as they sat down at the supper table, Jeremiah told Ruth, "Ask Clem what he named the pup."

Clem instantly threw in, "Boney!"

Ruth looked at the smiles on both faces looking at her, and they all three burst into laughter. "I guess that just fits!"

❖ ❖ ❖

Later that night as Jeremiah and Ruth were getting ready for bed, he knew he needed to talk to her.

"Here, let me brush your hair. You used to love for me to do that." Ruth handed him the brush without a word. "You've always had such beautiful, brown hair, Ruth. You still do. You're just as beautiful as the day we married."

"Oh, p'shaw! You know that's not so. Look at all these wrinkles and gray hair. My hands look like leather and so does my face."

"Ruth, I still see you like you were the day we got married. You seem tired and like somethin's on your mind. What's wrong, Ruth? You can tell me anythin'."

Ruth dropped her head a little but didn't say anything at first. Jeremiah continued brushing her hair. Finally she spoke, "I'm worried, Jeremiah. The taxes are due soon, and I'm afraid we just don't have it this time. Do we?"

"No, not yet, but I haven't given up hope. God's still in control of our lives and the taxes." He held his hand up, "I'm not preachin', Ruth. Just statin' a fact."

"I know, Jeremiah. I'm sorry I've been so cross lately. I've got so much to do that I'm wearin' down. I'm so tired all the time. Since we lost Moriah, I haven't been able to keep up with all the work on the farm and the work for other people, like the weavin' and sewin'. I don't resent it. I just can't seem to get it all done. I haven't brought in enough money to help with the taxes this year. What will we do?"

"Oh, that reminds me. We got a letter from Bess and Sam up in Virginia, the friends of Moriah's, and they said they was so sorry about Moriah. They also sent a dollar gold piece to Clem. That'll help a little, I reckon. It was sure nice of them. They probably can't really afford to do that. But you know, God directs folks to do things like that sometimes."

"It was nice of them, but it really won't help a lot. I just can't seem to get all this off my mind. The crops aren't doin' well this year either. My garden's dryin' up for lack of rain and from the heat. What'll we eat this winter, Jeremiah, if my garden doesn't produce? I've tried totin' water to it, but I can't hold out long enough to do much good. We need rain bad."

"Has God ever let us starve or even done without what we really needed, Ruth? Will He ever?"

"N-no, but it's scarey not knowin'. I know that's where faith comes in, and I usually have faith, but this time seems different. When I get this tired, it's hard to keep lookin' up."

"I know, Ruth. I don't mean to make you feel bad for not trustin'. My faith falls down a lot. You just don't always know it. Times are hard and gettin' harder, but somehow—somehow, we gotta keep faith in God. Come on, let's go to bed. A good night's sleep will help." They snuggled close in bed with Jeremiah's strong arms around Ruth and her head on his shoulder. Ruth always felt safe and protected in his arms. They lay there quietly listening to the tree frogs making noise and their own hearts beating.

Suddenly, Jeremiah sat up in bed and sniffed. "Do you smell smoke, Ruth?" He threw back the covers, jumped from bed, and ran to the open window. "Oh, Lord, no. The barn's on fire! Ruth, get Clem! Hurry!" Jeremiah grabbed his pants and pulled them on while he ran, hopping on one foot and then the other.

He ran to the barn barefoot and with no shirt, just suspenders holding up his pants. He threw open the barn door and saw that the fire was pretty far gone, but he felt he could get their two horses out if he hurried. The horses were frightened and didn't want to come with him, but he kept coaxing until he got Jackrabbit outside. Ruth and Clem met him there.

"Clem, jump on Jackrabbit and ride hard to Abe Fortham's place and tell him we need help. They'll pass word along to others. You know the way, don't you?"

"Yessir!" Clem called, already on his way, scooping Boney up in his arms.

"Ruth, get a bucket and use what little water we've got to try to douse what you can of the fire. I'm goin' back in to see if I can get Bitteroot."

"Be careful, Jeremiah! Please!"

When he entered the barn again, he noticed the roof was on fire and the area around Bitteroot was fully inflamed. He wasn't going to be able to save him! He turned to the cow stall and the same was true there. *I'm gonna lose'em both*, he thought. But he was determined to try. He kept trying to get close to Bitteroot's stall, but the flames held him back. The hairs on his arms and face, including his eyebrows, were singed off. He had to fall back. There was no hope! He stumbled outside before the smoke got to him.

Ruth threw the bucket aside and ran to Jeremiah. "Are you alright? Are you hurt?"

"I'm alright. Few singed hairs. I can't get Bitteroot or the cow. We're gonna lose'em." A spasm of coughing followed. "We're gonna lose the barn and everythin' in it, Ruth. This is a hard blow."

"How could this have happened?"

"I don't know. There was no lightnin'. We'll probably never know. Oh, Ruth, what'll we do now?"

Ruth didn't say it, but she thought how much he sounded like she had earlier. Aloud, she said, "Let's try to keep faith. God's still here, Jeremiah."

Jeremiah glanced up at her from the ground and replied, "Now I know how you feel. It is hard to keep lookin' up when bad things happen. But we'll make it. We have to."

By the time several neighbors arrived, the barn was engulfed in flames and a total loss. They all made a half-hearted attempt to save some things but could do no real good. They all knew how Jeremiah and Ruth felt because it could easily happen to them. They promised their help in raising a new barn when he was ready. As they rode away, Jeremiah called out, "Thanks to all of you for tryin' to help. It means a lot. Thank you."

❖ ❖ ❖

The next morning dawn found Jeremiah picking through the rubble left of the barn trying to salvage anything he could. He found a few iron implements that were alright. When Ruth woke up and discovered him gone, she went to the window and watched him as he stood and just stared at the remains of the barn. She could guess the feelings of hopelessness, loss, and heartache he was experiencing. Silent tears slid down her cheeks. Another loss. Another hurdle to be overcome. How many more would there be? How long could they hold on?

❖ ❖ ❖

The following week Jeremiah was out in the cotton field working when he noticed a thunderstorm blowing up. The clouds were moving fast and the lightning and thunder began. He began to make his way to the house since the barn had not been rebuilt yet. The wind was blowing hard, and he had a difficult time walking against it. Before he could get inside, the rain began to come down in sheets so hard he could barely see the house. When he reached the porch, Ruth and Clem met him. They knew how quickly bad weather could come and how devastating it could be in south Georgia. Twisters could come out of nowhere. They all watched the weather from the porch as hail began to rain down. The hail was almost as large as a small fist! It was as if a giant was pouring huge buckets of hail down on the fields.

Jeremiah's first thought was, *Everythin' is gonna be destroyed! If that happens, we're done for. Oh, God, save the crops. Watch over and protect us.* The hail was over in ten minutes. The rain continued for a while and the wind slowly abated. Jeremiah, Ruth and Clem in unison stepped off the porch to go have a look at the crops. As they got closer, Jeremiah began to run but came to a sudden halt. The view before his eyes was devastation. All the crops appeared to be destroyed!

Jeremiah fell to his knees and began to cry. Ruth and Clem knelt beside him with arms around him. "Oh, Ruth, what do we do now? Everythin'—is gone. All the work. Everythin' we had was tied up in these crops. We got nothin' left!"

"We've got each other and the Lord. We can start over. We can still work. Let's go back to the house, Jeremiah." She had to coax him up off his knees and back to the house. Clem, with Boney at his heels, followed them in.

❖ ❖ ❖

Later that night as Ruth slept, Jeremiah slouched in his chair in the parlor, looking and feeling more forlorn than he ever had in his life. He felt defeated. The crops were destroyed. There was no other way to raise the tax money in time. He fell to his knees in front of the chair.

"Oh, Lord God, I'm done in. I don't know what else to do. Lord, You know we need the tax money and we have no way to get it. Lord, please show me what to do. Ruth and me—we've both worked as hard as we can. We've done our best. What more can I do?" Tears began to stream down his face when he thought about how hard Ruth had had to work for these years. He had always wanted better for her, but she had always said she wouldn't have it any other way. "Lord, show us a way. Show us what to do. Oh, Lord, the only thing left is to sell out to the carpetbaggers and leave—maybe go west. Try to start over. If that's Your will for us, Lord, we'll do it no matter how hard it is." He knelt quietly for some time, listening for the Lord to speak.

Ruth had come into the parlor just before he finished his prayer. She also waited. When Jeremiah rose, she softly called his name.

"Oh, you startled me, Ruth. I hope I didn't wake you. I was just thinkin' and prayin'."

"I heard."

"Did you hear it all?"

"Most of it."

"Let's sit down, Ruth. We need to talk." After they were seated, he continued, "Ruth, things look bad for us. I don't need to tell you all the things we've lost in so short a time. It's as if the Lord is sayin' somethin' to us that I can't quite make out, but I know He'll show us His will in His time. He also expects us to do our part. I've thought and thought, and the only things I've come up with—and you aren't goin' to like it—is to try to sell some things we own, like furniture, the sideboard, the dinin' room table and chairs. Anythin' of value." He stopped when he saw the pained look on Ruth's face.

She dropped her gaze and was quiet for a few moments before she replied softly and with a lump in her throat, "I think that's a good idea, Jeremiah. The Lord expects us to be practical. Havin' the tax money and food in our stomachs is more important than some furniture. Why don't you go into town tomorrow and see what you can get for some of our things?"

"Why, Ruth, that's a good idea! I will. Maybe it will give us enough money to pay the taxes this year." Taking her hand, he whispered, "Thank you, Ruth. I know this is hard for you. I love you, woman."

"And I love you, Jeremiah." What she couldn't and wouldn't say to him was just how hard it would be to let her mother's precious furniture go. The only thing she hated worse was what he had mentioned in the last part of his prayer about leaving and moving west.

❖ ❖ ❖

The next day Jeremiah jumped off Jackrabbit's back, fuming and stomping around, before the horse had completely stopped. He had never been so angry. He was mumbling under his breath. A barefoot Clem and a growing Boney walked up and Clem asked, "What's wrong, G'amps?"

"Don't ask! I don't think I've ever been angrier or more insulted in my life. Do you know what that scum said to me?" Then he realized he didn't need to be taking out his anger on Clem. "I'm sorry, son. I'm just upset. Could you give Jackrabbit a good brushin' and some feed and water? She's been rode hard comin' back. I need to talk to your G'amma. Is she in the house?'

"Yessir, I think so." Clem's green eyes were big and round. He'd never seen G'amps like that before. He slowly led Jackrabbit away as he watched Jeremiah stomp into the house.

"Ruth, where are you?"

"In the kitchen, Jeremiah."

As he entered the kitchen, he practically yelled, "Ruth, you won't believe what's happened to me in town. None of the merchants will buy our furniture. They say they just don't have the cash either. That I can understand. But when I approached that sorry, no account, squirrely-eyed, little scalawag, Jonas Williams—." Ruth looked shocked and stopped what she was doing to stare at Jeremiah. "I know, Ruth, I said I'd never do business with him, but I was desperate. We're gonna lose our place if we don't have that unfair tax money. Well, I asked him first for an extension on payin' the taxes. You know what he said to me, whinin' like the no-account he is, 'Now, now, Jeremiah, you know I can't do that. I can't start doin' that for ever'body who comes in here askin', now can I?' Ruth, I swear I could've strangled him."

"Jeremiah, calm down. It won't help any to get so mad."

"I just can't take it, Ruth! Then I really humbled myself. I asked him if he would be willin' to buy our furniture. I know, I can't believe I asked either. He reminded me he had a fine house and fine furniture now. He didn't need our cast-offs. That I should just go on along, and don't forget to pay the taxes on time. Ruth, my blood boiled. I just stood there clenchin' my fists 'cause I was achin' to take him on. I'm sorry, Ruth. I let us down. I couldn't sell the furniture or anythin' we have." Once he had it all spewed out, he just slid down into a chair like the air had gone out of him. He put his head down on the table.

"Jeremiah," Ruth spoke softly as she stroked his hair. You did your best. You didn't let us down. God has other plans, that's all."

"Ruth, the only thing left is for us to sell our place if we can find a buyer and move. Try to start over. Maybe it's what God wants us to do. To be willin' to let go of everythin' we own and let Him lead us one step at a time. Can you do that, Ruth? Can you leave everythin' we've always known?"

"I guess we'll have to, Jeremiah, no matter how hard it is."

CHAPTER 11

Ruth noticed that Jeremiah had been rather quiet all day, keeping to himself while he worked. He had stayed close to the house most of the day except for the necessary chores outside. The weather certainly had not kept him inside because it was a clear, hot August day. The heat had never stopped Jeremiah before. She knew what was on his mind—the taxes. It was weighing heavy on his heart and mind. She didn't know what to do but pray for him and the situation. She did that as she moved about the kitchen preparing their supper, which consisted of smoked venison, cabbage, squash, turnip greens, cornbread, milk, tea, and plum pudding. As Ruth worked, she wondered to herself why she always cooked so much when there were only the three of them now. Of course, a working man ate a lot and growing boys like Clem could eat a person out of house and home!

Ruth went to the porch to call Jeremiah and Clem to supper, but she stopped to watch him as he made bullets, usually a chore he took care of on bad weather days or cold winter nights. He was showing Clem how to do the necessary job. Jeremiah melted pieces of lead in a big spoon held over a fire, then poured it carefully into the bullet-mold. He waited a minute or two before opening the mold, and when he did a new bullet fell out. He explained to Clem that the bullet right out of the mold would be too hot to touch, so they left it where it fell. When he had made all of his lead into bullets, he took his knife and scraped off the little bump created by the hole in the mold. He saved all the tiny pieces for use later. He let Clem drop all the new bullets into his pouch.

Ruth liked to watch her men work together. Jeremiah was so patient with Clem, showing him everything he would need to know. At some point, he would let Clem make the bullets himself, so he would really know how. There were many jobs on the farm Jeremiah was teaching Clem to do. She knew too that Jeremiah was preparing Clem for the future when he would be the man of the family as they grew older.

"Supper's ready! Come and get it!" Ruth yelled at them.

They both looked up, and Clem answered, jumping up, "Yes, ma'am!" He was always eager to eat. And, of course, Boney came running because he knew he'd get the leftovers.

Following grace, the three ate quietly for a while. Clem was not one to chatter like some children. He was quiet a great deal. Jeremiah was too quiet. Finally, after the plum pudding, he pushed his chair back and cleared his throat. "Ruth, Clem, I've reached a decision. I guess we all knew it was comin'. We don't have the tax money this year. We've tried everythin' we know to do. You know we've lost the crops this year, the barn, a horse and the cow. Nobody wants to buy our furniture. The only thing left is to leave here and start over somewhere—maybe Texas. There's lots of land there for the takin', I hear."

Ruth looked away and just sat staring at nothing while Clem looked from one to the other of them, trying to understand. "There are some things we need to talk about so we all understand what we're in for. This has been a very hard decision. My parents and their parents before'em farmed here. It's gonna be hard to give it up—especially to strangers, but we've no choice. I hear that in Mississippi the government has taken and then sold millions of acres of land because good, honest folks like us couldn't pay the taxes. The very thought of it makes my heart heavy. I know God is still in control, and I hope you know I've prayed and prayed about this. It seems God wants us to give up everythin' and move on. It's gonna be a time of testin' for all of us. There'll be hardships on the trip west. There'll be hardships when we get there. We won't be able to live in the way we're used to. We may have to do without some things at least for a while. Money will be scarce as hen's teeth, but together with God's help we can make it. We've seen it through other hard times." He paused and nobody said anything. Ruth was still looking at some distant point on the floor. "Surely, somebody has somethin' to say. Ruth, what are you thinkin'?"

Ruth waited for another minute before she spoke. "I—I don't know what to say. I've been afraid of this since I heard you prayin' that night. My heart—breaks with the thought of leavin'. Is there no other way, Jeremiah? Our children are buried here. We can't just—." She suddenly remembered Clem and didn't know how he would handle leaving his Ma's grave. He still sat quietly.

"Ruth, believe me, I have thought and thought, prayed and prayed. There is no other way that I can see or that the Lord has shown me. Do you know any other way?"

Ruth's head dropped and tears ran down her cheeks. She dabbed at them with the corner of her apron. "No-no, Jeremiah. I'm sorry. It's just so hard. How can we leave—everythin'? Our home, our land, our children, our household things. How can we leave our life?"

"We won't be leavin' our life, Ruth. Jesus is our life. He'll go before us and with us every step of the way. Maybe He's testin' us again to see how strong we can become with His help. We can do it, Ruth. Look at it as startin' a new life. We've done things just as hard before." Ruth started to shake her head. "Yes, we have, Ruth. We've lost all of our children. That was harder. These are only things. We have each other and Clem. We'll be alright. Clem, what do you think?"

Clem passed his hand across his forehead before he spoke. "I—I don't know. I don't want to leave. I love it here. Ma's buried here, but like you told me she's not really here. That's just her body out in that grave. She's really in heaven with Jesus and my Pa. Will they know where to find us in Texas?"

Jeremiah and Ruth were both shedding tears as they listened to Clem. "Oh, yes, son, they'll know exactly where we are! Ruth?"

"It seems I'm out-numbered and out-faithed. What do we need to do first, Jeremiah?"

Jeremiah reached for her hand and kissed it. "I'm sorry this has happened to us, but thank you, Ruth, for trustin'. Let's try to make the best of this whole situation and not live in the pit of depression." Ruth agreed, but in her heart she had grave reservations.

"The best time to leave is now, as soon as we can get things ready. Winter's not far off and it'll take some time to get where we're goin'. I'll go into town tomorrow to see what kind of deal I can get for some things we need. Maybe somebody will be willin' to do some tradin' for some things. We need to start goin' through things, sortin', throwin' away, givin' away, sellin' what we can, as quickly as we can so we can leave soon."

Ruth put her hands to her face and cried, "Slow down, Jeremiah! This makes my head spin. So much to do!"

❖ ❖ ❖

While Jeremiah was gone the next day, Ruth and Clem began the dreaded task of sorting what they needed and wanted to take, what they might be able to sell, and what they would give away. Ruth was overwhelmed but decided to take one room at a time and make piles or stacks for taking, selling or leaving. By midday the taking pile had grown far larger than the other two piles. She knew what Jeremiah would say: "Ruth, you know we can't take all that! You're gonna have to go through all of it again and leave some of that." He was right, but, oh, how she hated doin' this. To give up all her pretty things was just too much to ask! But she tried and by the time Jeremiah got home at dark, she and Clem had been through most of the household goods.

Just before dark they heard Jeremiah come up on the porch whistling. Ruth and Clem looked at each other and Ruth commented, "He's whistlin'. He must have good news!" They both met him at the door.

"Whoa! What's this? A welcomin' committee?"

"G'amma said it must be good news 'cause you was whistlin'."

Putting an arm around each of them, Jeremiah confirmed, "Well, yes and no. There is good news. Mr. Brownlee, the blacksmith, is tradin' us a horse and wagon, since we lost ours in the fire, in exchange for the sideboard and dinin' table and chairs. Said his wife would really like that." He looked at Ruth and waited for her reaction. She looked surprised first and then sad but didn't say anything. "It's better, Ruth, to let the things go to someone we know who will take care of them." She nodded once.

"What's the rest of the news, G'amps?"

"I was able to sell the farm but not for near as much as it's worth. I had to deal with carpetbaggers 'cause they're the only ones that have any money. I know, Ruth, but I had to. One of'em gave us $300 for it. He was the only one who would even talk to me, and, believe me, I talked to practically ever'body in town today."

"Oh, Jeremiah, I was so hopin' it would be more. Can we make it on that?"

"We'll have to, Ruth." When he saw her face, he hugged her and added, "We'll be alright. I promise. I'm still strong and not afraid of hard work. Also, Mr. Pike at the general store agreed to take some of our things to sell in the store. And he had a great idea. He says we ought to have a movin' sale one day here at the house and tell all the neighbors to come by and buy from us. He'd seen it done somewhere up North. So I put up signs in town for folks to come to our movin' sale day after tomorrow. Was that alright?"

"Jeremiah! How can we be ready by then?'

❖ ❖ ❖

Two days later the sideboard and dining table and chairs had been carted to Mr. Brownlee's house, and a horse and wagon, plus a piece of canvas he threw in, were at the Jakes' farm. Somehow Ruth, Clem and Jeremiah had gotten things ready for the moving sale which was then in progress. Ruth was thinking, *I can hardly stand to watch ever'body pick over my things I've collected all these years and some from my ma.* They had spread the goods throughout the house so people could see them, everything from kitchen pots and pans to linens ("But Jeremiah, we might need these things!" "We can always make more.") to clothes to foodstuffs that Ruth had preserved or dried ("But, Jeremiah—." "We can always grow more."). It was a hard day for all three of them, especially making conversation all day in reply to things like, "Now, that's pretty, but my ma used to make it with more lace." Ruth had to bite her tongue more than once. At the end of the day they had fifty dollars to add to their nest egg. They had really hoped for more, but folks around there didn't have any more money than Jeremiah and Ruth. Many times folks bought some little something just to help them out. Rev. Cameron, the pastor of their church, even came by and pressed a dollar into Ruth's hand just to help them out. They were grateful to everyone and to God for what came in.

The days following the sale were busy ones, trying to make final selections about what to take and what to give away, getting the wagon ready and finding a place for the necessities. Ruth soon learned how little she was going to be able to take. They were basically starting over, or as Jeremiah put it, God was showing them they didn't really need all those things to live anyway.

Jeremiah and Clem worked hard cutting and fitting hickory bows upright to the wagon box. Then they made a covering of canvas to go over the bows in such a way that it could be raised and lowered on the sides. Jeremiah commented, "Clem, this is the way my pa used to build a wagon. It'll still get us there."

Their neighbors and church friends threw them a farewell party at the church two days before they were to leave. They provided good cakes, pies and punch to eat and drink and many kind words and blessings, for the Jakes were well-loved folks in the community. Rev. Cameron stood at the end to say a few words.

"Attention, everyone! I just wanted to say a few words of farewell to Jeremiah, Ruth and Clem. We've loved these folks for a long time, and we'll all miss them, I'm sure. These are some of the finest folks I personally have ever known. They've always shown such love and faith to all of us. We wish them well and I'm asking you now to pray every day for them that their journey go well and that they prosper where they're going." There were several "Amens" and "Yessirs." "Let's drink one last toast to them and then let's pray." Following the toast, the Reverend prayed, "Heavenly Father, we come to you now lifting up Brother Jeremiah, Sister Ruth and Clem. We ask you to give them a safe trip. Watch over and protect them. We ask that Your blessing would be upon them as they start over in a new place. In Jesus' Name, Amen."

As the gathering broke up, almost everyone came by and shook their hands or patted them on the back with words like, "We'll be prayin' for you", "God watch over you all", "We love you", "Please write us and let us know how you are." Most of the women were crying, including Ruth. It was a sad time.

❖ ❖ ❖

Finally, the day of departure dawned, bright and cloudless in a late August sky. The wagon was packed with all they could safely carry. They had put two feather mattresses in the bottom of the wagon, one of which Jeremiah and Ruth would sleep on in the wagon while Clem would sleep on the other under the wagon. A trunk packed with clothes, linens, and Ruth's ma's handmade tablecloth she just couldn't leave behind was fitted into one end of the wagon bed. Another crate contained the necessary pans, cooking utensils and food. Jeremiah hung his gun, bullet pouch and powder horn on the wagon bow just inside the canvas where he could easily get to it.

When all preparation had been done and all was packed, Jeremiah and Ruth looked at one another solemnly. This was the only home they had known together for thirty-two years. Jeremiah had brought Ruth here after their wedding. It was hard to leave. They quietly walked through the house and looked in every room. Clem followed. Memories began to flood their minds of the laughter and antics of three small children, of the sicknesses they had brought them through, of good times and bad times, of laughter and tears, of skinned knees and learning to ride. So much to leave behind!

As they left the house for the last time, they still had not spoken. Without saying a word, they all walked to the family cemetery a short distance from the house under the large old magnolia tree. Ruth brushed the leaves and dirt off each of the three tombstones for the last time, wondering to herself who would take care of the graves of her children when she was gone. She read each inscription which had been impressed in her memory long ago. "Lydia Anabelle Jakes, William Jeremiah Jakes, Moriah Lilly Jakes Brown." Her throat was so tight she could barely speak. Not looking at anyone, she said, "Leavin' sure is hard."

It was quiet for a few moments as each one had his own thoughts. Finally, Jeremiah spoke, "Yes, Ruth. It's harder than I thought it would be."

They watched as Clem sat down next to his Ma's grave. Ruth was thinking, *Oh, how, I've dreaded this moment for Clem.* Clem laid his hand on Moriah's grave and bowed his head to pray. "Lord, watch over us as we move west. Keep us safe. Give us food and water when we need it. We love You and thank You. And, Lord, tell my Ma and my Pa where I'll be and take care of them till I get to heaven. Amen."

Jeremiah and Ruth were both weeping when he finished. No other prayers were needed. Simply and with child-like faith, Clem had said it all.

Jeremiah and Ruth climbed up on the seat of the wagon while Clem and Boney climbed in the back so he could look out of the hole left in the canvas where it was gathered. Jeremiah urged the horses on, and as they pulled away Ruth looked back one last time with tears in her gray eyes. Clem, with an arm around Boney, looked back until the house was out of sight.

CHAPTER 12

Once they were on the road, Jeremiah, Ruth, Clem and even Boney were quiet with their own thoughts for the first few hours. Jeremiah prayed; Ruth was sad and numb; Clem was feeling a little insecure. Finally, Jeremiah couldn't take it any longer and broke the silence, "We sure are a quiet bunch of folks. Cat got ever'body's tongue?" Nobody said anything. "Well, I tell you. I've been doin' a lot of prayin' and thinkin'. We've got to look at all this different if we're gonna make it now. I believe God wants us to see this as an adventure, a time to learn some new things and grow, and ever'body knows growin' usually ain't easy. But we can either make this movin' easy or we can make it miserable. I vote for makin' it easy by bein' happy and lookin' forward to seein' new lands and people. How do you vote, Clem?"

Clem passed his hand across his forehead and then said, "I vote with you, G'amps." He wasn't sure what he had just voted for, but he trusted G'amps a lot.

"Ruth, how do you vote?" He cast a sideways glance at her, knowing she held the key to the whole trip. If she perked up and tried to make things happy for them, it would make the trip a whole lot more pleasant. He could see written over her face the turmoil going on inside her. He knew it was hard for her because it was for him, too. Help her, Lord, help her to win, he prayed silently.

"I guess I'm out-voted again. I'll try. That's all I can promise, Jeremiah."

He reached over and took her hand, saying, "That's the way, Ruth! Thank you!" *And thank you, Lord,* he prayed. "I think we oughta sing. All of us. Let's see what we can do with this one." He started to sing:

>A penny for a spool of thread,
>Another for a needle,
>That's the way the money goes.
>Pop! goes the weasel!

All around the cobbler's bench,
The monkey chased the weasel,
Then the cobbler kissed his wife—
Pop! goes the weasel!

As they rode along they made up new verses to try to top one another. They laughed which helped them loosen up. Even Ruth finally joined in.

Oh, you Buffalo gals,
Aren't you comin' out tonight,
Aren't you comin' out tonight,
Aren't you comin' out tonight,
Oh, you Buffalo gals,
Aren't you comin' out tonight,
To dance by the light of the moon?

Once they had crossed the Flint River and were headed toward the Chattahoochee River which divided Georgia and Alabama, the knowledge that this was really happening set in. They were leaving everything behind and heading into the unknown. It seemed the trip was marked by rivers. Jeremiah had asked around and found out there were several rivers to be crossed before they got to Texas. He didn't really know how many. Their first experience of crossing a major river was the Chattahoochee. Jeremiah drove their wagon onto a raft provided for travelers made of logs tied together which had a guide rope attached to a longer rope stretched from one side of the river to the other. It was a strange feeling for all of them when they began to rock and sway in the river, but they crossed safely.

As they continued to travel across Alabama, the late August days were hot and humid and hazy. Jeremiah rolled the canvas up on each side of the wagon to let air pass through, especially at night, to try to keep as cool as they could. Sometimes Clem and Boney rode in the wagon, but often they walked beside it for exercise.

As day drew to a close, Jeremiah decided they would camp next to a creek for the night. He tied the two horses to the back of the wagon near their feed box and gave them some corn to eat. While Jeremiah and Clem gathered twigs and started a fire, Ruth began to make preparations for supper. Once the fire was going, Clem went to the creek for water. Ruth mixed cornmeal, salt and water and patted it into small cakes to be fried in the iron spider, which was nothing more than a large frying pan with short legs which could be set over the fire. She sliced salt pork, also to be fried, and then put coffee into the pot and put that in the coals. This would be supper. Ruth got out their three tin plates and cups, along with the forks and knives.

When Jeremiah returned thanks, they ate heartily, even though the menu was limited. There was not much conversation as would be common for people who spent all day every day together. The quiet was good too because they could listen to the sounds of day changing to night, such as a chorus of tree frogs and crickets blended with the throaty bass of the bullfrogs down at the creek. Clem and Boney tried to catch lightning bugs as they began to appear. It was fun to catch one in his hand and watch the glow between his fingers, even though it left his hands smelling bad. Jeremiah had showed him how to do it.

"Ruth, how would you feel about stoppin' here for a couple of days? Maybe I could do a little huntin' to round up some meat."

"Whatever you say, Jeremiah. It would be nice not to have to sit on that hard wagon seat for a day."

"That's what we'll do then. That sound good to you, Clem?"

"Sure, G'amps."

"Why don't we read Scripture and pray right now before we clean up?" All three settled into a more comfortable position as Jeremiah pulled out of the wagon the Jakes' family Bible. He opened it and began to read, " 'Now the Lord had said unto Abram, Get thee out of thy country, and from thy kindred, and from thy father's house, unto a land that I will shew thee.' That was Genesis 12:1. And then in Genesis 15:1, God said, 'After these things the word of the Lord came unto Abram in a vision, saying, Fear not Abram: I am thy shield, and thy exceeding great reward.' I know we're not in the same situation Abram was in, but it gives me hope and help when I read this. The Lord is with us every bit as much as He was with Abram. He knows where we are and where we're goin', which is more than I know, at least where we're goin'." Jeremiah gave a short laugh. "Our part is to trust Him to show us the way and take care of our needs as we go. And I believe He is. Let's pray." Jeremiah led in prayer for a safe journey and for the Lord to continue to lead them to where He wanted them to be.

Following the prayer, they all chipped in and cleaned up after supper, washing the cooking utensils in the creek. They bedded down for the night then, with Jeremiah and Ruth on one mattress in the wagon with the canvas rolled up and Clem under the wagon on the other mattress with Boney curled up beside him.

The next morning Jeremiah and Ruth were up at dawn doing the necessary chores. Jeremiah fed the horses while Ruth began to get breakfast consisting of bacon, pancakes and coffee. Clem woke up to the aroma of bacon frying. He jumped up to help, and Ruth sent him to the creek for water. Following breakfast, once again they read Scripture and prayed together.

On this particular day Jeremiah was going hunting for meat and decided to take Clem with him. This was something he needed to learn. Jeremiah took his powder horn, bullet pouch, gun and a sharp hatchet. They stayed within shouting distance of Ruth and were able to flush out several quail and finally a large rabbit. Clem was so excited because Jeremiah had let him shoot the rabbit. He couldn't have been happier if it had been a deer! These were times when Jeremiah would teach Clem about God's creatures and His world that He created. Jeremiah began to teach him how to skin a rabbit, which they discovered would take several lessons! At least, they would have fresh meat for a couple of days and Clem would have a fur cap next winter.

Thus would their days and nights be for many weeks to come. The variations would be rivers to cross, storms and rain, heat and humidity, getting stuck in the mud, hunting for meat, and, for Clem, learning to do many jobs on the trail.

Before long they crossed the Alabama River and learned from some folks they met on the trail that another river was ahead called the Tombigbee River. After they crossed that river, Ruth commented one day, "Jeremiah, it sure has been dry and hot. We need rain bad. I see some clouds off over yonder. You think it'll rain?"

"I don't know, Ruth. Only the good Lord knows." They both prayed silently for rain, and they watched the clouds. The clouds began to gather into thunderheads and move up on the horizon. Suddenly the wind began to whip the dirt and dust into dust swirls around the wagon, depositing a layer of dust over the contents of the wagon. Clem and Boney hopped up into the wagon bed and let down the canvas sides, thinking it was going to rain. The wind grew stronger and jerked Ruth's bonnet off the back of her head.

"Looks like we may get a thunderstorm, Jeremiah."

"I don't think so, Ruth. I think the wind's got in it and will blow it away." Unfortunately, that's what happened. There was no rain that day or for many days after that.

❖ ❖ ❖

As they passed into Mississippi, they began to see more homesteads and figured there must be a fair-sized town close by. They stopped at a farm to find out all they could about what was ahead for them. The farmer and his wife, Henry and Rebekah Jefferson, were friendly and invited them for supper and to spend the night. What a joy it was to eat at a real table and sleep in a real bed! At breakfast the next morning, Henry, who was a large, jovial man with almost leathery skin from working in the sun, gave them the information they needed.

"If I was ya'll, I'd stop in Hattiesburg for supplies. Thar's a good general store thar. Tell Pete I told ya'll to stop. He'll treat ya'll right. It might be good to trade them horses now, too, 'cause yore's are worn out. Where'd ya'll say ya'll was comin' from?" When he learned it was south Georgia, he let out a low whistle. "Them horses've got to be plumb tuckered out! Go see Charlie at the livery stable in town. Maybe he'll give ya'll an even trade for two fresh horses. Yore's'll be alright after a good rest."

"We can't thank you folks enough for your kindness to us, Henry, Mrs. Jefferson. How many more rivers before we reach Texas?" Jeremiah queried.

"The next one is the Pearl River. Not too big. But I heer tell they've had a passel of rain lately, so it's likely to be muddy as all git out. Take ya time and ya'll kin make it. I'd head for Natchez on the Mississip' River after that. 'Course ever'body knows the Mississip' is big, but there's a regular furry to take you across. Ya'll won't have no trouble thar, and hit shor' is a site to see. I ain't been beyond the Mississip' myself, so I can't tell ya'll anythin' past it. But ya'll kin ask folks thar to help."

After breakfast, the Jeffersons helped them to repack their wagon to accommodate the extra food and a couple of extra blankets they gave them. Jeremiah grasped Henry's hand and gave him a hearty thanks for all his help. Ruth hugged Rebekah and thanked her three times for the help they had been.

Once again they were on the trail west, wondering what they would see and experience ahead. A few days later they rolled into Hattiesburg to get supplies and hopefully fresh horses. Jeremiah let Ruth off at the general store in the center of town while he and Clem went on to the livery to talk to Charlie about the horses. Ruth felt a little funny going in by herself, but she squared her shoulders and went in. Like most general stores, there was a main room with a wood stove in the middle and two or three chairs where menfolk gathered from time to time to sit by the fire to spin yarns and tell tall tales. Shelves lined the side walls with quite a display of all kinds of goods. There was a counter that ran down one side. There were colorful calico and prints, barrels of nails and crackers, sacks of salt and white sugar, big wooden pails of candy, saws, plows, ax heads, all kinds of knives, boots, shoes. Ruth tried to think what she really needed. She decided on salt pork, salt, flour, cornmeal, and coffee. She had Pete, the owner, weigh out everything and get it ready. She told him she was waiting on her husband to come back and he would pay. She continued to wander around looking at the pretty calico and wishing she could get some other things, but money was hard to come by.

Finally, Jeremiah and Clem came into the store, paid the owner, and they went out together. When Ruth saw the horses, she drew in a breath. "Jeremiah! How much did you pay the man for these beautiful horses?" One of the horses was well-brushed and shinning black while the other was an off-white mare with black markings. They made a distinctive pair.

"Just traded the horses we had and one other little thing."

"What was the other little thing, Jeremiah?"

"Well, I told him I would build him a new corncrib out at his place." He raised his hand when she started to protest. "It won't take but a couple of days with Clem's help, and they are fine horses, Ruth. And he said we could stay at his place in the meantime. Not so bad a deal. We'll need these horses when we get to Texas."

Jeremiah hitched up the new horses and drove the wagon out to Charlie's sprawling farm. Once again they were able to enjoy a house and delicious, home-cooked meals, even though they slept in their own wagon at night. True to his word plus one more day, Jeremiah and Clem finished the corncrib, and once again they were on the road. Charlie's wife had also given them some fried apple pies, a little white sugar and corn meal which they really appreciated. Jeremiah reminded Ruth after they left how the Lord was looking after them. She had to agree.

As they approached the area of the Pearl River, it was obvious how it had rained in the valley. The river was swollen somewhat and the land surrounding the river was extremely muddy. The wagon immediately got stuck as they tried to approach the river. Jeremiah and Clem spent the better part of half a day getting the wagon out of the mud. They put their shoulders to the task, rocking the wagon back and forth, while Ruth took the reins and urged the horses on. Suddenly the wagon lurched up and out of the mud. They all shouted in happiness! Jeremiah and Clem were muddy from their heads down to their feet. They were so tired they decided to spend the night before crossing the Pearl. They pulled the wagon off to the side of the main trail but close enough to the water so they could take baths.

They made camp and had supper, consisting of corn pone and fried apple pies. Setting up camp had become a regular routine, and no one had to ask what needed to be done. Following supper, Jeremiah brought out the Bible as he did every night. "You know, I have to tell you what's on my heart tonight. God has been very good to us so far. He's provided people to meet our needs all along the way. We've had plenty of food and haven't done without a single thing we needed, have we? It makes me very grateful and humble before the Lord. There's a scripture that comes to mind—Matthew 6, starting at verse 25:

> Therefore I say unto you, Take no thought for your life, what ye shall eat, or what ye shall drink; nor yet for your body, what ye shall put on. Is not the life more than meat, and the body than raiment?
>
> Behold the fowls of the air: for they sow not, neither do they reap, nor gather into barns; yet your

heavenly Father feedeth them. Are ye not much better than they? .... And why take ye thought for raiment? Consider the lilies of the field, how they grow; they toil not, neither do they spin: And yet I say unto you, That even Solomon in all his glory was not arrayed like one of these.

Wherefore, if God so clothe the grass of the field, which today is, and tomorrow is cast into the oven, shall he not much more clothe you, O ye of little faith?

Therefore take no thought, saying, What shall we eat? or, What shall we drink? or, Wherewithal shall we be clothed? ...

For your heavenly Father knoweth that ye have need of all these things.

But seek ye first the kingdom of God, and his righteousness; and all these things shall be added unto you.

"Clem, do you understand what I just read?"

Clem passed his hand across his forehead and paused before he said, "Not all of it, G'amps. I know God gives us food and clothes and what we need. He—he takes care of us. Is that right?"

"Once again, Clem, you hit the nail on the head. Yes, He does all that and more and He expects us to put Him first in our lives."

CHAPTER 13

Clem woke with a start and quickly realized that Boney was licking him on the face with his sloppy wet tongue. He tried to hold him off and said, "Boney, boy, stop lickin' me, ya hear?" Then the sound of hard rain caught his attention and he realized it was pouring rain. Small rivulets of water ran under the wagon where he slept. He jumped up to try to save his mattress from getting too wet. He tried to roll it up and gather it in his arms, but then he realized he was on his knees under the wagon and had nowhere to go with the mattress. He couldn't stand up or even raise his head.

"Clem! Clem!" Ruth called from the wagon. "Get up here in the wagon before you catch your death of cold!"

"I'll help him, Ruth," Jeremiah responded. He jumped out of the wagon and rolled under it. He quickly saw the problem with the mattress. "Clem, hold Boney and climb up in the wagon as quick as you can. I'll take care of the mattress." Clem did what he was told, and in just a few minutes Jeremiah joined him.

"What'd you do with his mattress, Jeremiah?"

"Just never you mind. I took care of it. That's all that's important," Jeremiah answered, with a twinkle in his eye. He was always one to enjoy a little secret for fun. It poured rain, or "cats and dogs" according to Jeremiah, for the next two days. Jeremiah, Ruth, Clem and Boney did the best they could to make room for each other in the wagon and to devise new sleeping arrangements, especially for a wet dog who insisted on jumping from the wagon several times a day and returning with a shaking of his body from nose to tail which wet all of them! Ruth complained, "That dog has got to stay outside!" Jeremiah finally tied him under the wagon. Occasional thunderstorms raged around them with fierce lightning that seemed to split the sky and crashing thunder. There was no way to build a fire to cook meals, so they ate bits of cold food in the wagon. Everything was damp and miserable.

"Jeremiah, when do you think this rain is ever goin' to stop?"

"Why, Ruth, it was only a few days ago you was wishin' for rain. Well, here it is!"

"Jeremiah Jakes! Don't you make fun of me! We needed rain then; now we don't. Enough's enough!"

"You know back in south Georgia we used to say it was rainin' cats and dogs. I wonder what they say in Texas—rainin' mountain lions and panthers?"

"Well, Jeremiah, I'm glad you're in a good mood because I'm sick and tired of this rain and stayin' in this wagon and not havin' any hot food to eat!" Jeremiah was afraid Ruth was on the verge of tears, so his mind was thinking fast to come up with something for all of them to do to occupy their time.

"Ruth! Why don't you tell Clem some of the superstitions your ma and grandma had? He might find that interestin'. Do you remember, Clem, what superstitions are?"

Clem passed his hand across his forehead, trying to remember, and finally said, "Yessir! That's somethin' folks think is true but it ain't."

"Good boy! Now, Ruth, share some of the things your ma and her ma used to do for sick folks."

"Well, let's see." Jeremiah knew he had her mind off the weather, at least for a while. "My grandma used to say that 'like cures like'. Like she believed that the poison of tobacco kills poison in the body, and snake oil cures snake bite. I never believed most of the things she did like that and neither did my ma."

"What are some others, Ruth? I remember hearin' your ma talk about usin' onions to take up 'yaller jaundice'. Did you ever know anybody to be cured with all them things?"

"No, but Grandma sure believed 'em. I've seen her do this one. She used to take grease rendered from red earthworms and mix it with turpentine, asafeotida and red-onion juice to make liniment that she swore by. It sure did stink! And I remember her tellin' us about her grandma believin' that warts could be charmed off by tyin' an even number of knots in a horsehair or string and buryin' it, burnin' it or losin' it. Can you imagine how people believed such?"

"People can get real mixed up sometimes. The devil can help make 'em that way too. It would be hard to believe and trust Jesus and believe some of the things they did."

"Tell some more, G'amma!" Both adults laughed because Clem with Boney in his lap was sitting with his mouth hanging open taking it all in.

"Now remember, son, these things ain't true."

"I know, G'amps. I just like to listen to old stories."

"Well, Grandma used to believe that old women could cool fevers by the layin' on of hands or, even worse, that chills could be driven out by borin' a deep hole in the sunny side of an oak tree, blowin' your breath into it and pluggin' up the hole so the tree dies." They all laughed because they could see how ridiculous these superstitions were.

"Well, that's enough of that. Let's do somethin' more upliftin'. Jeremiah, why don't you lead us in singin' a hymn? You've got that nice baritone voice."

"Alright, let's sing 'Rock of Ages'."

> Rock of Ages, cleft for me, Let me hide myself in thee;
> Let the water and the blood, From thy wounded side which flowed,
> Be of sin the double cure, Save from wrath and make me pure.

"Sing another one, G'amps!" Clem's young eyes were lit up.

"Alright, let's sing 'Stand Up, Stand Up for Jesus' and you have to stand up when we sing the words 'stand up'. Come on, Ruth. It'll be fun."

> Stand up, stand up for Jesus, Ye soldiers of the cross;
> Lift high his royal banner, It must not suffer loss:
> From vict'ry unto vict'ry his army shall he lead,
> Till ev'ry foe is vanquished, And Christ is Lord indeed.

"Well, I don't know about you two, but I feel better. Why don't we rustle up somethin' for supper?" Ruth commented.

Jeremiah smiled at Ruth, reached over, took her hand and told her, "I love you, Ruth. Many women wouldn't go through this as well as you have."

"I love you, too, Jeremiah. That, and love for Jesus, is the only way I can go through this. By the way," she whispered in his ear, "where did you put that mattress?"

"Oh, there was just a piece of wood under the wagon that left some space for me to cram it in. That's all."

The next morning dawned bright and clear and still fairly warm for September. Jeremiah decided they needed to wait another day to let the river go down some and the mud to dry some. So they busied themselves with airing the mattresses, cleaning and rearranging the load in the wagon and hunting for some quail for a nice, hot supper which they all thoroughly enjoyed.

The following day at dawn they began crossing the Pearl River. Jeremiah had decided they would try to let the horses swim across pulling the wagon behind them. Ruth wasn't so sure.

"Jeremiah, what if the horses can't make it and we go down?"

"That's not goin' to happen, Ruth. If need be, I'll swim with them and lead them across if they get spooked."

"No, Jeremiah! That's too dangerous!"

"May not have a choice."

As the horses, which Clem had aptly named Blackie and Whitey, pulled them into the water, the wagon began to sway and float. Clem couldn't resist looking out the back of the wagon into the swollen river water, but as he did, Boney got a little too curious and jumped out! Clem cried out, "Boney! Come back!" And he started to jump in after him. Jeremiah called out, "Stop, Clem. Boney will be alright. Dogs can swim. He'll be fine. You just stay where you are. Do you hear me?"

"Yessir." But he looked and felt scared. *Please, Lord, let Boney be alright.*

It took some time for the horses to swim the river. At one point, Jeremiah thought he might have to swim and lead the horses on across, but they settled down and pulled them all up on the opposite shore safely. As they came out of the water when the wheels caught on solid ground, Jeremiah and Ruth said almost in unison, "Thank you, Lord!" And Boney was waiting safely for them on that side of the river.

❖ ❖ ❖

The trip from the Pearl River to the Mississippi was mostly routine, but they did meet quite a few people going in the same direction. When they arrived in Natchez, located on the Mississippi River, there was much activity in that waterfront town. Many boats were tied at the wharf as they began to look for the ferry to cross over the river. Jeremiah talked with several men on the wharf and learned where to find the ferry which was downriver a short distance. He found out in conversation that they would be crossing into Louisiana once they were over the river; then there would be two more rivers to cross before reaching Texas—the Red River and the Sabine River. He was told that he didn't have much further to go, for which they were all thoroughly grateful.

The trip across the Mississippi River was an adventure for all of them. Clem especially couldn't sit still. He wanted to be everywhere at once to see everything! This ferry was larger than the last one they were on, and it carried two wagons across at once. They had to pay to ride the ferry, but it was only ten cents. It took some time to cross as they once again swayed with the rhythm of the river. None of them had ever seen a river as wide or large as this one. Clem kept saying, "Look at that! Did you see that, G'amps? G'amma, can you believe how big this river is?" Then sometimes he would get quiet, moving his widened eyes in every direction trying to take it all in. He was fascinated by all the boats at the wharf and traveling up and down river. Once across the Mississippi, Clem and Boney sat in the back of the wagon watching the river until it was out of sight. He would talk about the Mississippi River and their crossing for many years to come.

Before long, they approached the Red River and crossed it uneventfully. After about another week on the trail, they reached the Sabine River which divided Louisiana and Texas. The crossing again was by ferry and uneventful, with the exception that they knew the end of their journey was near. This thought gave them excitement and also butterflies in their stomachs. They were uncertain how far to travel into Texas, what kind of land to expect, or where a good place would be to settle down. Jeremiah had talked to several men at the Sabine crossing and learned that east Texas was hot, humid, rainy and had bayous that sometimes had alligators and dense forests covering many, many acres. Jeremiah didn't want to tell Ruth and Clem too much of this to discourage them, but he also wasn't sure how much further they could all go. God would lead them to the right place to settle, and Jeremiah felt he'd know the place when they found it.

After they had traveled about fifty to seventy-five miles into east Texas, Jeremiah began to understand the description he had gotten of the land and climate, but they had been on the trail for seven weeks and were all exhausted and ready to stop somewhere, especially since it was October and winter was not far off. He began to observe more closely the surrounding area, looking for a stream and some relatively flat land to farm, all the while praying that God would direct them to the right spot. He also prayed that God would help him to see the possibilities in the land. Just as he was becoming discouraged, the wagon crossed a small stream, then cleared a grove of tall pines and came out into a fairly flat stretch of land. Jeremiah stopped the horses and stood up, scanning the area in every direction. He didn't see any houses or farms or smoke rising anywhere. This had to be it! He jumped down to the ground and began to walk and then run. When he was some distance from the wagon, he yelled. "Ruth, Clem, this is it! This is the perfect place for our farm. Plenty of land, a creek close by, and I think I see a grove—yes, a grove of pecan trees by that stream we passed through. Ruth, this is a good spot. We'd be hard put to find something better." He ran back to the wagon. "What do you think, Ruth? Could this be it?"

Ruth was standing in the wagon, also surveying the area. "It looks good, Jeremiah. Reckon we can grow cotton here?"

"I think so. I think we could grow a lot of crops here. What'd you say, Ruth? Clem?"

Ruth and Clem looked at each other and back at Jeremiah. "Jeremiah, I think this is goin' to be home. I like the looks of it. What about you, Clem? Do you like it?"

"Yes, ma'am. It shor' is pretty."

"I think we're here, Jeremiah."

"Of course, I need to ride the surroundin' area tomorrow and see if we're on somebody else's land or if we have neighbors. But this looks good." He kept repeating himself. "Come down from the wagon and let's thank God for leadin' us here safely." They all joined hands and Jeremiah prayed, "Thank You, Lord, for Your great provision of bringin' us here safely. We feel like this is the spot, Lord, where You've led us. Help everythin' to work out about the land. Take care of us here and help us to make it through the winter till we can plant next spring. We know that You will because You always are faithful. We praise You and thank You, in Jesus' Name. Amen."

"Ruth, let's pick a place for our house. How about pretty close to the creek and the trees to make it easier to fetch water and easier to haul trees to build the house? That'd also leave all this land for plantin'."

"I think that sounds good. What do we need to do first, Jeremiah?"

"Let's unload the wagon near the stream first." They drove the wagon closer to the bubbling, clear stream and the tall pine trees. After unloading the wagon, with Jeremiah on one side and Clem and Ruth on the other, they removed the wagon cover with bows and canvas and set it over their goods. They arranged their boxes and bundles and then made the beds under the cover since night was coming soon. Tomorrow was soon enough to start building the house. Clem cleared off grass in a spot outside the canvas for their supper fire and collected twigs and small branches while Jeremiah tethered the horses and brought water from the creek. After supper was cleared away, they sat by the fire for a while and listened to the night sounds which they observed sounded a lot like back home in south Georgia.

"Ruth, why don't you and Clem go on to bed? I'm goin' to sit by the fire a while longer." Clem was already asleep on his feet and Ruth was exhausted. They both quickly fell into deep sleep.

Jeremiah felt a strong need to be alone with his God. He walked a short distance away from camp and slipped to his knees in the brown grass of the field. He began to pray.

"Father, my heart is full of joy tonight that You've brought us here safely. Oh, God, You've blessed us greatly, more than we deserve." He raised his arms toward heaven as if trying to reach God. "Oh, praise You, God. Praise You! I thank You for givin' us the grace to come this far. Lord, give me the physical strength to start over. I'm not young anymore and I'm tired, but I know You can give me a physical touch. I ask You for that now, Lord. Touch Ruth physically, too. I know she's tired. Touch us all emotionally and help us not to look back so much as to look onward to what You have for us in this place. Help us take one day at a time and do only what we can in that day and not worry about the rest. Help us to live each day for You and let You work through us and in us to accomplish Your will."

Clem suddenly woke up at the sound of a hoot owl, and as he lay there he heard Jeremiah praying. He couldn't help but listen because he'd never heard his G'amps pray quite like that. He was crying and talking loud and then he heard his own name.

"Oh, God, I'm weak in faith. Help me keep the faith. I want to be faithful to You and Your ways. I want to be what You want me to be. I ask for Your mercy on this family. We've lost so many." He choked up with tears and wept openly to His God. "All of our children—gone. Lord, we don't understand why, but we trust You to do what's right. We know Lydia, William, Jeff and Moriah are all with You. We look forward to the day when we see them again. Now, Lord, we've lost our farm. Please have mercy! Help us to build a good life again right here. I don't ask You to take away all the problems, but just be with us and meet our needs through it all. I know it oftentimes takes sufferin' and hardship to grow us in faith. Help us remember that. Then, Lord, I pray for Clem. He's such a fine boy. Help him to grow strong in the faith and to become a man of faith as he grows older. He's already suffered more hardship than most children his age. Help him more than anythin' to come to know You personally and live his life for You in everythin' he does. Bless him, Lord, and keep him under Your wing. Thank You again, Lord, for all You've done for us and are goin' to do. Watch over us this night. In Jesus' Name, Amen."

Even as tired as he was, Clem lay awake quietly for a long time thinking about what he'd heard his G'amps praying for.

CHAPTER 14

The sun was beginning to warm the day before the Jakes' clan woke up on their first day in a new land. It was a beautiful October morning with a definite chill in the air early on, but it warmed up as the day went on. The oak and maple leaves were various colors of gold, orange, yellow and red, and many were already on the ground like a carpet. Jeremiah was the first to awaken, and as he did he noticed more of his surroundings than he had the night before. This is a beautiful place to settle, he thought. The tall, old pine trees, the creek, the pecan trees, and the glorious colors of fall. *This is all good, Lord. Thank you!*

"Wake up, Ruth and Clem! This is a glorious day! Let's get breakfast and then get busy. We've got a lot to do today. We've got a house to build!"

Clem jumped right up. He'd never been a boy to lag behind or be lazy. He worked hard. Ruth had a little more trouble dragging her older, tired body out from under the covers. Once they were all moving, breakfast was over quickly and plans were made for the house. Jeremiah first paced off the size of the house on the ground near the creek and the tall pine trees. Then he and Clem began the hard work of felling trees with an axe and carrying them to the house site. They were selective in choosing trees, so they wouldn't ruin their forest. Ruth helped carry the smaller logs. By noon, they had enough logs for the house when they stopped to eat.

As they were taking their noon break to eat, Ruth asked Jeremiah, "Did you see the beautiful, old cypress tree hangin' full of moss on the other side of the creek? I've always loved them."

"Yes, I did. When I was a child, I used to think they were really old trees because they had long, flowin' beards," Jeremiah snorted. "But, you know, cypress trees are ideal for a young boy to build a tree house in." He looked over at Clem, who perked up considerably as the thought sunk in.

"Really, G'amps! Will you help me build one?"

"Of course, I will, but first we have to build us a house and then a stable for the horses and then we'll work on you a tree house."

"Thanks, G'amps!"

"I'll tell you somethin' else, Clem," with a glance at Ruth. "I shor' do look forward to some fried catfish and pecan pies, don't you?"

"Yessir!"

Ruth smiled. "They will be good, won't they?"

"My mouth's already waterin'. But first we gotta build us a house. Come on, Clem. Let me show you how my daddy built a house without nails."

Jeremiah first built the foundation by half-burying four logs in a square with the ends notched and overlapped at the corners. He continued notching logs and with Ruth and Clem helping they raised the four walls slowly. By the time the sun was going down, the walls were up and a skeleton roof was on. They would still have to sleep in the tent that night, but the next day they'd move into the house. Following a supper of stewed jack rabbit with flour dumplings and gravy, they sat around the fire just inside the tent because the nights were getting cooler. Clem was exhausted and crawled into bed soon after eating. Jeremiah and Ruth sat by the fire talking for a while.

"It won't be a fine house like we had in Georgia, Ruth, but it'll keep us warm and dry. I wish it could be more for you, but we can add to it in time."

Ruth was very tired also but managed to say, "Jeremiah, it'll be a fine house when we're through. It's startin' over, but we'll be alright. This is all another test from the Lord, I think, to see how strong we are, or really how strong we can become, when we let Him take control and rest in Him. This family is made of strong stock, you know."

Jeremiah reached over, took her hand and kissed it. "You are the finest, strongest lady I've ever known. I love you with all my heart, Ruth. Where would I be without you? You mean more to me than I can tell you. My heart overflows with love for you, as much as when we married. Ruth, are you blushin'?"

"Oh, Jeremiah, you haven't said things like that in a long time! It makes me feel young again. I love you with all my heart, too, and always will." They sat companionably for a while holding hands. Jeremiah broke the silence.

"Did you notice how hard Clem worked today? He's growin' stronger every day. He's goin' to be a powerful man one day, Ruth."

"I noticed. I'm proud of him. Have you noticed lately that he seems to be thinkin' a little faster than he used to? I think he's goin' to be a fine man, too. I wish Moriah and Jeff were here to see him. They'd be so proud." She brushed away a tear with her apron. Jeremiah reached over and gave Ruth a big kiss and pulled her to her feet. "Come on, wife, let's get to bed. Morning comes early when you're buildin' a house."

❖ ❖ ❖

The next morning Jeremiah and Clem tied the canvas down to the roof skeleton until they could put on a good roof, then he cut square holes on each side of the house for windows and made shutters to keep out the cold. They then built a door and hung it with leather straps since they had no hinges.

While the men worked outside, Ruth worked inside sweeping wood chips and debris from the dirt floor. She walked on it as much as she could to make it hard. She dragged in the mattresses and made both beds on the floor. That was all the furniture they had for now, but Jeremiah would build some when he had time. She dug through her bundles and came up with four bent nails she had saved. She got Jeremiah to straighten them and drive them in the wall on each side of the windows. She ran a string from one to the other to hang her curtains on. She rambled through her things again and found her two pairs of white, lace-trimmed curtains and her iron, which she heated in the campfire, to iron her curtains and hang them. She stood back and surveyed her work. Not too bad. She could live with it, and it would be better when it had a floor and a roof.

For the next several days Jeremiah and Clem worked very hard to split logs into slabs to be used for the roof. It was very time-consuming work. They were finally able to remove the canvas and peg the slabs to the roof skeleton, overlapping them to keep the rain out. After this job was completed, they took the wagon to the creek and began picking up rocks for the fireplace. This was perhaps the hardest task they had, but after several days of back-breaking work they had enough rocks at the house. On the end of the house opposite the door, Jeremiah laid rocks in a box shape with the wall as one of the sides, smearing the clay mixed with water that Ruth stirred up for him between the rocks. This was another long, arduous job, but it finally reached the point of narrowing for the chimney.

Once the rocks were in place, Jeremiah cut through the logs inside the house for the fireplace, pegging a slab of green live oak on the ends of the logs and a slab across the top of those for a mantel. At last Ruth could cook inside the house. All of them were justifiably proud of the job they'd done.

The floor came next with more live oak logs to split into slabs and to smooth off the roughness. The boards were put into place, except in the fireplace and a small space for a hearth. With the weather turning cooler still, Jeremiah decided to chink the walls on the inside by driving thin strips of wood into the cracks and then filling every space with mud. That would keep them even warmer during the winter months.

After all these tasks were completed, Jeremiah and Clem decided to take a few days off to rest and to fish and hunt a little. They brought home several large catfish and a wild turkey which Jeremiah put on a spit to cook slowly all day in their new fireplace. The fact that this coincided with Thanksgiving was an extra blessing. On that day they enjoyed roast turkey with cornbread stuffing, baked beans with a little fat pork and molasses, fresh baked bread, and for dessert—a pecan pie!

"Let's join hands and thank God for all His blessin's," Jeremiah began before their meal. "Thank You, O God, for all Your blessin's on this family. Thank You for bringin' us here safely and givin' us this good land and strong backs to build this house. Thank You for the bounty of food before us. We are so grateful. We know it comes from You. Thank You for each member of this family. Keep us all strong and healthy this next year and, as always, close to Your side. In Jesus' Name, Amen."

Clem couldn't wait any longer. He jumped in and started dipping out the food and passing it around the table. He was so hungry! It had been a while since they had had a feast like this one. "This is so good, G'amma! All of it!" he said between bites. Ruth and Jeremiah just laughed. It was heartening to Ruth to see a boy eat so well.

After they had eaten for a few minutes, Jeremiah spoke up, "Ruth, I plan to get to the furniture just as soon as Clem and me get the stable built for the horses. That's the next most important job to get done before it gets colder. Don't know exactly what to expect from the weather here. And we've got to take care of those horses. I can always work on furniture during the winter when things slow down some. Can we make out till then?"

"Of course, we can. These wood slabs on the tree stump work fine for a table, especially with the tablecloth on it. And tree stumps are good enough as chairs for now. I do look forward to a wood frame bed, and I think it's time I made some new mattresses, too. Since I don't have enough feathers to stuff them, I'm goin' to make'em like my grandma used to. While I'm sittin' by the fire this winter, I'm going to cut shavin's off sticks of hazelwood if I can find any to stuff the mattresses with. I used to sleep on one at my grandma's, and I remember it smelled so good and slept good, too. They don't pack down like feathers do." Ruth had always been a resourceful woman, remembering and putting into practice things she had learned from her mother and grandmother for years.

"Ruth, you are so good with makin' things. Clem and I will start the stable tomorrow and it shouldn't take us too long. After that, I think I best go into town to take care of the paperwork on stakin' a claim on this land. Clem and I have walked it off and I can tell'em how much it is and where it is. There are some things I need to get in town, too. If you need things, make a list."

"Can I go, G'amps?" Clem queried around a bite of pecan pie.

"Not this time, Clem. I need you to stay here with your grandma to help her and look after the place."

"Yessir!" It made Clem feel proud to be counted on like that.

❖ ❖ ❖

It only took Jeremiah and Clem about four days to complete the stable for Blackie and Whitey. Clem had learned to love those horses and spent a lot of time brushing and petting them, and he was glad they now had a home, too. The day after they finished the stable Jeremiah announced after breakfast that he was going into town, the closest one being Victory ten miles away. He said it might take him two days to drive the wagon in, get what they needed and ride back.

"Will you two be alright while I'm gone?"

"Of course, we will. Clem's a fine young man, and he can take care of things and split wood. We'll be fine. The Lord will watch over us and you, Jeremiah."

"That He will, Ruth. That He will. Do you have a list of things you'll need this winter?"

"Yes, here it is. I hope it's not too much. Do you think we can afford some pork fat, salt, sugar, coffee, tea, flour and cornmeal?"

"I think so. We need'em, so I'll try to get the best deal I can. I hope to be able to get some chickens, and it sure would be good to get a plow for next spring's plantin'. We'll just have to see. Come on, Clem, and help me get the horses hitched to the wagon." Jeremiah left shortly after daybreak for the small town of Victory.

"Clem, help me wash up the dishes and then we'll go lookin' for some hazelwood so I can get started on those new mattresses. We'll also look for some good trees to fell for your tree house. How would you like that?"

"Oh, boy! Can I chop down the trees? And then can I go fishin'?"

"So full of questions! Yes, you can chop the trees and go fishin'!"

Ruth and Clem located some hazelwood and some good trees for the tree house which Clem chopped down. As they were dragging the trees back, Ruth began to notice a cold, sharp wind beginning to blow out of the north, and by the time they reached the house the storm had broken and it was raining and sleeting with an even stronger wind. They were drenched to the skin and had to dry off, wrap themselves in quilts and sit by the fire. Ruth began to worry about Jeremiah.

"Oh, I hope Jeremiah will be alright in this weather. I've never seen a storm like this. It was so quick!"

The next day with the storm still raging, Ruth began to look for him, but he didn't come nor did he come on the third day. By then, she paced the floor from one window to the other and then stood at the door looking out. She prayed as she walked, *Lord, please take care of Jeremiah. Keep him safe and out of harm's way. He's Your child and You know what's best, but, Lord, we still need him. Clem's still got a lot to learn I can't teach him. And I need him, Lord.* Her throat choked up. *Bring him home safely. Please.* She was praying silently, hoping Clem wouldn't notice how worried she was. One look at him told her he knew. His eyes were large and round with fear clearly written there.

On the fourth day, the storm had gone and the weather was back to normal. Suddenly, about midday they heard a wagon coming! It had to be Jeremiah! They both ran out to see. Jeremiah was driving the wagon up to the house with a chicken coop full of leghorns in the back, supplies piled up, and tied to the back of the wagon were three head of longhorn cattle. As Jeremiah jumped down, his two loved ones hugged him with a few tears from both.

"My, my, what a reception! I should leave more often. I'm sorry, Ruth, I got caught in the storm on the way to town, and it seemed best to wait it out there before I started back. I learned we'll probably have more of those. They call'em 'northers', and they say it can turn real cold in just a few minutes with no warnin'. Are you two alright?"

"Now that you're here we're fine. I was a little worried."

"She was a lot worried, G'amps, and so was I."

"Well, I'm here now and we're all fine. Clem, help me unload the wagon and see what a good deal I got on some things. I got everythin' on your list, Ruth, plus a few surprises. See the chickens. We can have eggs, Ruth, and milk and butter! I got a bull and two cows. And maybe best of all, I got a plow for spring plantin'!"

"Can we afford all this?"

"Yes, Ruth, the Lord just provided again!"

"How, Jeremiah?"

"Well, first let me show you one surprise I got!" He reached in the back of the wagon and pulled out two panes of glass. "I got us some real windows, Ruth. Now when spring comes, the flies and mosquitoes can't get in."

"Oh, Jeremiah, that's wonderful! I was so goin' to miss light comin' in the windows."

Clem helped Jeremiah begin to unload the wagon, carrying the precious supplies inside. On one of his trips back to the wagon, Ruth stopped him to inquire, "Jeremiah, just how did the Lord provide all this—exactly?"

"Well—I just agreed to do a little job for a couple of men in town."

"A little job? What have you promised to do now, Jeremiah?"

"I just promised the storeowner, Mr. Edwards, I'd build him a new stable and the blacksmith, Mr. Blackstock, I'd help some other men to build him a new barn. Clem can help and it won't take too long. And it's turnabout. If I help them, then maybe they'll help me. You see? It's the neighborly thing to do."

"Jeremiah, Jeremiah. You're gonna wear yourself out. You promised Clem a tree house first. Remember?"

"And we'll start that tomorrow." Jeremiah walked on to the house with his bundles and left Ruth standing there shaking her head.

CHAPTER 15

The winter weather turned out not to be so very different from that in south Georgia, except maybe a little wetter. There was a little snow and three "northers" to contend with, but Jeremiah learned to pack straw and leaves against the foundation of the house weighted down with rocks to try to keep out the cold. Keeping the shutters closed and a fire going all the time were the only things a person could do during a "norther" and just wait it out.

On sunny winter days, Jeremiah and Clem put up a tree house in the old cypress, and once that was finished they went into town to help build Mr. Blackstock's barn and finally Mr.

Edwards' stable. Those jobs took most of the winter, but these times afforded Jeremiah opportunities to learn about their newly adopted home of Victory, Texas, and to get to know people. It gave Clem opportunities to learn how to do many jobs related to building. Ruth passed the winter by shaving hazelwood to make new mattresses and knitting Clem and Jeremiah new socks and gloves. Jeremiah spent evenings with Clem's help building furniture for the house, including two bed frames, an oak table and four chairs, an oak cupboard, a few book shelves, a nicely carved mantel over the fireplace, and even a nice oak sideboard to replace the one they had to leave behind. Ruth was thrilled and often remarked that she didn't see how Jeremiah had the strength to work so hard. He accomplished a great deal that winter and was pleased with the results.

When they had time, the menfolk went hunting and brought home a deer that they smoked and enjoyed for much of the winter, several ducks and a Christmas goose. They spent Christmas simply with the exchange of small but thoughtful and loving gifts for each other. Jeremiah surprised Ruth with some calico cloth he had gotten at the general store back in the fall and some candy for Clem. Ruth had taken the best two shirts and pairs of pants Jeremiah and Clem had, took them apart at the seams and turned them inside out and resewed them to look like new. She had also taken up one of Jeremiah's old shirts for Clem. Clem's gifts to his grandparents were remembered by them for years because he made them. He built a box, smoothed and rubbed, for Jeremiah to keep the family Bible in. For Ruth, he took a slab of wood about a foot square and carved out the cross in it, also smoothed and rubbed. They were delighted and surprised, wondering how he had time to do this, until Jeremiah remembered seeing a light in the stable pretty late a few nights. It was a good Christmas, being together and sharing the simple things in life.

❖ ❖ ❖

One fine early spring day in 1876 when Clem was ten years old, a man happened across their path who would have an impact for the rest of their lives. His name was Josiah Jones, an itinerant preacher. It was common in those days for a traveling preacher to stop and spend a few days with a family, often helping with whatever work needed to be done for his room and board. They would all usually sit by candlelight far into the night talking, reading scripture and discussing it, and learning news from wherever the preacher had been. It was an exciting and wonderful time for Jeremiah and Ruth, and for Clem it was life-changing.

Jeremiah had made another trip into Victory to buy or trade seeds for planting, a few seed potatoes, and a few hoes. He had already plowed the fields for cotton, wheat, corn and the garden, and they were working on breaking up the clods of dirt with hoes to get the fields ready to plant. It was backbreaking work, but since they had no harrow it was the only way they could prepare the soil. Jeremiah vowed one day he'd have a harrow. It was on one of these days that Clem looked up to see a man approaching. It was uncommon because visitors were few, especially during planting season.

"G'amps, I see a man comin' yonder." Jeremiah looked up and watched this tall, rawboned man with a full head of dark hair and a stride that said he had a lot of energy.

"Good morning, folks!" he called as he approached. He walked directly up to Jeremiah and shook hands. "My name is Josiah Jones, and I'm a traveling preacher just passing through this area. Hello, ma'am, son." He tipped his hat in their direction.

"Pleased to meet you, Rev. Jones. I'm Jeremiah Jakes and this is my wife Ruth and our grandson Clem. Why don't we walk over to the shade here and get a cool drink of spring water?" They all stopped work and walked with him.

"Mighty good water. Mighty good! Looks like you folks have a lot of hard work to do here. Mrs. Jakes, why don't you take a rest and I'll take your place hoeing for a while?" Ruth looked at Jeremiah with a hopeful look. He smiled at her.

"That's good of you, Rev. Jones. Ruth, go on in and get us a good meal started for dinner." Ruth expressed her thanks as she handed her hoe to the Reverend. She certainly didn't want to turn down that offer, even from a preacher!

As Ruth mixed up biscuit dough, she watched them out of the window. This preacher was a hard worker! They were making better progress than if she had been the one working, and she could tell they were talking and getting acquainted, too. She was excited! This was the first time they'd had a visiting preacher to stay with them since they left Georgia.

They would be able to talk about the scripture and hear what the preacher had to say about it. Ruth had a wonderful thought, *Maybe this will be a special time for Clem! Maybe that's why the Lord sent this preacher our way!* She prayed a silent prayer that the Lord would speak to Clem sometime while the preacher was there.

The menfolk worked hard until dinnertime, ate heartily and then worked until dark before they came in for supper. During and after supper they became acquainted with one another.

"I'm from up in New York state originally, but I've traveled all over—from Boston to Virginia to Georgia and now to Texas. I plan on traveling on farther west if the Lord wills. It's a hard life sometimes, especially in bad weather and when I don't run into good folks like you who'll feed me." He gave a hearty laugh. "I do appreciate it, Mrs. Jakes. This is fine cooking! I hope I don't eat you out of house and home, ma'am!"

"Oh, no, sir, we've plenty more. I like to see a man eat as hearty as you do, Rev. Jones. Do you have a wife and family back east?"

"Call me Josiah. God's called me and given me a hard job to do, but I'm still just a man. A weak one at that. And, no, ma'am, I don't have a wife and all of my family are gone. It gets lonesome sometimes, but then God will send me to a family like yours. It helps a lot. How old are you, Clem?"

Clem was a little shy and hesitant around strangers. He passed his hand across his forehead and answered, "I'm ten, sir."

"Do you know the Lord, son?"

Now Clem was confused. He thought a while and replied, "Yessir, I think so. We talk to Him a lot."

Josiah glanced at Jeremiah and Jeremiah pushed back from the table and responded, "Brother Josiah, let's take a walk outside for a little fresh air." The two men rose to leave. "Clem, stay and help your G'amma clean up. Will you?"

"Yessir." Clem had always been obedient, respectful and loving. He never talked back or refused to do what he was asked.

Once outside, Jeremiah explained about Clem's slowness, how he had come to be with them, how he had lost both his parents, how he and Ruth had lost all three of their children and why they had come to Texas from Georgia. The preacher listened attentively and compassionately, for he knew what it was to lose family because he had lost his wife and son in a fire a few years before.

"You folks have surely had some hard times, Jeremiah. Has the Lord seen you through them all? Do you both know the Lord?"

"Oh, yes, Ruth and I have known the Lord Jesus personally for many years. And if it wasn't for Him, we couldn't have made it through all the hard times we've had. I admit it's hard when I start thinkin' about it. I try not to dwell on the bad times but remember the good. And I take comfort in knowin' that heaven is waitin' and so are my children and son-in-law. Maybe tomorrow you can share some scriptures and insight that might help all of us. Like I said before, Clem is a little slow in his thinkin', but he understands a lot, too. His mother and we have taught him about the Lord. He's watched us deal with a lot of hard trials and how we've tried to lean on the Lord. I believe he can understand and will be saved. His mother believed, and I agree, that the Lord's hand is on Clem for some reason. He's such a good boy, hardworkin'—well, you saw him out in the field today. He never quits or gets lazy. We're proud of him. Maybe you can talk to him about the Lord if you feel led."

"I will do that tomorrow, Jeremiah, and I will pray about it tonight."

❖ ❖ ❖

Daylight the next morning found Jeremiah, Clem and the preacher out in the field after a breakfast of flapjacks and syrup. They put in a hard day of hoeing and trying to cultivate the soil as best they could by hand, and at its end they had that job completed and could begin planting the next day. The preacher had proven to be a godsend in more ways than one. He was certainly an energetic worker. The planting was going a lot faster than they thought it would. As they worked that day, they all prayed silently for the evening when Brother Josiah would talk to Clem.

That night after supper, Ruth was a little nervous, but Jeremiah and the preacher were as calm as could be. Brother Josiah began to speak, "I know you folks have been through some hard times, and I'd just like to share some scriptures that might help you. God knows every trial you've been through, and in fact He planned them. There's a purpose for everything He allows because there's something He plans to do in you. Just trust Him and rest in Him. He will bring good from the bad. I read somewhere that a famous preacher named Charles Spurgeon said that when troubles are so hard you can only talk to God about them, then be thankful because you learn more about the Lord then than any other time. James 1:2-4 says, 'My brethren, count it all joy when ye fall into divers temptations; knowing this, that the trying of your faith worketh patience. But let patience have her perfect work, that ye may be perfect and entire, wanting nothing.' James goes on to say when God has tried and tested your faith, you shall receive the crown of life. Peter says in I Peter 1:7 that when our faith is tried it will bring praise and honor and glory to Jesus Christ. I think of a verse in Jeremiah 17:7-8, I believe, 'Blessed be the man that trusteth in the Lord, and whose hope the Lord is. For he shall be as a tree planted by the waters, and that spreadeth out her roots by the river . . . .' I think that means when we trust the Lord totally we will have roots that go deep that will keep us strong when the trials come like strong winds. Jeremiah, I think you and Ruth have had that kind of faith and trust in God through the strong winds of trials in your lives. I think God's purpose is to raise up two people of strong faith to pass it along to others and be an example to others of what God can do."

Ruth had begun quietly weeping early on as he spoke, and now she wiped her eyes on her apron. "Thank you, Preacher,

I needed to hear that and be reminded again of what I already knew. God bless you!" She wept more, but it was a cleansing type of crying—a release of wounds and hurts to her God.

Now he spoke to Clem directly.

"Clem, have you heard of the book of Jeremiah in the Old Testament?"

"Yessir. My G'amps is named after it." They all shared a laugh.

"Prob'ly so. Prob'ly so. Jeremiah 29:13 says, 'And ye shall seek me, and find me, when ye shall search for me with all your heart.' Do you know what that means, Clem?"

Clem paused and passed his hand across his forehead before answering, "I—I guess it means if we look we'll find something." He continued to look puzzled.

"Well, yes. In this case, what are we looking for? It says, '. . . if you look for ME, you'll find ME.' Who are we looking for?"

Clem just looked confused.

"It means, Clem, that if anybody, and that means you too, looks for God you can find Him, if you're looking with your heart. God wants you to find Him and give your life to Him and serve Him all your days, Clem. And if you really want to find the Lord, you can." Clem began to understand a little. The confusion left his face. "There's another verse that says, 'For God so loved the world, that he gave his only begotten Son, that whosoever believeth in him should not perish, but have everlasting life.' That means that God knows we're sinners, and He loves us so much that he sent His only Son, Jesus, into the world to die for our sins—to take our punishment. And if we believe this, we will live forever with Him in heaven. Do you want to go to heaven, Clem?"

"Oh, yessir! I want to see my Ma and Pa and be with them." Ruth's tears came a little harder.

"Clem, are you a sinner? Have you ever committed a sin?"

Clem thought a minute, then slowly said, "Yes—sir. I took a piece of candy at the general store one time and never told anybody. That was wrong." He sat with his head down. Jeremiah and Ruth were astonished and it showed on their faces, but they waited. "But the next day I took it back and told the owner I was sorry." He hesitated. "He let me keep the candy 'cause he said I was h—honest." Jeremiah's and Ruth's eyes both glistened. They were so proud of this green-eyed grandson of theirs, with the cowlick pointing to the sky in the crown of his head!

"Yes, Clem, that was a sin. Do you know how Jesus died?"

"Yessir, He hung on a cross with His hands and feet nailed and He died there with people makin' fun of Him."

"And do you know why He died like that?"

"No—no, sir. Not 'zactly."

"He took your sins—your stealing that candy and all the others—and my sins on Himself to be punished in your place and my place. We can't go to heaven as dirty sinners. We have to be cleaned up, and the only way is to believe in your heart that Jesus died for your sins and rose again from the grave. Jesus has taken all your sins on Himself and all you have to do is believe it. I heard a story one time of two boys at school. One of them got into a fight and the teacher was going to whip him, but the other boy knew that his friend hadn't had anything to eat in two days and probably couldn't withstand the whipping. He stepped up and said, 'Let me take his punishment, teacher.' And the teacher did because she understood. See, Clem, that's what Jesus did for us. Someone had to be punished for sin and God sent His Son Jesus to take that punishment in our place, just like the boy in the story. Do you understand what I'm saying?"

Clem nodded. "God must love us a whole lot." Ruth's heart swelled within her because she saw that he really did understand.

"Would you like to ask Jesus to come into your heart and take away your sins so you can go to heaven, Clem?"

"Oh, yessir!"

"I want you just to talk to God and tell Him what you want, Clem. Can you do that?"

"I think so." He squirmed around until he was on his knees. "Dear God, I've sinned. I took that candy. And I was mean to Blackie one day too. And I got mad at You when my Ma died." He dropped his head and started to cry. "I'm sorry. I want to go to heaven to see my Ma and Pa. Forgive me, God, and come in my heart, Jesus. I want to serve You and be what You want me to be. I need Your help. I can't do it by myself 'cause, you see, I'm kinda slow. But I know You're real smart. You can help me when I can't do it. Thank you, Jesus. In Jesus' Name, Amen. Is that alright?"

There were three adults weeping when Clem finished praying. He had touched all their hearts with his simple, honest confession and prayer. Ruth wiped her eyes on her apron and threw her arms around Clem. "Oh, thank You, Jesus! He's saved! He's saved! We'll all be in heaven together now."

The preacher was deeply touched by Clem's simple prayer. When the preacher got his emotions under control, he said to Clem, "Clem, you aren't slow at all. You're smarter than a lot of old folks I know!"

❖ ❖ ❖

The itinerant preacher stayed on for a few more days than he intended to spend time with Clem, teaching him as much as he felt he could, and helping plant the fields and the garden.

Once the cotton, wheat and corn fields were planted, they concentrated on the garden, from which they would have to eat all the next winter. They planted beans, carrots, onions, squash, cabbage, turnips, sweet potatoes and white potatoes. Ruth cut the potatoes into sections with an eye in each piece while Clem took them to the men who dropped them in the plowed rows. They let him drop some of them as well as some of the carrot seeds. Clem loved being able to help the men do their work.

Every chance he got the preacher would talk to Clem about living the Christian life—how he needed to pray and go to church. He knew Clem couldn't read, but he encouraged Ruth and Jeremiah to read to him from the Bible a lot. He knew of people who couldn't read but had learned much of the Bible by memory.

At night the preacher continued to share many things with the whole family. Some of what he shared was news from back east. "Brother Jeremiah, some of the best news I've heard in a long time is the revival still going on back east. There was a preacher named Charles Finney, who only died last year that had a lot to do with it. He was a lawyer, a minister and a college president. In 1857-58, these noon prayer meetings started in Boston and New York, and from those came sweeping revival in the northern states with as many as 50,000 people being saved in a single week! Can you imagine? Sometimes so many people came to the prayer meetings that they had to make rules limiting prayers to five minutes to give everybody a chance to pray! Even the newspapers reported the meetings and the revival that spread. The preaching was simple and practical, and people of every class were saved. It was one of the most wonderful experiences of my life to sit, or more likely stand, in some of these meetings and to hear Charles Finney preach. There's nobody can quite touch him when he preached. It was sad to see him go, but the revival movement is still being felt up North."

"My, my, Brother Josiah, it's a wonder to behold what the Lord can do! I wish I could see such a revival myself."

"Jeremiah, you could. Just start praying for it!"

❖ ❖ ❖

Jeremiah grasped Brother Josiah's hand in a firm and heartfelt handshake. "This has meant so much to us, for you to be here. Not the work you've done, though that was greatly appreciated, but the words of faith and encouragement you've given us. Your words will encourage us for a long time. And especially, we are grateful for what you've done for Clem. The good Lord brought you here because His time for Clem was at hand." Jeremiah choked up and couldn't go on.

"Don't thank me, Jeremiah. Thank the Lord! He's the one Who does all things. Thank you and Mrs. Jakes for taking me in and feeding me so well and, ma'am, thank you for the sack of food you've given me to take. You are both so generous. God bless you many times over. And, Clem," putting his arm around the young shoulders, "never forget what happened to you the night you asked Jesus in your heart. Don't ever let the devil try to discourage you or tell you you're not saved. You see that tallest pine tree over there. Take a piece of wood and carve on it your name and the date you were saved and nail it to that tree. If the devil ever tells you that you aren't a child of God, go point to it and tell him you are and he better leave you alone. Trust God, lean on Him, especially when times are hard. And never, never forget that He loves you," putting a finger on Clem's chest, "with a love that will always last. You are special because you are a child of God. Remain loving, obedient, respectful and faithful like you are now, and you'll grow up to be a fine man of God, Clem Brown."

"Thank you, sir." They watched the tall, dark-haired preacher walk energetically down the road, whistling "Amazing Grace." He turned once and waved before he disappeared from sight behind a line of tall, loblolly pines.

Two days after the preacher left Ruth and Jeremiah watched Clem nail the reminder of his salvation to the tall pine tree.

CHAPTER 16

It was the summer of 1882 when Clem became a young man of sixteen, tanned from working in the sun, with broad shoulders and distinct muscles in his arms, shoulders and legs. He was no longer a boy and worked alongside his grandfather in every respect. He was a handsome young man, though only five feet tall. Clem would never become a tall man. His green eyes were more lively than they used to be, even though he was still slow in his thinking and reactions. His hair was still unruly and, of course, the ever-present cowlick stood up in the crown of his sun-lightened dark hair.

As Clem worked with his grandfather to pick the last of the cotton on this late August day, he slapped at Texas-size mosquitoes lighting on his sweaty skin. It was one of the hottest days of the year. The heat was so intense that it was almost like a solid wall, and breathing was sometimes difficult due to so much water in the air.

Jeremiah straightened up and looked out across the few, white-speckled rows of cotton remaining to be picked and could see waves of heat rising above the ground. "Clem, this must be the hottest day I ever saw! I'll be glad when this cotton is finished. Won't you?"

"Yessir! The creek sure would feel good about now."

"Hmm. We don't like much finishin' up here. When we're done, why don't we take us a little dip in the creek?"

"Yessir!"

"What was your G'amma gonna do today, Clem?"

"She was gonna pick huckleberries, I think. Maybe she'll make us a pie for supper. That'd be good!"

After a refreshing dip in the creek, Jeremiah and Clem enjoyed a scrumptious meal of cabbage and meat, squash, turnip greens, soda biscuits, cornbread, tea and huckleberry cobbler. It took a lot of food to fill up Clem as he grew older. Jeremiah pushed his chair back and drank a glass of "pot likker", as most folks called the liquid left when turnip greens were boiled. He always believed it made him feel better.

"Ruth, come sit down a few minutes and talk to us. You look hot and tired. Clem will help clean up after we've talked a bit."

"I suppose you're right. I've never been so hot! I'll be glad when fall comes and it cools off some." She wiped the sweat from her face with her apron and then propped her face in her hands, looking tired and worn out.

"I will too, Ruth. Did I tell you a coyote carried off another chicken last night?"

"No! That makes three! If I could get my hands on that coyote, I'd—."

"Well, don't get upset. There's no way to ever catch the sneaky devils. This time I didn't even hear Boney barkin'. I guess I was so tired I slept through it or maybe he did."

"Well, let's clean up, Clem. I've got sewin' to do."

"That woman is always in such a hurry, Clem."

"What did you say, Jeremiah?"

"Oh, nothin'." When Ruth walked away, he added, "She's ill, too. I wonder if she's sick. This ain't like her. Why don't you let me help her clean up, Clem? Maybe I need to talk to her."

All three pitched in and cleaned the table and put away the food. Ruth washed dishes while Jeremiah dried them and put them away. They worked quietly for a while and then suddenly Ruth exclaimed, "I am so hot! Just look at me sweatin'! I've never seen the like."

"I hope you aren't gettin' sick. Here let me feel your forehead. Ruth, you're burnin' up with fever! We better get you to bed!"

She shook off his hand and responded, "I'm alright. Just let me finish these—." Ruth crumpled limply to the floor like a rag doll.

"Ruth—." Jeremiah scooped her up in his arms like a child and headed to their bedroom. "Clem, come quick! Your G'amma is sick with fever and she's collapsed." He talked as he laid Ruth on the bed and began to undress her. "Ride over to the Posey's and bring Mrs. Posey back. Maybe she can help. Hurry!" Almost to himself, he said, "Oh, how I wish we had a doctor close by!" The closest one was a hundred miles away.

Clem sped out to the stable and saddled Blackie in record time and headed to the Posey's as hard as he could go with Boney keeping pace with him.

Once Jeremiah had Ruth's dress off, he gathered up all the cloths he could find and a bowl of cool water and began to bathe her with cool cloths. Almost as soon as he put one on her it would be hot. Her skin was hot to the touch. *Oh, Lord*, he prayed, *touch Ruth and bring this fever down. Help us know what to do. Please, Lord, spare her life. We need her so. I need her. I love her. Please, Lord.*

By the time Clem arrived with Mrs. Posey, who was a round, fleshy woman with sad, caring eyes that had seen much misfortune in her fifty years, not only was Ruth bathed in sweat but the bedsheets were also. The fever was raging very high in her, and frankly Jeremiah had never been so scared. He had no idea what else to do.

"Mrs. Posey, what can we do? She's burnin' up with fever. I've put cool cloths on her, but it doesn't help. What else can we do?" Tears began to roll down Jeremiah's face.

Mrs. Posey began to take charge. "Mr. Jakes, you got to pull yo'self together for Miz Jakes' sake. She needs you right now. You got any ice?"

"No, ma'am," Clem spoke up.

"Clem, ride back to our house and git Mr. Posey to help you brang back some ice, and when you git it here chip it off in little pieces. We'll put it in some cloths and put it next to her skin. Mr. Jakes—Mr. Jakes, you hear me?" She took him by the arm and shook him gently. "Mr. Jakes, do you know where you can git some willow bark?"

He looked up through his tears with a blank look on his face.

"Mr. Jakes! I said git up and git me some willow bark. I wanna make willow bark tea. Some folks say it'll brang down a fever. Now git! You hear me?"

"Yes, ma'am." Jeremiah numbly rose to his feet with his eyes glued to Ruth. "Take care of her, Mrs. Posey. Please."

"I'll do the best I kin. Now go."

Jeremiah dragged himself to the door, and then as if suddenly realizing that he had something concrete to do that might help his wife, he ran to the stable to get Whitey, and not bothering to saddle her, took off in the direction of the woods. By the time he had returned with the willow bark, Mrs. Posey had water brewing into which she dropped the willow bark. While it was steeping, Clem and Mr. Posey returned with the ice, and they all set about chipping ice to fill cloths which they laid on and next to Ruth's skin. When the tea was ready, Mrs.

Posey used a spoon to let some of the tea trickle down Ruth's throat. After a while, Ruth seemed to rest better.

"Mr. Jakes, I done all I know to do. I think now we got to pray to the good Lord for His help. I'm gonna stay fer a while. Mr. Posey's goin' home to do the chores and then he'll come back to see if we need anythin'. Why don't you try to git some rest? It's gonna be a long night."

"No, ma'am, I'll stay right here with Ruth. Thank you both for all you've done."

Thus began one of the longest nights Jeremiah had ever known. This night would be followed by two more days of fever and delirium. He talked to her, prayed for her and cried more than he ever had in his life. Clem and Mrs. Posey stayed by his side. During the night Mrs. Posey gave Ruth more willow bark tea, and they continued to pack her in ice as long as it lasted.

On the second day, Ruth began to cry out in her delirious state while tossing about and twisting the sheets in her hands. "Jeremiah! Jeremiah!" she cried over and over. He was always there to smooth her brow and speak words of love to her. "I'm here, Ruth. I'm here. I love you, darlin' Ruth. I'll never leave you. Clem is here too and Mrs. Posey. We're all prayin' for you. Jesus is very near. Just rest in Jesus, Ruth." He laid his head on the bed with his arm across her and prayed, "Oh, Jesus, this is Your child here sufferin' and burnin' up with fever. Please touch and heal her. Give her Your strength. Help her to rest. Oh, God, please spare her life! I can't live without her!" He dissolved into tears. Clem had never seen his grandfather like this and finally cried himself to sleep.

By the third night after the fever began, it left and so did Ruth. She left this world for a far better one in heaven. Jeremiah was so numb that all he could do was sit and hold Ruth's hand and stare at her face. "She was only 59. Why did she have to go so soon? We'd only been married 42 years. Why, Lord? Why?"

Mrs. Posey and Clem had to move Jeremiah bodily from the bed and into the kitchen where Mrs. Posey made tea and made him drink some. She instructed Clem to keep Jeremiah there while she prepared Ruth. Jeremiah sat with his head on his arms on the table, not speaking or crying, just numb.

The next three days were difficult, and even though Jeremiah talked with people who came by, ate and lay down to sleep, he neither slept nor cried. Mrs. Posey commented that she'd never seen a man so distraught in her life. They buried Ruth under the old cypress tree because that was the spot Clem chose. Jeremiah seemed unable to make decisions as he stumbled through these days. When the funeral was over and the people all went home, Jeremiah and Clem were left to go on with life. Neither one really felt like it. Clem was hurting, too, but there was no one to console him. Jeremiah was in another world of emotional pain and loss. Three days after the funeral Jeremiah began to cry and couldn't stop for a week. Every time Clem looked for him he was either staring out the window toward her grave, lying on their bed crying, or sitting at the grave. Clem did not know what to do, besides worrying and praying, and he did both.

One rainy, muggy, hot day, Clem once again saw his grandfather at the grave. He was soaked to the skin, but it didn't seem to matter to him. He felt he could be closer to Ruth there than anywhere, and it would take him months to realize that he was close to her everywhere he went because she would always be a part of him. But, for now, Clem knew he had to do something to try to help Jeremiah. He needed his G'amps and, in the child's part of his heart, he was afraid he'd lose him, too. Clem wandered around inside the house trying to think what he could do. Suddenly, it seemed, he noticed the family Bible on the shelf. Something began to stir inside him and he thought, *Yes, I gotta talk to G'amps like he talked to me when Ma died.*

Clem picked up the Bible and headed to the grave just as it stopped raining. When he reached his grandfather, Jeremiah was a pitiful sight with his clothes soaked, his hair wet and stringing down his face, and lying prostrate on his wife's grave. Clem got on his knees and touched Jeremiah on the arm.

"G'amps? G'amps? It's me, Clem. I know how sad you are. I am, too." Silent tears ran down his cheeks. "I miss her, too, but like you told me when my Ma died, G'amma's with Jesus now and she's happy. One day we'll get to see her again. You told me that, G'amps. She's already got to see my Ma and Pa and Uncle William and Aunt Lydia. I wish I could be there." Jeremiah sat up slowly as if in a daze and looked at Clem, the first time he had really seen him since Ruth became ill.

Clem opened the Bible as if to read, but of course he couldn't read. Nonetheless, he began to give Jeremiah some scripture. "Do you remember the travelin' preacher tellin' us that when your faith is tried it'll bring glory and honor to Jesus? I think God still loves us, G'amps. He just needed to take G'amma on to heaven. It was her time to go. We just gotta trust Him and rest in Him. I've heard you say that lots of times. Well—." Clem ducked his head. "Well, I think this is the time to trust Him. Don't you?" Jeremiah sat up and brushed the wet hair from his face. The tears had slowed down. He was listening.

Clem continued. "I remember the preacher tellin' us that in the book of Jeremiah in the Bible it says when we really trust the Lord it's like puttin' down deep roots to keep us strong when the hard winds blow. G'amps, you've always been a man of faith and deep roots. And the preacher said that you and G'amma were two people of strong faith who would pass your faith along to somebody else. I hope that's me 'cause I'm tryin' real hard to trust. You told me before when Ma died not to get hard or bitter against God and not to give up. I wanted to give up when she died and die, too. Is that how you feel?"

Jeremiah had to clear his throat before he spoke weakly, "Yes, Clem. I'd like to die, too."

"But, G'amps, I still need you. What would I do without you?" Jeremiah's face began to reflect an inner inkling of understanding. "Do you remember the story you told me about your Pa, how he believed the scripture that says 'Though He slay me, yet will I trust in Him.' I've always remembered it. You said you had come to believe that, too. G'amps, you just gotta trust. That's all I know to say. You gotta trust Him. Trust Him." Finally, Clem broke down in sobs. "I'm sorry, G'amps, I can't say it right."

Jeremiah rose, went to Clem, pulled him to his feet, and threw his arms around him. "You said it just right, son. Thank you." They both stood, embracing and crying until they lost track of time. They finally began to walk toward the house, with Jeremiah's arm across Clem's shoulders. "Clem, I don't know what I'd do without you. You've helped me see things a little clearer. I've got a long way back. Promise you'll help me."

"I'll help you, G'amps, any way I can."

❖ ❖ ❖

Later that night Jeremiah was sitting outside thinking and trying to pray after Clem had gone to sleep. He felt as if he had been on a long journey and had only just started back. He needed to pray, but it was a difficult thing to do. Finally, he slipped to one knee and began to pray, "Lord, please forgive me for not trustin' You. I've never had anythin' hurt so bad as losin' my—Ruth. It still hurts." He broke down into sobs once again, but the difference this time was the cleansing effect it had on him. "Lord, it seems like I just can't go on now, but I know I've got to, for Clem's sake and for Yours. I want people to see You in me and see me trustin' You. Help me, Lord. It's so hard. I miss her so much. I miss her close at night. I miss her pretty smile. I miss her laugh. I even miss that apron she used so many times to wipe the tears from her eyes. We'd been together forty-two years. Buried three children together. Lord, what will I do without her? Please help me. Help me." Jeremiah stayed in a bowed position for a while listening for God inside his heart. Finally, he felt a release and the most warm, loving feeling in his spirit he knew was from the Lord.

As he stood to his feet, he continued in prayer, "Lord, I've still got a long way to go, but I'm gonna be alright now. Just keep holdin' me up, Lord." He looked up into the starry night and said, "Lord, Clem is gonna be alright, too. He may not seem real smart, but he knows more than most people about faith and trustin' You. Thank You for him and bless him, Lord."

As he turned to go into the house to sleep his first full night alone in their bed, he whispered, "Ruth, I love you. I always will. One day soon we'll be together again. Look for me. Tell the children I love them."

CHAPTER 17

Harvest time was upon Jeremiah and Clem just after Ruth died, and perhaps it was good because it kept them extremely busy. The weather was cooling and the oaks and sycamores were beginning to add color to their world. Life was still a struggle each day and each night for Jeremiah as he sought the Lord often when the grief welled up in him to the point of almost causing physical pain. Clem cried much more than Jeremiah ever knew. He also missed his "G'amma" tremendously. They talked a lot about her which helped them both, and they took one day at a time and, at first, one hour at a time. But they were going to be alright given enough time and prayer. They had learned through much sorrow that death is a sad but necessary part of life.

Haying time had come, and Jeremiah borrowed two scythes from Mr. Posey. Jeremiah and Clem worked side by side cutting great swathes of the wheat, laying it smoothly on the ground in windrows to dry before it was bundled. Clem was slow at first, but as he learned how best to do it he picked up speed. Using a scythe was hard work, and they worked from sunup to sundown for two days to finish the haying. Clem usually went to the house early to get their supper started, and Jeremiah would come later to help finish. Their meals were not quite what Ruth used to cook for them, but they were filling. The day after they finished cutting the hay they bundled it and used the wagon to haul it to the stable where for another two days they flailed it to remove the grain from the chaff. Once that was done they used large, shallow winnowing baskets and tossed the grain into the air. This was done so that the breeze would blow the chaff away and the grain would fall into the basket. They felt good about getting this task accomplished because it meant bread for them and food for the horses during the coming winter.

The night they finished haying they sat at supper a little longer and talked while finishing their best attempt at rabbit stew. "Well, Clem, it's finally done. But no rest for the weary. Tomorrow we got to start harvestin' the vegetables so we can eat this winter. When that's all done, we'll take some time off to fish and hunt and just plain rest. How does that sound?"

"Sounds real good to me, G'amps. I never been so tired."

"I know, son. Me, too. But you worked like a man out there. You stayed with me. I'm proud of you and thankful for your help. You're almost grown, Clem. It's hard to believe." Jeremiah paused long enough to sip hot coffee out of his saucer. "Ruth never did like for me to drink out of my saucer, but it's a good way to cool my coffee some before I drink it." They were quiet for a few moments as they always were after Ruth was mentioned. Jeremiah broke the silence, "Clem, did I tell you that I saw a panther the other day? You remember when I rode into the woods to check the traps along the creek. Well, I had gotten pretty far back in the woods when I heard him up on a knoll. He was lookin' down on me, and I just knew I was a goner, but he just turned and ran off. Mean-lookin' critters. I don't care if I never see one of them again."

Clem passed his hand across his forehead before he spoke, "I never saw one. What do they look like?"

"Well, he was black all over, had ferocious teeth and must have been six or seven feet long. He could easily chew you up and spit you out. You know there's a lot of animals here we didn't have back in south Georgia, like bobcats, panthers, wolves, and somebody told me something about a flyin' squirrel! Imagine that—a squirrel that flies!"

"I never heard of such. How does it fly?"

"I don't know, Clem. Oh, by the way, I need you to go into town tomorrow to the livery stable and see about gettin' some leather straps. I need to do some mendin'. And while you're there, go to the general store and get some salt, coffee—and let's see, what else? Oh, a little sugar. Anything you need?"

"No, sir," mumbled Clem. He was looking down at his plate, so Jeremiah didn't notice his reluctance.

"Take Blackie and come straight back. I need you to help me dig potatoes and beets."

"Yessir." Clem's face was so long he could've tripped over it, but Jeremiah still didn't notice. He was thinking of tomorrow's chores.

❖ ❖ ❖

The next morning about eight o'clock Clem was saddling Blackie as slowly as he could. He really didn't want to go to town. He had a reason, but he was ashamed to tell his grandfather. So he mounted Blackie and rode very slowly into Victory. As he entered the edge of town, which was made up of only four or five stores including the general store, the livery stable, a dress shop for ladies, a saloon, a jail and across the street facing the stores a new church just being built, he saw them—a group of young men about his age and a little older—just hanging around in front of the general store. They were all boys who had quit going to school when they reached a certain age or just hated school. They had such dubious nicknames as Slim Jim, Bobcat Bob, Coyote Carl, Possum Pete and Fatty Frank. The worst one in the group was definitely Slim Jim. Their mission in life was to ridicule people and generally cause trouble around town. He slowed

Blackie to a walk. *Why do they have to be in front of the general store?* he wondered to himself. He decided to go to the livery stable first. After concluding his business there, he led Blackie by the reins up the street, hoping they wouldn't see him. *Oh, no, they see me!*

"Hey, look, there comes the dummy. Hey, dummy! Whatcha know? Nothin'!" They all roared with laughter, slapping each other on the back.

"Yoohoo, half-wit. Do you know what your name is?"

"What does it feel like to be stupid, dummy?"

"You must be dumb. You never even went to school. They couldn't make it simple enough for you, huh?"

Slim Jim, who was the tallest of the group at just over six feet tall and lean but with large hands and feet, was the only one who hadn't said anything yet. His plans were usually more devious and harmful.

Clem's head dropped as it always did when this happened, and he started to walk on into the general store when he tripped and fell flat of his face in the doorway. He looked back and saw Slim Jim with his foot still sticking out in his way and with a smirk on his face. The gang of boys laughed uproariously and mimicked Clem. He felt ashamed and weird but, most of all, angry. He went on in and gave Mr. Edwards the list of what he needed.

Mr. Edwards spoke up, "Don't let'em get to you, Clem. They're the dumb ones. You're very bright. I heard your grandpa say so. Just ignore them."

After gathering his purchases, Clem slowly lifted the box and turned to go. He stopped when he saw the boys making faces at him through the glass in the door. The last thing he wanted to do was walk back through that group of ruffians.

"Go on, Clem. Don't pay'em any mind. Hold your head up and go on."

Clem did what Mr. Edwards said or at least he tried. "Bet you never had a girlfriend, did ya? Do you know what a girl is, dummy?" The boys continued their harangue until he was out of hearing distance.

Clem was quiet the rest of the day as he helped Jeremiah dig potatoes, pull beets and carrots and carry them to the root cellar under the cabin. Jeremiah was so busy he didn't notice that Clem was quieter than usual. When they sat down to supper that night, Jeremiah asked Clem, "Did you get everythin' in town we needed, son?"

"Yessir." Clem could only get out a word. His humiliation and anger was about to make him sick. He'd never had to deal with anger like this before and it scared him, but it was too hard to admit what happened to his grandfather.

"Guess what I saw today, Clem! A copperhead snake! I sure did! On the edge of the cabbage patch. Probably the last one of the season since it's gettin' cooler. Did you know snakes go underground in the winter?" He paused realizing Clem didn't seem too interested. "You must be perty tired tonight, Clem. Why don't you go on to bed and I'll clean up the dishes?"

"Yessir." Clem dragged himself out of his chair and over to his bed. He undressed and climbed under the covers. He felt bad not helping G'amps with the dishes since he was tired too, but he hated even worse not being able to talk to him about what happened in town. There had never been anything he couldn't say to his G'amps. Somehow this was different, but he didn't understand why. As he lay there replaying in his mind what had happened and hearing again the cruel remarks, his anger rose again, his fists clenched, and the tears began to seep from his eyes. He didn't know what to do.

❖ ❖ ❖

The next day Jeremiah and Clem finished digging the potatoes, pulling beets, carrots, turnips and onions. They laid all these vegetables except the onions in the root cellar where they would keep well over the winter. They braided the dry tops of the onions together into long braided ropes of onions and hung them in a back corner of the house. Their next day's task was to bring in the cabbages and beans which were also put in the root cellar. Harvesting time was always a busy time in any household.

The main task remaining was pulling the corn. Clem didn't like this job too well because he usually got scratched up and jabbed in the eye at least once. While they each took a row and a bushel basket, they worked quickly to fill the basket and return it to the wagon at the edge of the corn field. As Clem worked, he thought and prayed about the boys in town and about his anger. *Lord, I don't rightly know what to do. Please show me what to do. I'm mad and I wanna punch'em, but I know that would be wrong. I just can't say the right thing to them. Help me, Lord.* The Lord would hear and answer those prayers in a most unique way.

❖ ❖ ❖

A week later Jeremiah and Clem were busily fixing supper and talking over the harvest and how fortunate they had been that year.

"We've put away a lot of vegetables and grain, Clem—enough for us and the horses anyway. The Lord has been good to us again."

"Yessir, He has."

"What would you like to do tomorrow, Clem? I think it's time to take some time off from all this hard work. Fishin'? Huntin'?"

Clem wasn't really listening because his mind was still working on his problem in town. He sat with his head down silently eating.

"Clem?" A little louder, "Clem? Where's your mind, boy?"

"Huh, oh, I'm sorry, G'amps. What'd you ask me?"

"What would you say to some huntin' or fishin' for a few days?"

"That'd be great! Can we go huntin' tomorrow?"

"Sure can. I know a new place we ain't been before. We'll leave out at first light. That okay?"

"Sure is!" Clem was excited partly because he knew they'd be far from town and the boys there, but he also loved to spend time with G'amps when they went hunting and fishing. G'amps would tell him stories of the old days when he was growing up, how he met G'amma and they married, about their children which included his Ma, how his parents met and married and had him. He'd heard all the stories before, but he loved hearing them again and again.

❖ ❖ ❖

Sunrise the next morning found Jeremiah and Clem leaving the cabin with a sack of food and their guns, heading for the deep woods of east Texas oaks, pines, firs and junipers. They were both excited to spend the day together doing what they loved to do, especially knowing the harvest was behind them. Sometimes they simply enjoyed watching the wildlife and discovering animals and plants new to them because they had great respect for God's creation. As the day wore on, they saw possums with their young and 'coons. Jeremiah wished for a good 'coon dog, with no offense to Boney, who was enjoying the day immensely. They saw deer, foxes, badgers, some minks, muskrats, a skunk from which they quickly fled, and even an otter.

"Shh, Clem. Look! A beaver's dam. I've never seen one so big!" They stood at a distance and watched beavers working to build a dam in the creek, gnawing off four—or five-inch thick trees in about fifteen minutes and dragging the logs to the creek where they fitted them together as well or better than a man could have done. Jeremiah and Clem crouched under a thick pine-thicket for close to an hour, watching the beavers at work. Some of the beavers were as long as four to five feet while most were smaller. When the dam was across the creek and about three feet high, Jeremiah whispered, "My knees have plumb give out. Let's move on, Clem."

When they were a short distance away, Clem spoke, "G'amps, that was sumthin'! I never saw beavers workin' like that before."

"Yeah, I always heard people say all my life 'busy as a beaver' and now I know what it means. I know some people who could take a lesson from the beavers, don't you?" slapping Clem on the back. "You know it's hard to tell how late it's gettin' in these thick woods, but we best be shootin' us some meat, I think, and gettin' on home. Let's get serious about this now. Be on the lookout."

In the next two hours they shot a possum, a 'coon, two squirrels and a skunk ("Just to put him out of his misery!" Jeremiah claimed.). As they continued on through the woods, they suddenly came into a clearing and found a cabin with smoke rising from the chimney and other signs of life. Jeremiah called out, "Hallo, in the cabin!"

An answer came in the form of a gunshot fired over their heads! Jeremiah pulled Clem down fast flat on the ground. "What in the world is goin' on?" Jeremiah cupped his hands around his mouth and yelled, "We're friends and don't mean any harm. We're just out huntin', my grandson and me." They heard the cabin door open and chanced a look up. The shortest, scrawniest, most bearded, old man they'd ever seen was standing in the door. His wrinkled face looked like the ground in the summer when it hasn't rained in weeks and is full of cracks and was about the color of nutmeg.

"Stands up real slow-like and trow down dem guns. And ah means bidness." Jeremiah and Clem did what they were told, too afraid not to. "What is youse doin' on mah land?" Jeremiah found his tongue finally and spoke, "My grandson, Clem, and me was out huntin' and the truth is we seem to be kinda lost in these thick woods. Maybe you can tell us how to get back out of here and to home."

"Ah 'spect ah kin. Lived here all mah life—me and mah kin. Whur youse cum frum?" When Jeremiah told him where they lived, he told them how to get back, never once lowering his gun. They figured they weren't about to get an invitation to supper! "Ah gahrontee youse git back if youse foller what ah say. Now git! And watch out for the haints in these hare woods. They's ever'whur. Watch out specially for that woman haint in that tree yonder."

"Yessir, we will and thank you for the information," Jeremiah thanked him while taking Clem by the arm to lead him quickly away from there.

The wizened, old man called out one last warning, "Youse better watch out for 'old coffin-head', biggest rattler ever was growed. He lives round hare."

Jeremiah and Clem, whose eyes had grown large and round during the encounter, moved as quickly as they could in the direction the old man indicated. They didn't talk for a while, partly because they were concentrating on finding their way out and partly, in truth, out of fear. When they were finally back in familiar territory, they stopped, looked at one another and sat down on a log. Jeremiah started shaking his head after a few minutes to catch his breath. "I've never seen anybody like that before. Was you as scared as I was, Clem?" Clem's big, round eyes said it all and he only nodded. "When we catch our breath, let's make tracks outta here."

When they reached their cabin, besides the game they already had they had collected two ducks and a goose. They were tired but felt good about the meat they had brought home. That night by the fire they discussed the day's events. "You know, Clem, we've had some adventures today. Some I've never had before and you'll be tellin' your grandchildren about someday, I'll bet. 'Specially that old man. I'll ask in town tomorrow to see what I can find out about him—what sort of fellow he is and about those haints' he was talkin' about. He sure don't like company, that's for sure. Scared me enough not to ever go back. How about you, Clem? You want to go see him again?"

"No, sir. Not ever again. Maybe we can hunt in a different place next time."

"I think so, Clem. I think so," Jeremiah laughed.

"G'amps, did you say we'd be goin' into town tomorrow?"

"Yeah, I need to get some nails and salt pork I forgot the last time you went in."

Clem's heart fell to the pit of his stomach. What a way for this adventurous day to end!

CHAPTER 18

As dawn gradually spread across the gray sky, Clem stood at the window watching it rain. Hope swelled in his heart that the trip to town would be postponed. That thought made him feel much better. That is, until Jeremiah got out of bed. He started grunting and groaning as soon as his feet hit the floor.

"Oh, my. Boy, my knees are hurtin' bad and doggone it if my big toe ain't throbbin'! It must be rheumytism or somethin'. I never had such a hurtin', Clem. I don't know if I can even walk. Come and let me lean on you." Clem helped him to stand and try to walk, but it was with great pain. "It must be all that walkin' in the woods yesterday and now the rain. Boy, I tell you I'm in misery. Help me sit down at the table. See if there's any willow bark in the place where your G'amma used to keep it and make me some tea. She used to swear by it."

Clem found the willow bark and brewed tea for Jeremiah. Once he had drunk it, he directed Clem, "Son, I think you'll have to go into town without me. I hate for you to go in the rain, but if you'll look in the corner beside the fireplace you'll see why I need you to go now." Clem looked and there was a leak in the roof allowing rain to spatter on the floor. Without a word, he got a pan and set under the drip with a resulting "ping", "ping" as each drop hit the metal bucket. Each "ping" felt to Clem like a knife in his heart because he knew he couldn't refuse his G'amps. They needed nails to fix the roof leak and he'd have to go to town. Oh, how he hated that!

Clem took as much time as he could with breakfast, cleaning up, and getting Jeremiah settled. He stretched every task as long as he could—changing clothes, getting a slicker and a hat, saddling Blackie, asking G'amps what else they might need in town. Finally, Jeremiah's patience ran out, "Clem, quit dawdlin' and get goin'. The rain has slacked. Now's a good time to leave. Why are you takin' so long leavin' anyway? A body would think you didn't even like to go to town, but I know you do."

"I'm sorry, G'amps. I guess I'm just tired from yesterday, too." He immediately felt bad because this wasn't the whole truth, but somehow he just couldn't seem to tell him why he hated going to town.

Clem, Blackie and Boney finally set off toward town. Clem rode so slowly even Blackie and Boney became impatient. Boney kept running ahead, stopping, looking back and barking at Clem, as if to say "Come on! Hurry up!" Even Blackie seemed in the mood for a good run because Clem had to keep holding him back, but not Clem. The longer it took him to get to town the longer he could postpone the inevitable. He prayed and he thought and he thought some more. His hand passed across his forehead many times, but he was oblivious to it. He stared off at some distant point, more or less giving Blackie his head finally. As a result, he approached town before he was aware of it or prepared for it. As he raised his head and focused in, the first person he saw was Slim Jim coming out of the general store, alone at least. Clem slipped down off Blackie and began to walk slowly, leading Blackie by the reins. Boney was by his side.

Slim Jim saw Clem also and his mind started working on what he could do to ridicule him. When Clem was within earshot, Slim Jim yelled, "Hey, stupid. Forgot what you come to town for?" Slim Jim stood watching Clem slow his pace. He walked slower and slower while anger built inside. Clem was a little frightened because he had never felt so angry, like a volcano about to erupt. Slim Jim continued cruelly, "How'd you find your way to town, dummy? Take ya all day to get here? Ha! Ha! Ha!" Slim Jim slapped his knee and laughed even harder, too busy laughing to see Clem's face change from fear and dread to anger and then to rage barely under control. Then Slim Jim made his mistake. "Where'd they find you, dummy, under a rock? Bet you didn't even have a ma! You probably hatched out of an egg! Your ma was probably a chicken, 'cause you sure are an ugly ducklin'!"

Clem's face went through a metamorphosis. Rage boiled over and he bellowed "Aagghh!" as he charged Slim Jim with his head down like a bull. He hit Jim in the midsection, knocking him to the ground. They rolled over and over in the mud, each trying to best the other one by getting on top. They were actually pretty evenly matched, so finally they just mutually separated. They both stood with arms akimbo, waiting for the other one to do something. Slim Jim pointed suddenly behind Clem which caused him instinctively to turn, giving Slim Jim the opportunity he needed to land a fierce blow on Clem's chin, knocking him to the ground. Before he could get up, Slim Jim was all over him, punching him in the face. Clem tried to push Slim Jim off of him but didn't have the strength, even though Clem was a strong young man through years of work on the farm. For self-preservation, he used all the strength in his legs to lift Slim Jim and toss him over his own head to land with a hard thud in the muddy street.

The wind was knocked out of Slim Jim momentarily, but he quickly recovered. Clem was on his feet and ready this time with the first blow to Slim Jim's face, knocking him down again. The free-for-all continued while town folk gathered to watch. Finally, the town sheriff, Tom Brackett, a short, plump, balding fellow, heard the ruckus and came running.

Sheriff Brackett waded into the fight and started pulling them apart. "Alright, alright, enough! I said enough! You both wanna end up in jail? Huh? We can arrange that." Clem settled down immediately, but Slim Jim wasn't finished and kept trying to swing at him. The Sheriff let go of Clem in order to take hold of Slim Jim by both shoulders and push him away, which caused him to land on the ground on his backside. This provoked some laughter from the crowd gathered to watch which only served to make Slim Jim madder.

"Alright, folks. Back away. Let's don't start this over again. Git up, Jim."

"My name is Slim Jim."

"Your name is mud, boy. Don't push me. The jail is jist right over yonder. It's empty and I'd be happy to put you up for the night. Now, you two, what started this?" He looked to Clem first, but he only dropped his head and said nothing. The sheriff looked at Slim Jim.

"That dummy hit me first 'cause I wouldn't move outta his way."

"Is that right, Clem?"

"No, sir."

"Well, Clem, what did happen?" Clem remained mute. He knew the truth, but he couldn't bring himself to say in front of everybody what Slim Jim had said. He was embarrassed and angry at himself, too.

At that moment the owner of the general store, Mr. Edwards, came out and spoke to the sheriff, "Sheriff, I saw the whole thing from the store. Jim here makes fun of Clem every time he comes into town. Clem hasn't done anything wrong. He's a good boy. You know his grandpa, Jeremiah Jakes. Good folks. Jim and his gang make fun of Clem, and my guess is Clem had taken all he could take. Clem swung first, but my guess is Jim said something to start it."

"Ain't so! I never said nuthin' to that dummy!"

"Oh? Well, what'd you call what you just called him?" Sheriff Brackett offered. Slim Jim just looked down. "I suggest you both git along home. You both look like you been hit by a grizzly. Alright, folks, the show's over. Let's all get about our own business. Jim, I wanna see you in my office after you wash your face. Clem, you git on home now. Guess I don't have to tell you to tell your grandpa because it's written all over you." Clem and Slim Jim were muddy from head to toe, clothes torn, noses bleeding, lips bleeding and swollen, and black eyes beginning to form.

"Yessir," Clem answered. Slim Jim went over to the horse trough, dunked his head and came up spitting water and blood from his lip and nose. Then he turned to followed the Sheriff to his office. Clem turned to go and then remembered the nails and other things he was supposed to get at the general store. After making his purchases, Mr. Edwards let him clean up a little in back of the store. Mr. Edwards had taken a liking to Clem and wanted to help him.

"Clem, don't worry about Jim. The Sheriff'll have a talk with him, I'll bet. Just tell your grandpa the truth and he'll understand."

"Thank you, Mr. Edwards, for your help."

Clem turned toward home but stopped to pet Boney for a minute who had been yapping ever since the fight started. "Good dog, Boney. You wanted to help me, didn't you?" Clem tiredly mounted Blackie, cringing a little from the pain all over his body. He did feel like a grizzly had chewed on him a little. He urged Blackie into a brisk walk, but as his mind went over what had just happened he pushed Blackie into a run and called out, "Come on, Boney! Let's run!" The wind pushing against him and blowing his hair seemed to help clear the cobwebs and troubles from his mind. He couldn't help wondering what G'amps would say.

Clem slowed Blackie to a walk before they reached home, suddenly afraid to face G'amps. He was hoping to have some time to clean up better before G'amps saw him, but that was not to be because Jeremiah was heading out of the stable as he rode up. Clem couldn't meet him eye to eye, but he felt his eyes on him.

Jeremiah took in the whole situation with one look. *Lord, the boy's been fightin'! I don't reckon he's ever had a fight in his life! What caused this?* "Clem, are you alright? Are you hurt bad?"

"I'm alright."

"What happened, Clem? Do you want to tell me about it?"

"Maybe later."

"Come on in the house and let me see if you need some tendin' to."

"Yessir." Jeremiah cleaned Clem's wounds as best he could while Clem sat quietly but tensely. Clem wasn't sure what G'amps would say or do. He'd never whipped him before. He'd never had to. What would he do now?

"Clem, how about you and me go fishin'? Right now. In the rain. Best time to go. The fish come up to meet you in the rain. I'm feelin' some better. What say?"

Clem looked up sharply. *Did I hear right? Did G'amps just ask if I'd like to go fishin'?* "Uh, uh, sure, G'amps. I need to change clothes. My shirt and pants got tore. I—I d-don't know how to fix 'em. I'm sorry, G'amps. I'm sorry about everythin'."

"It's alright, Clem. I'll fix your clothes. I'm pretty good with a needle, so your G'amma said. Go on and put on some of my pants and a shirt. I'll get our cane poles and we can dig some worms. They come up to meet you when it rains, too."

They were soon on their way to the creek with their cane poles and a jar of worms. They found a likely spot up the creek a short distance where the creek started widening.

"Looks like a good spot, Clem. Set down here and let's see what we can catch." They each chose a comfortable spot to sit on the creek bank, baited their hooks and threw in their lines. They sat quietly a while. Jeremiah was letting Clem settle down and rest before they talked.

"You know, Clem, I always say that fishin' is one of the best things to do to relax, pass the time and talk. Do you feel like tellin' me yet what happened in town today?"

Clem's head dropped. He really didn't want to talk about it. He didn't even want to think about it! He waited so long Jeremiah wondered if he had fallen asleep. "I guess so." Another long pause.

"Go ahead, Clem. You can talk to me about anythin'. I know you're not one to fight for no reason. I'm not goin' to punish you, if that's what you're worried about. You're too old for that. It might help to talk about it."

Clem cleared his throat which suddenly seemed tight. "Well, G'amps, there are some boys in town who—." His throat grew tighter and he was afraid he would cry. "Who make fun of me. They call me names. They say I'm a dummy and stupid and half-wit. It makes me so mad."

"Has this been goin' on for some time?"

"Yessir."

"Go ahead."

"Well, there is this one boy, Slim Jim, who tripped me goin' into the general store last week. He's meaner than the rest. Today when I went to town, he's the first person I saw comin' out of the general store where I needed to go. I couldn't get in the store without comin' face to face with him. He started callin' me names and makin' fun of me as soon as he saw me. I don't know what happened, but I just got so mad I jumped him. I was so mad it scared me. We fought for a while till the Sheriff came and stopped us."

"Clem, what did this boy, Slim Jim, look like after it was over?"

"'Bout like I did, I guess."

"Good. Give as good as you get, I say. What did the Sheriff do?" Clem cut his eyes to look at Jeremiah.

"Well, he took Slim Jim to his office and told me to get on home. He said he figured you'd know what happened by the looks of me."

Jeremiah sat quietly for a while, thinking and fishing. "You know, Clem, if it makes you feel better, it makes me mad, too, that these bullies call you names. In fact, it makes me want to go into town and—well, never mind. You are none of the things they're callin' you. You're as smart or smarter than they are, and you're a heap better feller than they are. Have you prayed about what to do?"

"Yessir. A lot."

"Well, what did God tell you to do?"

"I—I don't know."

"You're a good boy, Clem, always have been. God loves you and has His hand on you. We've always told you that. If you keep prayin', He will give you an answer in His time. That's a promise. There's a scripture that just came to mind from Jeremiah. I quote Jeremiah a lot, don't I? It says, 'Let them be confounded that persecute me, but let not me be confounded: let them be dismayed, but let not me be dismayed: bring upon them the day of evil, and destroy them with double destruction.' Now, I don't really believe we ought to wish bad on those boys, but don't you be so upset and dragged down by it. The Lord will fight your battles. He promises that. Trust Him to show you a way to solve this problem. And I tell you what, let's both start prayin' He'll show you that answer soon because I know those things they say hurt. Let'em roll off your back, son. They aren't true. Hold your head up and be as strong as I know you are. Just don't start any more fights, but if they start it you help'em finish it. Do you understand?"

"Yessir."

"Alright then, let's get down to some serious fishin'!"

By nightfall, Clem and Jeremiah felt a lot better, but there were about a dozen catfish that had given their lives in the effort!

CHAPTER 19

One winter day Clem was splitting wood at the old tree stump they used for that at the side of the house when he happened to glance up while he wiped sweat from his face. He actually heard it before he saw it. There was the sound of a horse but also a tinkling and a clanging. Clem completely stopped work to see what in the world could be making such noises. When it came into view, he thought his eyes were deceiving him. He wiped them again on his sleeve, but it was still there—a wagon unlike any he had ever seen. It was painted red on the sides and white on the top, and in black letters painted on both sides were the words

"Matthews Moving Emporium." It was an enclosed wagon, and from the sides hung all kinds of pots and pans, tin cups and plates, just about anything you could want. Clem was spell-bound. He'd never seen anything like it. As the wagon drew closer, he called, "G'amps! G'amps! We got company."

Jeremiah stepped outside the stable to see who this company might be. "Bless pat, if it ain't a peddler. You ever seen one, Clem?"

"No, sir. Sure is a strange lookin' thing."

"What he has inside is even stranger. Wait'll you see. They try to sell you everythin' they got. This should be fun. Come on, Clem."

Jeremiah and Clem were waiting on the peddler when he pulled his team into the yard. "Good morning, folks! Beautiful day, ain't it?"

"Well, if you don't mind cold weather, then I guess it is. What can we do for you?"

"It's not what you can do for me but what I can do for you, my fine man." He stepped forward and shook hands with Jeremiah and Clem and introduced himself. "My name is Malachi Matthews."

Jeremiah responded in kind, "I'm Jeremiah Jakes and this is my grandson Clem. What've you got for sale, Mr. Matthews?"

"The important thing is not what I have for sale, Mr. Jakes, but what I might have to help you folks. As you can see, I have all sorts of pots, pans, plates, and cups. For the womenfolk, I have fabrics, laces, hats, shoes, clocks, kitchen hardware, scissors, razors, pins and needles, perfumes and jewelry." His voice grew louder and more persuasive as he talked. "Are your womenfolk at home, sir, so I could show them what I have?"

"Our womenfolk have gone on to be with the Lord, Mr. Matthews. We won't be needin' any of that stuff."

Mr. Matthews softened. "I'm sorry, Mr. Jakes. Truly I am. I lost my wife and child years ago in a fire during an Indian raid. My heart goes out to you."

"And mine to you, Mr. Matthews. Thank you. What else do you have for sale?"

"Well, I do have some firearms and hunting knives you might be interested in as well as some medicines such as Turlington's Balsam, which, sir, has fifty-one different ailments it's good for all listed on the wrapper! One of the most popular items I sell! Would you like to try some?" He rambled inside the wagon and brought out a bottle for them to see.

Jeremiah took the bottle and read some of the ailments listed on the back. Handing it back to the peddler, "Don't think so."

"I have other medicines like Bateman's Pectoral Drops, good for coughs and congestion in the lungs. No? Well, there's one other thing I didn't mention. I have store soap for sell. It's so much better than the kind most folks make, the old soft brown soap? My soap is harder and in a bar shape, and it's wrapped, too! Would you like to try some, Mr. Jakes?"

"Don't think so. We menfolk don't mind what kind of soap we use, do we, Clem?"

"No, sir."

The peddler was trying hard to make some kind of sale. "Say, young man, would you like to see the hunting knives I have?" He jumped back in the wagon and soon emerged with three different knives for Clem to see. "I have a good choice. Just look at the handles. This one is bone—hand-carved. They're all sharp as a razor! Wouldn't you just love to have this one, Clem?"

Clem took it and really looked it over. He was thinking, *I really would love to have this knife, but I know G'amps can't afford to buy it. Better give it back.* "I don't guess so, mister." Jeremiah was wishing in his heart that they could afford the knife, but he knew the money just wasn't there. Maybe one day.

"Well, it looks like I can't persuade you folks to buy anything today."

Jeremiah hesitantly answered, "Well, there is one thing we could use."

"What's that, Mr. Jakes?"

"How much are your needles? The last one of my wife's needles is bent and dull."

"Well, it just so happens I have a small packet of needles for three cents. How's that?"

"Clem, go in the house and get three cents. Mr. Matthews finally made himself a sale." Clem was back quickly with the money.

"Thank you, Mr. Jakes. Good to do business with you," spoken while he climbed back onto the seat of his brightly colored wagon.

"Thank you, Mr. Matthews, and I hope business is better wherever you're goin'. Times are hard for a lot of folks nowadays."

"That they are. That they are. Well, God bless you folks," spoken as he urged the horses on.

"And God bless you, too."

❖ ❖ ❖

At supper one night a few days later as Jeremiah and Clem shared beans and fat pork, Jeremiah brought up the knife. "I'm really sorry, Clem, that we couldn't afford the knife you wanted from the peddler, but money is something we have little of. Maybe one day we can get you one."

"Don't worry about it, G'amps. We got knives. I don't have to have a fancy one like the one he had. I understand."

"You know, Clem, you're really a fine young man, and I appreciate you understandin'."

They were quiet a few moments before Jeremiah spoke, "Clem, I need to ask you to go into town for me tomorrow. I wouldn't ask if I didn't need for you to because of what happened the last time you went. I'd understand if you said no. I've got to get started mendin' the fences and I need some more barbed wire. If you'd rather, I'll go. Just say the word."

Clem was quiet for a few moments while he stared at his plate. He finally drawled, "I—I'll go. I have to face'em sometime."

"Clem, I suggest you spend some time in the stable tonight prayin', son. That's where the answer is. God holds the answer to everythin'. Ask Him what to do, Clem. Tell Him everythin', about how the boys treat you and how it makes you feel—the anger. He already knows, but He wants you to ask. Will you do that, son?"

"Yessir, I will. Right after supper."

❖ ❖ ❖

As soon as supper dishes were cleared away, Clem wordlessly made his way to the stable. He stood for a while watching the stars and thinking. After a while, he slid to his knees in the hay, clasped his hands and stared at the heavens, almost as if straining to see God. The words began to tumble out. "Oh, Heavenly Father, I have to go to town tomorrow. I don't want to go. Those boys will be there and they'll make fun of me again. Lord, they call me mean names—dummy, stupid, half-wit. They trip me and fight me. What can I do? I get so mad like last time that I punched Slim Jim. Why do they hate me? What have I ever done to them? Lord, show me what to do! G'amps says you have all the answers to everythin'. Please, please show me the answer to this. Should I call them names back or fight'em every time they call me names. I really don't know what to do. I'm gonna have to trust You to show me in Your time and way. Lord, thank You. In Jesus' Name, Amen." He laid on his face in the hay and cried to let out the emotions swirling inside and so G'amps wouldn't see him cry.

Little did Clem know that Jeremiah was inside the house on his knees crying and praying for the situation.

Morning came, no matter how hard Clem tried to pretend it hadn't. Breakfast was eaten in silence. Clem got ready to go in silence. As he mounted Blackie, Jeremiah put his hand on Clem's arm and said, "God is with you, Clem. He'll give you the answer."

"Yessir. I know He will." Clem rode off at a slow pace. Jeremiah stood watching him ride off with the weight of the world on his shoulders while he cried and prayed for Clem. "Lord, I would give my right arm if Clem didn't have to face this, but he has to grow up and become a man. We all have to handle what seem to be impossible situations to learn to trust You. This is Clem's. Be with him, Lord, and show him how to handle it." With tears dripping off his chin, he added, "Lord, if I could only take this on myself I would, but he has to do it. Help him."

Jeremiah went back inside and poured himself another cup of coffee to wait. He didn't really have a need to work on the fences today. He wanted to create a situation when this problem in town could come to a head and be resolved. Clem was about to do the hardest work of the day and maybe his life.

As Clem approached town, he saw four or five of the boys, including Slim Jim, so he slowed Blackie to a walk. He felt better about the situation, but he still didn't know what to do. As he rode closer to the general store where the boys were gathered, an idea slowly began to form in his mind, so that by the time he got to the hitching rail he knew what he was going to do. Slim Jim and the others began to laugh when they saw him. He never gave them a chance to call him names or do anything to him. Instead he held his head up, put a smile on his face and walked right up to them. He looked each boy in the face around the circle and said, "God loves you." He walked on into the store, inquired about barbed wire and came out. The gang of boys had moved down the street and didn't say a word to him as he came out and rode off.

Clem swung up into the saddle, held his head high and rode out of town without looking back. He couldn't have been happier, and he couldn't wait to tell G'amps! The closer he got to home the faster he rode and the broader his smile grew. Jeremiah heard him coming before he saw him because Blackie was pounding the dirt. When Clem rode into the yard with a big smile on his face, Jeremiah knew it was good news. Clem jumped to the ground and began jabbering so fast Jeremiah had a hard time keeping up, but he finally got the jist of it. Jeremiah threw his arms in the air and shouted, "Amen! Thank you, Lord!" He threw his arms around Clem in a big bear hug and said, "Son, let's go duck huntin'! Want to?"

"Sure! Oh, they were out of barbed wire, G'amps."

"No matter. Another time. Duck huntin' is more important right now. We gotta celebrate!" They stood grinning at each other for several minutes. "Go get the gun, Clem, and I'll put

Blackie up. Throw us some food in a bag too. No tellin' how long we might be gone."

"Yessir!"

As Clem walked off, Jeremiah brushed his hand across his eyes to wipe tears away and silently thanked the Lord for the unique way he handled the seemingly impossible situation. Only the Lord could do that.

For all the years that Clem would go into town after that, he couldn't know then that he would never have problems with those boys again.

CHAPTER 20

Jeremiah was sitting at Ruth's grave one March morning in 1884, just talking things over with her, as he did sometimes. He really missed being able to talk to her and to get her opinion or advice. He didn't do this in a morbid way but simply out of loneliness. While he could talk with Clem, it just wasn't quite the same.

"Oh, Ruth, I wanted to tell you about our boy, Clem. You wouldn't believe the man he's grown into. He's eighteen now—a man in every way. He's a hard worker, dependable, honest. He's had some hard knocks, but he's learned from them. There's a depth to his spirit that amazes me sometimes.

He definitely has a walk with the Lord. Moriah would be so proud of him and you would too, my love. We're doin' alright on the farm. We've claimed some more land and we're tryin' to put up a barbed wire fence around our property. It's a lot of hard work, especially when someone comes along and tears it down about every other day. There's a lot of conflict right now between the cattlemen and the homesteaders. I don't want to get into all that. I just want to run my farm and mind my own business. So—I guess we just keep puttin' up the fence they keep tearin' down." He rubbed his hand through his almost white hair. "I'm gettin' old, Ruth. I'm tired." He stopped talking and looked out across the fields. In the distance he could barely see a field of wild bluebonnets in bloom. "Ruth, the bluebonnets are in bloom, but as pretty as they are they can't hold a candle to you, my love. I still miss you so bad and I wish you was here. I know that you're happy in heaven, so I really can't wish you back. I believe it won't be too much longer before I'll be seein' you again and Moriah, Jeff, Lydia and William. Look for me. I still love—."

"G'amps! G'amps! Mr. Logan is here to see you," interrupted Clem.

Jeremiah glanced toward the house and saw Joshua Logan dismounting his horse. "I've got to go now, Ruth. I still love you."

Jeremiah rose, brushing a lone tear from his cheek, and strode briskly to greet Joshua Logan, who was a huge man with hands almost as big as hams, legs as big as small trees and a head full of curly black hair with a big shaggy mustache over his lip. His family had moved into the same area about the time Jeremiah and Ruth had. Joshua's farm was about three miles from Jeremiah's, and as a result they had gotten to be good friends over the years.

"Good morning, Joshua. How are things over to your place?" Jeremiah gave him a hearty handshake. Joshua returned his handshake which was rather like shaking hands with a bear!

"Well, Jeremiah, things are tol'able. Always some kind of work to do, ain't that so? Naw, I just wanted to talk to you about an idea I heard about that might help us both if you're interested."

"I'm always interested in a good idea, especially from a friend. What's on your mind, Joshua?"

"Well, I heard in town the other day that a company has started usin' cotton seeds as fertilizer and cattle feed. There was a couple of men askin' around to see if any cotton farmers in the area would be interested in sellin' cotton seeds. Have you ever heard of it?"

"As a matter of fact, I have heard of it, but that's all. Don't know much about it."

"I never knew cotton seeds was worth anythin' except to throw away, but to get paid for'em sure sounded good to me. I don't know how much they pay, but anythin' is better than nothin'. What'd you think, Jeremiah?"

Jeremiah rubbed his beard before he spoke. "Well, it sounds good. Do you think it could be a trick or is it for real?"

"I talked to Edwards at the general store after these two fellers left, and he says it's on the up and up. They'll be back next Saturday to sign up any farmers interested. They come back at the end of summer durin' cotton-pickin' time to get the seed. I think I'm gonna sign up. What about you?"

"Well, it sounds good. I'll think on it and pray about it by Saturday. I'll probably sign up too."

"The way times are now we have to bring in a few dollars however we can. Long as it's legal, o' course. How's Clem comin' along with keepin' his honeybees?"

"He's doin' real good. He's got five hives right now, but he plans to set up more in time. He's still learnin' how to handle bees. He gets stung pretty often, but he's learnin' better all the time. He's sellin' a little honey to Mr. Edwards at the general store, and like you say it brings in a few dollars. Truth to tell, Joshua, I'm so proud of Clem I could just bust sometimes. He's doing real good. He's a hard worker, and the way he's headin' he's goin' to be a successful farmer—better'n me. He wants to grow sugar cane and eventually sell logs to the lumber mills in Beaumont. He's young and has the energy that I don't have anymore. I think he might just make it."

"You're lucky, Jeremiah, to have him. I wish I had a son or grandson as good as Clem to help me out. It's hard goin' it alone sometimes. I don't know about you, but I'm gittin' old or at least I feel like it. I don't admit that too often, but it's true."

"I know just what you mean, Joshua. I was just tellin' Ruth—I mean—I was just thinkin' that myself this morning. Truth to be told I'm gettin' tired. Don't know how many more years I can hold out to work this hard. But I figure there's a better place I'll be goin' to where I'll never be tired again."

"Amen on that, Jeremiah! Amen! Well, I got to get me on home. Speakin' of work, I got to get to it. Guess I'll see y'all Saturday week at the church-raisin'."

"Sure will. Lookin' forward to it. So long, Joshua." Joshua threw up his hand as he rode away.

❖ ❖ ❖

On the planned Saturday Jeremiah and Clem gathered their tools and headed for the site of the new church they were helping to build in town. All of the men and women in the surrounding area were there, the men to build and the women to do odd jobs and to provide a feast at noon and leftovers at supper. They all planned to put in a full day. The church building had been begun about six months previously by men individually or by twos and the work had been haphazard over that time. Weather and thieves had wreaked some havoc on the partial building that had been done. Finally, it was decided by everyone wanting the church that they'd have to take it more seriously and apply themselves as a body and get the building done. They decided they'd all meet every Saturday and work until the church was ready for services, which they figured would be about three Saturdays. On that particular Saturday fifteen men, twelve women and an assortment of children showed up. A lot could be accomplished in a day with that many hardworking men on the job.

The church was located right in the town of Victory across the street from the general store and the saloon. It was the only building on that side of the street; therefore, it was aiding the town in growing and even in having a street. Up until the church was started, all the businesses or offices were in a straight line, so one would be hard put to say there was a street in Victory until now.

The men had started about seven o'clock and by noon had the church framed in. They stopped for the noon meal, rest and fellowship. It was during these times that neighbors got better acquainted. All these men were farmers and cattlemen who worked long, hard hours, and that explained why times like those were so pleasurable.

The women had laid out a feast. There was fried chicken, ham, roast beef, fried quail, boiled potatoes, cabbage and meat, baked beans, baked Hubbard squash, stewed pumpkin, fried apples and onions, boiled turnips, mashed potatoes, gravy, creamed carrots, johnny cake, cornbread, homemade bread, salt-rising bread and butter, pumpkin pies, dried berry pies, plum cake, and homemade ice cream. The men had thrown together some boards over sawhorses for the food before they started work. Jeremiah was the first one to notice, "Whoa, men, we better eat a lot in a hurry! The tables are bowin' in the middle with the weight of all that good food!"

The men filled their plates high and accepted big glasses of iced tea. The children followed with the women. The women tended to gather together as well as the men and children. The children ate fast so they could play. The adults lingered so they could visit.

"Well, Clyde Posey, it sure is good to see you here. I thought you was ailin'," Joshua Logan threw in, calling the men's attention to him.

"I was, Joshua. Some kind of gout the doctor thinks. It still bothers me a little, but I wanted to help with the church," responded Clyde. "How have you been gittin' along, Joshua? Did you hear about the two fellers who came to town last Saturday to sign up folks to buy their cotton seeds?"

"Sure did. I signed up and so did Jeremiah here. Did you?"

"No, I didn't 'cause I don't raise enough cotton anymore to make it worthwhile. But I tell you, if somebody comes along and wants to buy the weeds that grow up in my garden and fields, I'll be glad to sell 'em!" Clyde laughed. The men in hearing distance had a good laugh, and a few "Amens" were heard.

Clem was busy eating while listening to the men and, as usual, had not said much. "Clem, you gittin' enough to eat?" Joshua asked, smiling.

"Yessir!"

"I hear you git bee stung pretty regular, Clem. I heard of a new remedy for bee stings the other day. Wanna know what it is?"

"Yessir. It might help."

"Git rid of the bees!" Joshua laughed and slapped his knee. The other men joined in the merriment.

Clem wasn't sure how to take it, brushing his hand across his forehead. He didn't know if he was being made fun of or not. When he didn't laugh, Joshua added, "I was only joshin' you, boy. You know I think the world of you."

This served to embarrass Clem a little, but he responded, ducking his head, "Yessir, I know that. I think I'll get some more fried chicken. G'amps sure can't cook it like this!" All the men laughed, poking Jeremiah in the ribs, and saying things like, "Can't fry chicken?", "Where'd you learn to cook, Jeremiah?", "Bet you can't boil water!", "No wonder you and Clem's eatin' so much! You're probably half-starved!" Clem left the group to return to the food tables and left Jeremiah to take the ribbing, which he did well. He did, however, call out after Clem, "Thanks a lot, Clem. I'll get you later, boy!" Clem smiled as he walked off.

Clem walked the length of the tables to find the fried chicken and was pretty intent while looking at the food. As he reached for a chicken leg, another hand also reached for the same leg. Clem looked up slowly and said, "I'm sorry." He looked into the eyes of a lovely, short young lady who had long auburn hair hanging loose about her shoulders, beautiful soft, green eyes and a tiny waist. When she spoke, she had a soft voice, "No, I'm sorry. I guess we wanted the same leg." They paused and didn't know what to do next. "I don't think I've ever met you. My name is Susannah Brady. My parents are George and Martha Brady, sitting right over there under the tree. We live about eight miles in that direction," indicating southwest. "We've lived there about a year. I'm so glad we're building the church so we can get to really know folks, aren't you?"

She had talked so much Clem hadn't taken it all in. He brushed his hand across his forehead before he replied, "My name is Clem Brown and we live about ten miles south of here."

"Do you have family, Clem?" Susannah asked.

"Yes, ma'am. G'amps. The tall man with kind of red and gray hair sittin' over there with the men."

"Well, it's a pleasure to meet you, Clem. I hope to see you again sometime. You can have the chicken leg. I've decided to get some dessert."

"It's nice to meet you, too, Miss Susannah." Clem took the chicken leg and wandered on back to the men.

By the end of that day, the walls of the church were up, and plans were made to meet again the next Saturday to put on the roof. As it turned out, it rained the next Saturday, but they worked the following four Saturdays and completed the building. The last Saturday one group put on the finishing touches of whitewash inside and out while another group built pews and the pulpit. The ladies washed windows and hung curtains. Also, during the time of building the church, a committee of men looked for a preacher for their congregation. They finally found a preacher named Samuel Jennings who was willing to be their pastor. They couldn't pay him much, but they promised him they would provide him with all the food he could eat, and they would build a parsonage next door to the church where he could live.

The Sunday finally arrived for the first church service. Jeremiah and Clem had taken their Saturday night baths and got up Sunday morning eager to get to church. They dressed in their best and slicked down their hair, or at least Clem tried to slick down his cowlick. They rode ten miles to church which started at ten o'clock with Sunday school. Different men in the congregation would take turns teaching the Sunday school lesson, and this Sunday Joshua Logan taught a lesson from the book of Matthew, chapter 5. Preaching followed by Pastor Jennings, who was a rather short man with an open, smiling face and bright blue eyes. He was a lively man who radiated love to everyone he met. He preached his first message from I John 2:1-11, emphasizing keeping God's commandments and loving the brethren. Most folks complimented Pastor Jennings on his sermon as they filed out of church.

A typical Sunday at Victory Community Church included dinner-on-the-grounds after preaching, weather permitting. At that time, spring was bursting out all over and it was a beautiful day. Lunch was spread on the tables, and as always there was a country feast. This was a good social time for the families in the area. The older children ate in a hurry and began a game of baseball.

Jeremiah and Clem were talking with one of their neighbors, Frank Gershom, about raising sugar cane, which Clem was interested in doing.

"It's hard work, Clem. I won't lie to you. It grows best close to or even in the water, and it grows in big clumps of stalks with individual stalks that may be a half inch wide or even sometimes three inches, if it has a good year. It can grow twenty feet tall or taller. It's hard to work with, Clem. It's ready to cut after six to seven months in these parts. You cut it with long, sharp knives close to the ground, strip the leaves off the stalks, and then chop the stalks into short lengths to be ready for processin'."

"How does a body get started with raisin' sugar cane, Frank?" Jeremiah queried, wondering if Clem really wanted to take on this much more work.

"Well, I tell you what, Clem. Next time I cut mine I'll save you some stalks. What you do is cut the stalks so that you have a joint in the cane where the buds are. You plant the buds. It's pretty simple. I can also put you in touch with the folks that buy mine, if you're interested."

"Thank you, Mr. Gershom," replied Clem. "I really think I would like to try it."

"You're welcome, Clem," responded Frank. "Anytime I can help let me know. Think I'll go back for seconds. How 'bout you?"

"Maybe later, Frank," added Jeremiah. "Thanks again."

After Frank left, Jeremiah looked Clem in the eyes and asked, "Are you sure you want to take on that much more work on the farm, Clem? Ain't there enough to do? Or are you just younger than me and have more energy?"

"Well, G'amps, I would like to try it. You've always said that you wished you had raised more than just cotton back in south Georgia. That we might still be livin' there if you had d—d," Clem stuttered.

"Diversified. You're right. I did say that. And it's true. If you raise many different crops to sell and lose one or even two, you still have others to rely on. That's a bright move on your part, Clem. I just don't want you to take on more than you can handle. Think about it and pray about it first."

"I will, G'amps."

As the social began to break up and folks began to gather their food and put it in the wagons, Clem and Jeremiah were busy with getting the team ready to go when Clem looked up and saw a green-eyed young lady with long auburn hair sitting in the wagon next to theirs. Their eyes met, and Clem tipped his hat. Susannah spoke, "Hello, Clem. It's a beautiful day, isn't it?"

"Hello, Miss—."

"Susannah. Susannah Brady."

"Hello, Miss Susannah. It is a beautiful day."

As the wagon began to move, Clem looked away while Susannah watched him. Jeremiah happened to look back and saw Susannah looking at Clem. He smiled and poked Clem in the ribs and confided, "There's a real pretty girl lookin' at you, Clem."

"Yessir."

CHAPTER 21

Jeremiah woke early one morning and lay in bed listening to a mockingbird outside his window. "Beautiful," he whispered. Ruth always loved mockingbirds. Before he could arise, the pain started. *Oh, this is a bad one.* He broke out in a sweat and turned pale. The pain increased in the center of his chest and down his left arm. He lay there until it passed, which took about half an hour this time. *It's worse and it lasts longer*, he thought.

Jeremiah pulled himself out of bed when the pain subsided, and after sitting on the side of the bed for several minutes he pulled his clothes on. He didn't want Clem to know about it just yet. He hadn't even been to the doctor who was new in town. Maybe today he would have to go, but he still wouldn't tell Clem why—not yet.

Clem had breakfast ready when Jeremiah got up—good pancakes, sausage and scrambled eggs. "Good morning, Clem. Did you rest well?"

Clem glanced up as he answered, "Yessir. Did you?"

"Oh, pretty fair. Us old folks don't need as much sleep as you young ones. Breakfast looks good. My favorites."

Clem noticed how pale and sweaty Jeremiah was. "Do you feel bad, G'amps?"

"No, I'm fine." They ate breakfast in silence, although Jeremiah picked at his food more than he ate. Jeremiah didn't want to have to admit to Clem how sick he felt, and Clem didn't want to push him.

After they finished breakfast, Jeremiah asked Clem, "What are you goin' to work on today, Clem?"

"Thought I might plant the sugar cane Mr. Gershom gave me. Did you need me to do somethin', especially if you're sick or somethin'?"

"No, I'm fine. Go ahead and plant your sugar cane. Look forward to seein' how it grows. Lot of hard work. Are you sure you still want to do it?"

"Yessir, I want to try it."

"Good enough then. Hope it goes well. I think I'm goin' to ride into town and get that harness fixed and pick up a few things, like flour and salt pork. Can you think of anythin' else we need?"

"No, but do you want me to go with you? You look kinda weak."

"No, I'll be fine. May be comin' down with somethin'. Thanks anyway. See you when I get back. Don't work too hard—I really mean it."

"Thanks, G'amps. I'll watch it."

An hour later Jeremiah was riding into town on Whitey. His plan was to see the new doctor to find out if he could do anything for him. First, he dropped by the livery and got his harness repaired; secondly, he stopped by the general store for a couple of things; lastly, he went to the doctor's office which was in a new building next to the church. He read the name on the door as he entered, Dr. Hiram Purvis, M.D.

The outer office was empty, and Jeremiah wasn't sure what to do, so he sat down in one of the several chairs there. He decided he'd just wait and see if the doctor came out. He had waited about fifteen minutes when a door opened and the doctor and a woman came out.

"Mrs. Jones, don't worry. I don't think it's serious. Just take this tonic three times a day for about five days, and I think you'll be fine."

"Are you sure?" As the doctor nodded, she went on, "Well, thank you, Dr. Purvis. Here's some money on what I owe you. I'll pay more when I can."

"I understand, Mrs. Jones. You pay as you can. Goodbye now."

The short, fair-complexioned, bespectacled doctor turned back to Jeremiah and shook his hand. "Good morning. I'm Dr. Purvis. How may I help you, sir?"

"I'm please to meet you, Dr. Purvis. I'm Jeremiah Jakes. I live about ten miles south of here. I may be wastin' your time. There may not be anythin' wrong, but I've been havin' these pains in my chest."

"Come on in the examining room, Mr. Jakes." The doctor led him into the next room. After thoroughly examining him, the doctor sat down across from Jeremiah with a thoughtful expression on his face. "Mr. Jakes, how long have you been having these pains in your chest?"

"Oh, I'd say about three or four months."

"Do you have pain down your left arm also?"

"Yes, I do."

"Have the pains been getting worse?"

"Yes. This morning before I got out of bed was the worse I've had. I broke out in a sweat and felt weak, but it passed. Mostly."

"Mr. Jakes, I'm going to be honest with you because I think that's better than sugar-coating the truth. You have a heart problem which you probably already figured out for yourself. How severe, I don't know. Only time will tell. Based on your symptoms, you could have a heart attack at any time and die. I'm just being honest which I think you deserve to know. I can't predict how long you have. Only God knows. We really don't have any treatment for heart trouble, but let me give you some medicine called laudanum that will help with the pain."

"I don't want to take that stuff. I've seen what it can do to folks."

"I think it would be best if you keep some with you. The pain can sometimes be unbearable. You may reach the point where you'll wish you have some to lessen the pain. Please take it."

"Alright, but I don't plan to use it."

"I suggest you don't do any hard physical labor with your arms. It will bring on the pain and probably a heart attack. Do you have someone who can do the work for you?"

"Yes, my grandson already does a lot of it. Bless him. What will he do when I'm gone? He won't have nobody. I don't mind it for myself because I look forward to goin' home to heaven to see my wife and children, but Clem will be alone."

"I don't have any answers for that, but I do know God knows every need we have. He'll take care of Clem—and you. So don't worry."

"Are you a believer then, Dr. Purvis?"

"Yes, I am. In this business, I could never do it alone. I ask for His help every day. Let me pray for you right now." Dr. Purvis and Jeremiah both bowed their heads while the doctor prayed a heartfelt prayer for Jeremiah and his heart problem as well as Clem.

"Thank you, Dr. Purvis. It's wonderful to have a doctor who knows the Lord! How much do I owe you?"

"You know, Mr. Jakes, when I settled in the small town of Victory, I felt God called me here. I also felt that He would have me charge patients only what they could pay. So you pay me only what you can afford to. The Lord takes care of me."

Jeremiah reached in his pocket and handed the doctor a dollar. "Thank you, Dr. Purvis. Wish I could afford to give you more."

"That's more than enough. Take care of yourself and I mean that. You could live a good while longer if you don't work too hard. Do you understand, Mr. Jakes? Send for me if you need me."

"Thank you, doctor." Jeremiah walked out into the bright sunshine, squinting his eyes. *Well, Ruth,* he thought, *it may be quicker than I thought.* What about Clem?

He rode back to the farm slowly, thinking deeply and talking to the Lord. "Lord, I'm not afraid to die. I know I'll be with You and my family, especially Ruth. But, Lord, I am concerned about Clem. Can he make it on his own? There's so much work on the farm. Lord, I know Your time is close for me to come home. Prepare Clem. Give him courage and strength and wisdom. And, Lord, I've not prayed this before, but send him a helpmate to love him and support him. We know You're in control of all things, so we trust You to do what's best for all of us. In Jesus' Name, Amen."

That night at supper Jeremiah decided he had to tell Clem, and it was not easy. "Clem, I went somewhere today I didn't tell you about. I went to see the doctor in town." Clem's head jerked up and his eyes widened. "He says—he says I have a bad heart. He doesn't want me to work too hard physically because it could cause a heart attack. He gave me—."

Clem jumped up, and his chair fell over backward. "No!" he yelled. "It's not true! It can't be!"

"Clem, calm down. I've known for some time that somethin' was wrong, and I figured it was my heart. I just didn't want to worry you, and really I didn't want to believe it either. But the Lord's in control and He'll do what's best for all of us. You believe that, don't you?"

Clem was crying. "I guess so." He ran out of the house to the stable and threw himself into the hay to cry, very much like he had done for his mother and grandmother. When the sobs subsided a little, he prayed, "Lord, it's not fair. I've lost everybody in my life but G'amps. You can't take him too. I'll be all alone. I need him. I need him." He lay there for an hour devastated by the news G'amps had given him.

Early one morning a few days later Clem was feeding the chickens while Jeremiah was using a pitchfork to put hay in the stalls of Blackie and Whitey. Suddenly Jeremiah grabbed his chest and fell to the ground. He weakly called to Clem. Clem finally heard him and came running.

"G'amps! What's wrong?"

"Heart—heart—," Jeremiah gasped. "In the—house." Clem managed to get Jeremiah into the house and then into his bed. He was weak, pale and sweaty and had a hard time getting his breath. Clem got a cool cloth and wiped Jeremiah's face and neck and then gave him some water to drink.

"I'm goin' for the doctor, G'amps!"

"No—wait," he responded weakly. "No use. Nothin' he can do. Stay with me, Clem."

"But the doctor might be able to help, G'amps."

"No. Nothin' he can do. I want to tell you what a fine young man you've turned out to be, Clem. Your mother and grandmother would be so proud of you and I'm sure they see and know."

"Don't talk like this—like you're about to—."

"Clem, I really think God's time has come for me to be with Him and your G'amma and your parents. It's alright, Clem. You'll be alright. There's nothin' on the farm you can't handle now. You're a hard worker and I'm proud of what you've accomplished. You'll make a go of the farm better than I ever did. I'm tired now. Let me rest." Clem sat by the bed and held Jeremiah's rough, calloused hand with his own rather rough hand. Clem prayed silently while Jeremiah slept. About noon, Jeremiah woke up long enough for Clem to feed him a little broth, and then he fell asleep again.

Clem began to pace the floor and pray. "Please, God, don't take him now. I still need him. Heal him and let him live. Oh, God, please." He kept repeating the same words over and over because it was all he could think of.

Jeremiah woke up and Clem was at his side in an instant. "How do you feel, G'amps?"

"Very—tired. I love you, Clem. You've been like a son to me."

"I love you too, G'amps. You've been like a pa to me. Thank you for everythin' you've done for me." Tears were streaming down Clem's face. Jeremiah clutched his chest again and squeezed his eyes shut while grasping Clem's hand with his other hand. Slowly Jeremiah's grip was released on his chest and in Clem's hand while his face relaxed. When Clem looked at his face, he almost looked as if he had a smile on his face. Clem knew he was gone.

Clem numbly walked to the window thinking about what he should do. His tears dried and he came to the conclusion that he needed help. He went out to the stable to saddle Blackie and then headed for Joshua Logan's farm.

Joshua Logan and his wife Abigail, who was a petite woman with light blue eyes in direct contrast to her husband, followed Clem in their wagon. There was no need to hurry now, and Clem was so numb he more or less let Blackie lead him home. When they reached the farm, Joshua and Abigail followed Clem inside reverently as people tend to do when there is a death. Abigail began to cry openly, and even Joshua felt a tear or two roll down his cheeks when he saw his closest friend laid out in death. Clem didn't cry. Abigail hugged Clem and cried, "I am so sorry, Clem. Don't worry about anythin'. We'll help you. We'll always be here for you."

"Thank you, Mrs. Logan."

Joshua shook Clem's hand and echoed his wife's sentiment, "Clem, I'm sorry too. I just can't believe it. What happened?"

"A heart attack. He just went to the doctor a few days ago and the doctor told him if he worked hard physically it could cause a heart attack. But G'amps wouldn't slow down. Thank you for comin'. What are we supposed to do?"

"Don't worry, Clem. We'll take care of things."

"I want to help."

Joshua and Clem washed Jeremiah, dressed him in his best clothes and laid him out on the bed. Abigail straightened the house, washed the breakfast dishes, and swept the floor since she knew people would be bringing food and stopping by to pay their respects.

"Is there anythin' else we can do right now, Clem?" queried Abigail.

"I don't know. What about a coffin, Mr. Logan?"

"I'll take care of it, Clem. Don't worry."

"I want to help build it, Mr. Logan."

"I understand, son. I'll bring all the lumber over here this afternoon and we'll work on it together. How's that?"

"Fine, sir. Thank you."

As the couple climbed on their wagon, Abigail reassured Clem. "We'll get word to Pastor Jennings and I'm sure he'll come."

That afternoon Clem helped Joshua build the pine coffin and set it up in the front part of the house. Pastor Jennings came and talked and prayed with Clem. As word spread in the community, people began to stop by to leave food and give their condolences. Clem was numb and endured the many kind things people had to say. He knew they meant what they said, but he just wanted to be alone in his grief. As usual Clem had little to say. There was a lot of food brought which the ladies took care of, and soon the table was full to overflowing.

Joshua Logan took Clem aside and volunteered, "Clem, I want you to know that if you ever need any help on the farm I'll be glad to help."

"Thank you, Mr. Logan, but I think I can make it on my own."

"Will you promise me you'll ask if you do need me?"

"Yessir. And thank you."

"There's a good turnout of folks. Jeremiah was a good neighbor and folks thought highly of him."

"Yessir." Clem was at a loss for words.

Joshua wandered off, and Mr. and Mrs. Posey came to him to tell how sorry they were and to offer their help. Clem responded the same way he had to Joshua Logan. They were followed by Frank Gershom and his two sons. Once again he had offers to help him. Mr. Edwards, owner of the general store, and Mr. Blackstock, the town blacksmith, gave their condolences. Even Sheriff Brackett came by. "Jeremiah was one of the finest men I ever knew, Clem. I'm real sorry this happened. Can I help you with anythin'?"

"No, sir. I don't think so."

"If you ever do need help with anythin', you just call me. Alright?"

"Thank you, I'll remember that."

An older couple walked up that he didn't recognize, but they introduced themselves. "You probably don't remember us. We're new in the church. I'm George Brady and this is my wife Martha, and I think you may have met my daughter Susannah. We just wanted to say how sorry we are for your tragedy, and if we can help please let us know. I'm good at figuring and keeping books if you ever need help with that."

"Thank you, sir."

Susannah took Clem's hand to shake it and softly said, "Clem, I don't know if you remember me, but we've met twice before. I'm so sorry about your grandfather." She was softly crying and wiped her green eyes with a handmade, linen handkerchief.

"Yes, I remember you. Thank you all for comin'."

Pastor Jennings came over to talk with Clem about the funeral the next day. "Clem, did Jeremiah have a favorite hymn or scripture that you know of?"

Clem was thinking hard. "Well, he was always quotin' Job. Especially the verse that says 'Though He slay me, yet will I trust in Him.' He had learned it from his pa and through some hard times he went through." He passed his hand across his forehead before he spoke, "I don't know about a hymn. He liked so many."

"Well, that's fine. We'll choose one."

Finally, the day passed and everyone went home. Clem was exhausted emotionally and physically. He turned down all offers to stay the night with him. He assured everyone he'd be fine. He was so numb and tired that he went straight to sleep and didn't wake the next morning until it was full daylight.

When he awoke, it took him several minutes to remember what had happened. He was still tired and numb. First thing he did was to go to Jeremiah's coffin. "I love you, G'amps, and I really miss you. I wish you could come back. I still need you, but I know you're with G'amma again and my Ma and Pa and William and Lydia. Tell them hello from me. Say a special prayer for me that God will watch over me real close. I really need His help now."

The graveside service was that afternoon at two o'clock at the family cemetery. Jeremiah would be laid to rest next to his life partner, Ruth. There were so many people there that Clem was amazed. People were standing everywhere to pay their last respects to a good neighbor and friend. Pastor Jennings led everyone in singing "Amazing Grace", and then he read some scripture including Jeremiah's favorite verse in Job and made some remarks about what a fine man he was and what a strong faith he had. He would be missed by all. Clem threw in the first clod of dirt. And before he knew it, it was all over. People went back to the house to eat again, and Clem felt that he just couldn't take much more of all the social doings. He just wanted to be alone.

While folks were eating and socializing, Clem sneaked out of the house and walked down to the creek. He didn't know he was being watched by Susannah Brady, who almost went to the creek also to try to console him but thought better of it. She lifted him up in prayer where she stood. She didn't realize then how many prayers she would pray for this man in the years to come.

CHAPTER 22

The air was beginning to feel crisp several days after Jeremiah's funeral while Clem was splitting wood. He had been at the task for more than an hour and had worked up a sweat despite the coolness. His thoughts traveled from how much wood he needed to split to the crops he needed to harvest to his rumbling stomach. He even had a fleeting thought of Susannah Brady at the funeral, especially how she had cried softly for practically a stranger. As he continued to split wood, he noticed big drops falling on his tanned, muscular arms and hands. His first thought was rain and then sweat, but as he reached up to wipe sweat he realized they were tears running down and dripping off his chin and nose. After his initial tears when Jeremiah died, he couldn't cry through the funeral and talking with all the people who came to the house. It seemed as though numbness set in and he couldn't really feel anything, but now suddenly and unexpectedly the tears and emotions he had held in began to flow. He dropped his axe and headed to the family cemetery under the old cypress tree where there were now two graves.

Clem sat down by Jeremiah's grave and realized what it meant to be all alone in the world. He spoke aloud through his tears, "I don't have anybody, G'amps. Ever'body's gone but me. I don't like bein' by myself. Oh, G'amps, I miss you and G'amma! What am I gonna do?" He laid his head on his arms on the fresh dirt on Jeremiah's grave and finally released all the pent up emotions that he had had ever since Jeremiah died. He was wracked with sobs for a while as he thought about having nobody. Slowly the sobs turned to tears and finally to soft crying. Finally, Clem called out to the only One left to talk to, "Oh, God, what am I gonna do? I'm all alone now. G'amps is gone. He's always been there for me. Now there's not even anybody to talk to!"

Clem was quiet for a while until a strange thing happened. He felt compelled to get up and walk away from the graves, which he did. He stood there looking up toward the deep, azure sky wondering what was happening. "Lord, are you tryin' to tell me somethin'?" He didn't hear words like the prophets in the Old Testament, but he sensed the Lord was speaking to him. He felt a strong warmth and love inside such as he had never felt before. He fell to his knees and softly said, "Lord, You're here and I'm not alone, am I? You've always been with me and You always will be. I can always talk to You. Thank You, Lord. Praise You, Lord." He was quiet for a while just listening. He continued to pray, "Lord, help me with all the work there is to do. Guide me in what I should add to the farm work. Help me to build a fine farm here. That's my dream." He fell quiet again. "Lord, I've never thought to pray for this before, but could you send me a wife to love and take care of? I guess it'll have to be somebody special for the likes of me since I'm kinda slow and can't read and write, but You know all that. Send me what and who I need, Lord, and I thank You for lovin' me and takin' care of me all my life and for the rest of my life. Help me keep faith always and trust You with all my heart and help me have the courage to go on. Amen."

Clem threw himself into the work on the farm, harvesting the crops that year which produced a good yield. He added ten more beehives and watched his sugar cane every day to see when it would mature. He also began to selectively cut trees to take to Beaumont to sell for lumber as well as continuing his cotton, corn and wheat crops. He remembered what Jeremiah had told him about not taking on more than he could do, but he also remembered the idea of diversifying that Jeremiah had always wished he had done. Clem just felt it was good sense to have several cash crops in case something happened to one of them like cotton, then he would have others to fall back on. In fact, he felt rather proud that he had thought to plan this way, and he just knew everything would be alright for him.

The experience Clem had at Jeremiah's grave of being filled with God's love and warmth was a turning point for Clem. He began to go back to church and made it a point to talk with the other men and tip his hat to the ladies. A sense of being part of the community as an individual, not just as Jeremiah's grandson, was growing in Clem, and it made him feel more a part of the adult community.

❖ ❖ ❖

In 1889, Clem was twenty-three years old, and though he was still short at five feet six inches, he was muscular, tanned, confident young man. He was still soft-spoken and often hesitant before he spoke, which actually reflected his thoughtfulness. However, when he did speak, people tended to listen because he showed wisdom in his thinking. People knew that he worked hard and had done well for himself, so they trusted his opinions. He had consciously worked on giving up the habit of passing his hand across his forehead and replacing it with tugging his hat brim or his ear if he wasn't wearing a hat. He was faithful to church and helped his neighbors when they needed it as they did for him.

One late spring day Clem was in town on errands, and as he passed down the newly laid board sidewalks in the growing little town of Victory, a conversation took place between Mr. Edwards at the general store and Joshua Logan, Clem's closest neighbor.

"There goes one of the finest young men I know, Joshua. Wouldn't you say so?"

"I sure would. Clem works hard on his farm and is always willin' to help somebody else. He's helped me time and again. He's turned out a good crop of sugar cane for the last five years and cotton and corn and honey. Did you know he now has twenty-five beehives? He's also cuttin' timber which he hauls to Beaumont to sell. Sometimes I think he's workin' too hard. Wonder what Jeremiah would say about that. You know, I still miss ol' Jeremiah. There was another good man."

"Yes, he was. Clem has sold me the finest honey in this whole area because he takes care of it so well. It's clean and pure. He sure is faithful to church too, ain't he? He's always willin' to help out any way he can. You know, the one thing I think Clem's missin' in his life is a good wife."

"Why, Edwards, I never knew you noticed things like that!" Edwards ducked his head and blushed a little, but Joshua went on, "As a matter of fact, my Abigail was sayin' the same thing the other day. He needs a good, lovin' wife to come home to and share life with. Course Abigail wanted to start fixin' him up with somebody right off the bat, but I told her Clem's got to do it for himself. As shy as he is, if anybody was forced on him, he'd run like a scalded pup.

We've got to pray this one into happenin', don't you think?"

"Knowin' Clem, you're right. The Lord knows who would be right for him. Say—what about Susannah Brady? She's pretty as can be and kinda shy herself. You ever met her, Joshua?"

"I've seen her with her parents. She is a pretty one, but like I said I know Clem well enough to know we better stay out of it and let the Lord handle it."

"You're right. I just want the best for him. He's suffered at lot in his life, losin' ever'body—both his parents and his grandparents. That's tough."

❖ ❖ ❖

Joshua Logan came riding into Clem's yard as fast as he could go and almost threw himself over his horse's head in his efforts to stop. Dust and dirt flew up in every direction, even into Clem's face as he stepped out of his cabin.

"Well, Mr. Joshua, you're sure in a hurry. What's wrong?" he asked, as he brushed dust off himself.

"I'm sorry to cover you with dust, Clem, but my prize heifer, dang her hide, has got herself stuck in a bog. I'm gonna need help gettin' her out. Can you help me?"

"Sure thing, Mr. Joshua. Let me saddle Blackie right quick."

"Bring some rope, Clem."

In only a few minutes, the two rode out about as fast as Joshua had ridden in. When they got to where the heifer was stuck, Joshua suggested they both use their ropes to lasso her and try to pull her out. After several attempts to throw the ropes around her neck, they successfully had her lassoed.

Joshua and Clem tied their end of the ropes to their saddles and began to use the horse power to pull her out.

"Alright, Shotgun, pull and pull hard," Joshua urged his horse with his knees. Clem and Blackie pulled as hard as they could. The cow wouldn't budge. They slacked off and tried it again. The horses were straining, but so far the heifer didn't move. "Man alive, she shor' is stuck. Clem, reckon you could ride over to Clyde Posey's and see if he could come help?"

"Be glad to." Clem untied his rope and dropped it to the ground before he took off in the direction of Mr. Posey's farm.

Soon Clem and Clyde Posey rode up to find Joshua resting under a large elm tree and the heifer with her head sticking out of the bog. Joshua jumped to his feet and cried, "We gotta hurry. She's sinkin'. Glad you could help, Clyde. See if you can lasso her."

Within minutes, Clyde had her lassoed, and with all three using the strength of their horses, they began to see her rise a little. They kept a steady pressure on the ropes, and within half an hour they had her on firm ground.

As Joshua took his rope off her, he spit out, "Dang heifer. She's always gittin' into somethin'. She keeps it up and I'll shoot her!"

Clyde and Clem laughed. Clyde threw in, "I don't think you'd shoot your prize heifer, Joshua!"

Joshua laughed then. "I don't guess I really would at that. Thanks to both of you for helpin' out. I couldn't have done it without you. If you ever need help, just let me know. And I mean it now."

"I'll remember, Joshua. By the way, are you two comin' this Saturday to help paint the church and plant some trees?"

"I am," Clem answered quickly.

"Just can't pass up that good food, can you, Clem?" Joshua kidded him. "I plan on bein' there, too, if this heifer stays put."

❖ ❖ ❖

Clem was digging on his ninth hole to plant poplar trees around the Victory Community Church when he looked up and saw Susannah Brady heading toward him with a glass of lemonade in her hand. Why it happened at that particular moment he never knew, but the handle of the shovel he was using broke which put him on his backside on the ground about the time she reached him! His face turned all shades of red as he jumped up brushing himself off. The men who saw it happen cackled like hens! When word spread around, all the men were laughing so hard some of them rolled in the dirt laughing. Clem wanted to run off or get swallowed up by the earth! *Did they have to make so much out of it right in front of Susannah? What would she think?*

"Are you alright, Clem?" Susannah almost laughed. A smile played at the corners of her mouth. She tried hard not to laugh at him, even though he did look funny. Clem began to look around and finally saw the humor in the situation and began to laugh at himself. Then Susannah laughed out loud, too.

"Would you like some lemonade, Clem?" she laughed.

"Yes, Miss Susannah, I believe I do. Let's walk over to the wagon." He wanted to get out of sight of all the men laughing at him. "How are you today, Miss Susannah?"

"Oh, I'm fine, Clem. Are you alright after your—uh, fall?"

Clem ducked his head and turned red again. "Yes, ma'am, I reckon so. Been usin' that shovel all mornin'. Can't figure why it broke like that. Guess it was just wore out."

Susannah changed the subject, "The church is looking nice, isn't it? And the trees around it will give some shade in the hot summertime. The ladies are washing the windows and putting up fresh curtains. We've—that is, the ladies—have decided when we get time and can afford it we're going to put cushions on the pews to make them softer. What do you think, Clem? Is that a good thing to do?"

"Sounds good to me. If Pastor Jennings preaches a long time, it might help out." Clem spoke it with a twinkle in his eye, which seemed a lot like what Jeremiah would have said and done.

Susannah laughed and added, "I guess I'd better go help the ladies with the food. It's not long till dinner. See you later, Clem."

Clem stood where he was watching her walk off and thought how much he enjoyed hearing her laugh. He glanced up and decided he'd better get back to work before the men started kidding him about Susannah. He gulped the lemonade, got another shovel, and started digging holes again.

When dinnertime came, the ravenous men went through the line first, followed by the children and women. Clem had sat down on the porch steps to eat, and shortly Susannah came over and interrupted Clem's eating, "May I sit with you, Clem? It seems to be the only place left."

He jumped to his feet to make room for her and answered, "Yes, ma'am. I'd like that." They settled in and quietly ate for a while.

"Clem, were you born here in Texas?"

"No, ma'am, I was born in Virginia. My pa died before I was born. He was shot up in the war and came home but just never got well. After I was born, my mother moved us back to south Georgia where she was from to live with my grandparents. I lost my mother a few years later in an accident. When times got really hard there and we couldn't pay the high taxes anymore, G'amps—that's what I always called my grandpa—decided to sell out and we moved here with only what we could bring in our wagon. My G'amma—that's what I called her—really didn't want to leave all the things she'd collected through the years—even some furniture and other things her mother and grandmother gave her. But we had to leave it all behind. Oh, I'm sorry, Miss Susannah, I'm talkin' too much!"

"No, Clem, I love hearing about your family and your life. And I'm sorry about you losing both your parents. That must have been really hard. Tell me more. Then I'll tell you about myself."

"Well, alright. I just don't want to tire you out."

"You're not tiring me out at all! Please go on." Clem looked at her. Sincerity was etched across her face, and her face had a softness to it he hadn't noticed before. Her soft green eyes showed interest in what he was saying, and her long, auburn curls lay about her shoulders with the sun highlighting it. Clem couldn't have put these thoughts into words if he tried, but the lovely young woman beside him surely made an impression. He was caught lost in thought when Susannah repeated, "Go on, please, if you don't mind talking about it."

"Oh—uh—no, I don't mind. Where'd I get to?"

"Your grandparents decided to move here, and your grandmother hated leaving her nice things behind."

"Oh, yeah, they had an auction to get rid of all our things. Anyway, we had quite an adventure gettin' here. We crossed seven rivers. The Mississippi River was so big and wide!" Clem became more and more animated as he brought back memories of their trip. "It was so dirty, too. There were ferries that took our whole wagon and horses across. For a young boy, that was a real adventure. We got stuck in the mud once, and we floated the wagon across one river and didn't know if we'd make it or not. I remember my dog Boney jumped out of the wagon to swim across. I thought he was gonna drown and I started to jump in after him, but G'amps stopped me. He said Boney would be alright and he was right. By the way, that's Boney over there, the dog eatin' any scrap that comes his way." Susannah lightly laughed and Clem whistled for Boney who came to him slowly. "He's anythin' but Boney now, but he's also old. Don't really know how old. He's lost some of his teeth and he can't see too good anymore, but we love each other. Gonna miss him when he's gone." Boney snuggled up under Clem's arm and started to eat from his plate until Clem moved it away. "Boney, don't eat outta my plate!"

Susannah laughed again. "No, he's sure not Boney now. Here, Boney, have this piece of chicken." She handed it to Boney who sniffed it, took it in his mouth, plopped down and began eating it. Susannah and Clem both laughed. Clem realized suddenly how much he loved Susannah's laugh and that they laughed together a lot.

"Enough about me. Tell me about yourself, Miss Susannah."

"Well, our lives aren't as full of adventure as yours, really kind of dull, I guess. You've met my parents. They're good people and I guess they've always spoiled me some since I'm an only child. By the way, you didn't say, but do you have any brothers or sisters?"

"No, no brothers or sisters."

"Well, I used to get lonesome playing by myself until my Papa came home. He used to make up fun games to play with me. He always worked in a bank, keeping books and doing figures and that kind of thing. He was always my best playmate, besides my dolls. I grew up helping Mama in the kitchen and with the cleaning. She always tried to make a game out of everything we did together. She hasn't been well for the past five years and has to not overdo. That's why she's not here today. I worry about her." Tears glistened in her eyes.

"I'm sorry, Miss Susannah. I'll pray for her, if you'd like."

"Yes, I would. Thank you, Clem. Anyway, the bank in Philadelphia where my Papa worked for sixteen years went out of business and he lost his job. He decided we'd move west and perhaps he could start a small bank with our savings. He would like to do that here in Victory. I hope it works out. I really like it here, don't you?"

"Yes, I do. I'd like for you to see my farm sometime. Me and G'amps have worked hard to make it a good farm. I'm kinda proud of it." He lowered his head because he felt like he was bragging.

"I'd love to see it sometime. Right now I guess we'd better get back to work. Everybody else has."

Clem looked around and sure enough the men were painting and planting trees. He blushed when he realized they were watching him and Susannah. He jumped up and headed for the tree planting. Susannah called after him, "Will I see you in church tomorrow?"

"Yes, ma'am. I'll be here."

As he went back to work, one of the young men his age, Johnny Morgan, called out, "Pretty little girlfriend you got there, Clem!"

Clem knew he meant it good naturedly, but it still embarrassed him. "Oh, hush, Johnny." He couldn't keep himself from casting a glance in Susannah's direction.

CHAPTER 23

"Is this seat taken, Clem?"

"No, ma'am, Miss Susannah. Have a seat." Clem jumped up and slid over some. "Are your parents here?"

"Yes, but they're sitting with Mr. and Mrs. Logan over there. You just looked lonely sitting here by yourself. Do you mind?"

"No, Miss Susannah." Clem started sweating and he couldn't understand why. The weather wasn't that warm.

Clyde Posey taught Sunday school that morning. There was a short break before preaching, and then the service began with a few hymns. Clem and Susannah shared a hymn book, which made Clem more nervous. He'd never sung in front of anybody but Jeremiah. Susannah had a clear, strong soprano while he just kind of stumbled through. He loved listening to her sing. Pastor Jennings preached a good message, but if anybody had asked Clem what the sermon was about he couldn't have told them. He was so aware of Susannah next to him that he couldn't concentrate, and he knew the boys and men would tease him unmercifully.

A dinner-on-the-grounds was planned after church. "Clem, my parents and I would like for you to join us for dinner today. Would you like to eat with us?"

"That would be fine, Miss Susannah, but are you sure your parents won't mind?"

"Oh, no, it was their idea to ask you. Come on." When Clem hesitated, Susannah added, "We all want you to come, Clem. You'll like my parents. They're very nice people."

When the tablecloths were spread and food was laid, Susannah brought Clem over to meet her parents. "Papa, Mama, this is Clem Brown. Clem, these are my parents, George and Martha Brady."

Clem swept his hat off and turned it round and round in his hands. "I'm pleased to meet you, Mr. and Mrs. Brady."

George Brady stood up and extended his hand, "It's our pleasure, Clem. We're so glad you could join us. We've heard a lot about you from Susannah. This is my wife Martha."

Clem nodded and said, "Pleased to meet you, ma'am."

Martha extended her hand also. "It's good to know you, young man. Please have a seat and help yourself to our dinner. Susannah insisted on cooking more than we could ever eat today." It was Susannah's turn to blush.

As they ate, they learned more about each other. Mr. and Mrs. Brady asked a lot of questions of Clem in a friendly way. They just wanted to know more about the young man their daughter was so obviously interested in. He was all she'd talked about for weeks. Clem repeated the story of his life he had already told Susannah and then warmed to his favorite topic of his farm. He was justifiably proud of it and even told them about some of the improvements he planned to make in time. "I'd like to add maybe two rooms or even more to the cabin and maybe dig a well close to the house. I live near a creek, but it would be easier if I had a well close to the house. One day I might even put a pump in the kitchen. I plan to put in more sugar cane, corn, cotton and wheat when I'm able to do it. I don't want to put in more than I can handle though."

Susannah's parents were impressed with Clem. He obviously was a hard worker and had plans for his farm which already sounded fine to them. They enjoyed a delicious dinner as they talked and got acquainted. He learned more about the Bradys—how the bank where Mr. Brady worked had failed in Philadelphia and they, actually Mr. Brady, decided they'd move west with hopes of opening a bank of their own. So far they hadn't been able to do it because they had spent the last year building a house and furnishing it. That had used up a lot of their money and now they'd have to save for some time to be able to finance a bank. Clem got the impression that Mrs. Brady was a little selfish wanting a house first, and it didn't seem quite right to Clem to build a fine house and furnish it before Mr. Brady had a good job but he didn't say anything.

George Brady answered one question Clem had in his mind. "I'm working now for several businessmen in town keeping books for them—Mr. Edwards at the general store, Mr. Blackstock who is the blacksmith, Mr. McDougall at the livery. I'm talking to a few others too. One of these days we'll have enough saved to start the First National Bank of Victory." Mr. Brady had a big smile on his face at the thought. It was easy to tell this was a dream he cherished.

"Clem, let's take a walk by the creek." Susannah made it more of a statement than a question.

Mrs. Brady threw in, "Yes, you two run along. The homemade ice cream will be ready by the time you get back."

Clem rose to his feet and slapping his hat on the back of his head, he responded, "Sure, Let's go, Miss Susannah." They headed to the creek, and Clem knew everybody would be watching them. By the time they reached the creek, his neck was beet red.

It was cool and green at the creek, which was a relief to Clem. They walked quietly for a while until Susannah asked, "Why do you always call me 'Miss Susannah'?"

"Well, I don't know. I guess just bein' respectful."

"Would you mind calling me just Susannah?"

"Of course not. If it's what you want."

"Oh, I've got a good idea, Clem. Let's take our shoes off and wade in the creek! It'll be fun. Come on." She started taking hers off.

"Well, alright, but it's gonna be cold."

Susannah was the first in the water, shrieking and jumping up and down. "Oh, it's so cold!"

"I told you so." Susannah reached up and pulled Clem into the water beside her. "Yep, I told you so." Clem was jumping from one foot to the other.

"You look so funny, Clem, like you're dancing or something!"

"So do you, Miss—I mean—Susannah! We better watch out for copperheads and water moccasins."

"Not this early in the year surely. Let's walk down the creek a little ways or are you chicken?"

"No, ma'am, I'm not chicken, but there's lots of holes you could step into and places where snakes can hide."

"Are you sure you're not just chicken, Clem?"

"Just tryin' to look after you. That's all."

Susannah stopped and looked back at Clem. "That's really sweet, Clem."

"Well—uh—uh—." Clem was totally flustered.

They walked down the creek a distance and had no mishaps, so they turned back to where they'd left their shoes and dried their feet as best they could on the grass. "Well, I think it's time to go, Clem. I hear Mama calling. That was fun. Let's do it again sometime. Come to my house sometime and I'll show you around."

"Alright, if it's okay with your folks."

"They'd love to have you come, Clem. I'll let you know when."

❖ ❖ ❖

About two weeks later on a Saturday night Clem was bathed, dressed in his best shirt, pants, polished boots, and brushed hat, and on his way to Susannah's house on Blackie who was also rubbed down till he shone. Clem wasn't really sure why he had done all that he had, but somehow it just seemed an important thing to do. He was nervous and self-conscious. He kept asking himself why he should be nervous. After all, he had already met Susannah's parents and talked with them. As he rode along, he prayed, "Oh, Lord, help me not be so nervous. I know I'm not very smart, but they seemed to like me. Lord, help me just to be the person I am and not pretend to be somebody I'm not. You made me this way and so I just ask You to give me the grace and faith to handle this tonight. Thank you, Lord. In Jesus' Name, Amen." *I feel better already*, he thought.

Clem arrived a little early at the Brady home which was located within walking distance of the town. It was a two-story, white, colonial home with green shutters. A porch went around the entire outside of the house! Clem began to feel uneasy with such an elaborate house compared to his. As he dismounted and tied his horse to the hitching post out front, he wondered if he had made a mistake in coming. He might mess up in front of these fancy people. He slowly went to the front door and knocked.

George Brady opened the door and warmly welcomed Clem. "Come in, my boy! Come on in. We are so glad you could come have supper with us. Susannah has talked of nothing else. Mrs. Brady has looked forward to it too. Come on in the front room here where the fire is. My old bones need some warmth even this late in the spring. Here, lay your hat on this table."

"Thank you, Mr. Brady. Your house is beautiful and so big. I mean—uh—well."

"That's alright, Clem. It is big, bigger than I wanted, but sometimes you have to please the womenfolk. Have a seat here. Supper will be ready in a few minutes I'm sure."

Some of the furniture and other things reminded him of his grandparents' home back in south Georgia, maybe newer and a little fancier, but not too different. It made him relax a little.

Mr. Brady broke into his thoughts by leaning over and whispering in his ear, "Relax, boy. You'll do fine. We're just simple folk at heart, no different than your own grandparents."

"Thank you, Mr. Brady. That helps."

Susannah practically ran into the room. "Clem, you're here. I'm so glad. Supper's ready. Come on into the dining room." Susannah took her father's arm and Clem's and propelled them into the dining room, where Clem was once again startled by the wealth displayed—china, crystal, silver, the chandelier, the great mahogany table, chairs, china cabinet and sideboard.

Clem was warmly greeted by Mrs. Brady and they sat down to supper, which consisted of ham, chicken and dumplings, squash, cabbage, creamed carrots, yeast rolls. All of this was followed by pumpkin pie and plum cake for dessert. Clem was afraid he wouldn't know which fork or spoon to use, so he watched Susannah and did what she did.

Conversation at the table was slow. Clem was more quiet than usual, concentrating on his manners. Finally, Mr. Brady brought up the subject of gardening which Clem knew something about. "Clem, I guess you know a lot about gardening, don't you?"

"Well, yessir, I've done my share of gardenin'."

"Maybe you could help us get started with it here. I want to plant a garden this year if we can and it's not too late. Not too big."

"I'd be glad to help, sir. It's a little later than most folks plant, but you can still make a crop. It'll just come in a little later, that's all."

"What do you grow in your garden, Clem?" queried Mrs. Brady.

"Besides the acreage in wheat, corn and cotton, I usually plant cabbage, carrots, squash, beans, onions, white and sweet potatoes, peas. And last year I planted watermelon and had a few good ones."

"How does a busy, young farmer like you have time to put up all those vegetables?"

"Well, my G'amma—that's my grandma—taught me how to do it. And it is hard at harvest time to get it all done, but somehow I manage. I guess the good Lord just helps me."

"Amen!" came from Mr. Brady.

"Clem, let's go sit on the porch. Will you excuse us, Papa and Mama?"

"Surely, go on. Your mother and I will clean up."

"Thank you, ma'am, for the supper. It was really good. My own cookin' don't hold a candle to yours."

"Thank you, Clem. Susannah helped. She made the plum cake."

"It was very good, Susannah. One of my favorites."

"Thank you, Clem. Let's go." She took him by the arm and ushered him out to the front porch, grabbing a shawl on the way out.

They sat on the porch swing, quietly swinging for several minutes. "Clem, aren't the stars beautiful? When I was a child, I used to think of them as embroidered with sparkly thread on black velvet. Silly, I guess."

"No, it's not. Have you ever looked at the figures some of the stars make? My G'amps showed them to me. Come on. I'll show you. I only know two of them, but there are lots more. Look right up there." Clem extended his arm. "That's the big dipper because it's shaped like a dipper. Can you see it?"

"No. Show me again." Susannah moved right next to Clem to follow the direction he pointed in which caused them to brush shoulders. Susannah didn't seem to notice, but Clem was keenly aware of her nearness. He'd never been that close to her, but she smelled so good, like lavender, and her hair was so shiny and soft looking he wanted to reach out and touch it, but he held back.

"Oh, I see it now, Clem." She turned to look at him and they were face to face. They looked in each other's eyes for only a moment, each of them thinking how green the other's eyes were. Clem practically jumped back when he realized how close they were standing and went back to the swing. Susannah smiled a little at how sweet and innocent he was. *I'm probably his first girlfriend*, she thought. *I'm so glad! Thank you, Lord! He's only my second boyfriend and my first serious one.*

"Where's the second one, Clem?"

"Oh, I forget."

Susannah came back to the swing. "When I was a little girl, I had a swing hanging from a tree limb, and I used to swing so high I thought I could reach the sky. I thought about jumping out when it was at its highest to see what would happen, but I thought better of it." Susannah giggled.

"I remember when I was real little my G'amps taught me a rhyme to get a doddle bug to come out of its hole. Let's see, it was, 'Doodle bug, doodle bug, fly away home. Your house is on fire, and your children are alone.' He would turn a stick around and around in the hole while he said this and the bug would come out. Course I know now the rhyme had nothing to do with it, but I went around saying 'dooda bug, dooda bug' for months." They both laughed.

"I would've liked your G'amps, I think. And I'm sure your G'amma too."

"They were both fun, except G'amma could be stern sometimes, but I guess she had to be. They both loved the Lord and really depended on Him. They taught me to do the same. G'amps was a man of faith which he had learned through trials and hard times, but he never turned away from the Lord. When G'amma died, he completely broke down but he came back. He lived his life on the scripture, 'If the Lord slay me, yet will I trust Him'. He was strong in his faith."

"Something tells me he passed some of that faith on to you."

"Oh, I don't know. I guess so. When G'amps died, I didn't think I could go on. I was all alone and really shook up. But God spoke to me—." He choked up and finally went on. Susannah reached out and took his hand. "He filled me with a warmth and love I can't explain. I knew then I was not alone and never would be. God is always with me and always will be."

"How did your mother die, Clem?"

"Well, I was eight years old. One day Ma went for a horse ride. She always said she liked to ride fast and feel the wind blow her hair and against her face." Clem reflected for a moment. "This day she rode across one of the pastures to a creek. G'amps figured that a snake must have spooked her horse, and she was thrown and landed in the creek and hit her head on a rock. It was several hours before G'amps found her. She'd lost a lot of blood and then she developed pneumonia and died. Before she died, she told me to trust God completely and be faithful to Him." He looked down. "I try to do that."

When Clem looked up at Susannah, tears were trickling down her cheeks. "That touches me, Clem. I'm so sorry about your mother."

"Thank you, Susannah. I try to remember to live by what my parents and grandparents taught me, but I'm sure not perfect," laughed Clem. "I think it's gettin' late and I need to get on home." They stood and he realized they were holding hands. He dropped his. "I really enjoyed myself, Susannah. Please tell your mother supper was really good. You're easy to talk to, and I've never found it easy to talk to people outside my family. Goodnight, Susannah."

"Goodnight, Clem. I'm so glad you came and I want you to come again and again. You're welcome anytime."

"Oh, why don't you and your parents come to see my farm after church and dinner next Sunday? It's not fancy like your house, but I'm proud of it."

"Oh, we'd love to, Clem. I'm sure it'll be alright with my parents."

"Good. Well, goodnight again." He kept hesitating twisting his hat in his hands. Finally, he stepped over and kissed her lightly on the cheek, then turned and mounted Blackie and rode swiftly out of sight.

Susannah stood on the porch with a smile, hugging her arms to herself. "God, I think he may just be the one."

❖ ❖ ❖

A couple of Sundays later, George Brady and Susannah followed Clem out to his farm after church and dinner-on-the-grounds. Martha Brady was not feeling well and had not gone to church.

Clem proudly showed Mr. Brady and Susannah his corn, wheat and cotton acres which had begun to come up. He showed them his sugar cane, beehives, cattle and his vegetable garden which only had a few green sprouts coming up. He also showed them the creek with the pecan grove, his tree house from childhood and the family cemetery under the old cypress tree. He saved the house till last because there wasn't much to see, especially after seeing their beautiful house.

"The house ain't much to see. Just a one-room cabin really. G'amps and I worked the farm more than the house, I guess."

Mr. Brady spoke up, "I admire what you've done here, Clem. You put in the ground what was most important. A house doesn't matter if there's love and God's presence in it." He reached out and shook Clem's hand and patted him on the back. "You've done a fine job here, Clem. I guess we had better get home and see about Martha. She's not been feeling well for some time. I worry about her. Are you ready to go, Susannah?"

"Yes, Papa." He knew how it was to be young and in love, so he went on to the wagon and left them alone.

"Clem, I love your farm and your house. I never dreamed it was so big. You have worked very hard for all this," waving her arm around. You're a fine man, Clem Brown." She reached over and lightly kissed him on the cheek. "Goodbye, Clem. See you soon."

Clem was a little stunned, but he managed to walk Susannah over to the wagon and help her up into it. "Mr. Brady, I'll get over to your place this week and get that ground broken for your garden."

"Well, thank you, Clem, we'd appreciate that. Goodbye now."

CHAPTER 24

Clem looked back at the sod he'd turned over with his horse and plow and thought to himself, *Won't be too hard. Not the roughest sod I've seen. Shouldn't take too long to get this done.* Clem was preparing the soil to plant a garden for Mr. Brady, which was only twenty by twenty feet. Mr. Brady felt it would be large enough for the three of them, and he wouldn't have time to take care of any more than that.

"Susannah, you can't help with this." Clem, with Susannah's unwanted help, was using a hoe to break up the clods since he had no harrow.

"Yes, I can, Clem. I'm not too soft to work hard. I need to learn about these things."

"It'll blister your hands when you aren't used to it which turns into calluses if you keep doin' it. Do you want your hands to look like mine?"

"I don't know. Let me see yours." He stuck his hand out. "Hmm. I see what you mean. I sure don't want my hands to be that big!" Susannah threw her head back and laughed while Clem just looked exasperated.

Later in the morning Susannah brought Clem some lemonade and freshly baked bread. She had kept up a running chatter the whole time he'd been there. "I want to learn how to plant a garden. Then you can show me step by step what we need to do when the plants come up."

"Have you never had a garden before, Susannah?"

"No, remember we were city folks. We didn't have enough ground to have a garden. I like the idea of raising our own food."

"I like to work with the soil, get my hands in it and get dirty."

"Okay, here." Susannah grabbed two handfuls of dirt and dropped them on his head. She shrieked with laughter.

"Now just wait a minute. You're playin' dirty."

"Playing dirty—now that's funny!"

"Okay, remember you started this." Clem grabbed a handful of dirt and threw it at her and it hit her on the skirt of her dress.

"Oh, look what you did, Clem Brown! My new dress!" Then she pretended to start crying, so Clem would come closer to see about her. When he did, she rubbed a handful of dirt on his cheek! "I got you that time!"

"Susannah, Clem, look at the two of you playing like children. Don't you think you need to act more your age?" Mrs. Brady happened to look out the window in time to see the dirty work.

"Yes, Mama." Susannah genuinely looked contrite. "Clem, how old are you? I never have asked you."

"I'm twenty-three. How old are you?"

"You aren't supposed to ask a lady her age, but since I haven't been acting like a lady I'll tell you. I'm twenty."

Clem had never been around a lady who teased like Susannah and hardly knew how to handle it, but he was beginning to enjoy it. It brought needed laughter into his life.

❖ ❖ ❖

In his spare time, Clem began digging a well close to his house with the help of Joshua Logan and Clyde Posey. It took them several days, but soon Clem had fresh water just a few steps from his door.

The day they finished the well Clyde had gone on home and Joshua and Clem were talking. "I plan to build a bedroom on that end and a separate kitchen on the back of the house. What do you think, Mr. Joshua?"

"Great idea. You can use the big room you have as a sittin' room. The kitchen bein' in a separate room is a good idea, keeps cookin' smoke and smells out of the house better. Course you'd have to build another fireplace." He scratched his head. "Or you could build the kitchen right behind the fireplace in the front room and build an openin' from the fireplace you've got into the kitchen. I've seen it done. It'll work. And I tell you somethin' else that would be good is buildin' a pantry off the kitchen to keep your food supplies in. Abigail likes that. It'd also be good to build a woodshed off the kitchen with a door to the outside. Then you could store your wood there, so it wouldn't get wet and you wouldn't have to go outside to get it as often."

"That all sounds good but a lot of hard work. I'll just have to work on it a little at a time till it's done. With all the farmin' chores to do, it's hard to find time to do extra things like buildin'."

With a twinkle in his eye, Joshua added, "Specially when you plant a garden for a certain young lady in town. These young ladies can take up your time, Clem." Joshua started laughing.

Clem ducked his head and couldn't keep from grinning, but he never said anything.

"Tell you what, Clem, I'll be glad to help you build on to your house when I can. And maybe we can round up a couple other men to help. Can't get a better offer."

"I really do appreciate that. I know you have as much or more to do than I do. Thank you, Mr. Joshua."

"Well, what are friends for, Clem? You help me and I help you. That's just bein' neighborly. Besides, there might be weddin' bells one of these days and you need to have your house ready. Ain't that right?" Joshua didn't even wait for an answer but mounted his horse and threw up a hand as he rode off.

❖ ❖ ❖

Clem carried the picnic basket in one hand and took Susannah by the elbow with the other as they walked to the wagon. He set the basket in the back of the wagon and helped Susannah up on the seat. He climbed up beside her. Mrs. Brady called after them, "You two be careful today."

"Yes, ma'am," they both answered.

Susannah put her arm through Clem's and laid her head on his shoulder. "I have been so looking forward to this day, Clem! The sun is shining. It's warm. The berries are ready to be picked. A lunch is packed. And I am with my favorite person in the whole world." She glanced up to see how he would react.

Clem grinned from ear to ear and then reached down and kissed her lightly on the lips. It wasn't the first time they had kissed on the lips, but Susannah was surprised he did it in public. *Oh, how I love this man!* she was thinking. *I wonder what Clem's thinking. I know he loves me by the way he acts, but I wish he'd tell me so.*

Lord, I love this woman, but how can I tell her about me—how slow I am and I can't even read and write? I may lose her and I can't live without her. Clem surprised himself with the sudden realization that he really felt he couldn't live without her. He wanted to spend the rest of his life with her! *Lord, you've answered my prayers and I know now she's the one, but how do I tell her the truth about me. And Lord, I don't have much to offer her. I don't have a big, fancy house like she's used to. But, Lord, if you brought her to me, then it will all work out.*

They drove several miles out of town to find the huckleberries Clem remembered seeing there. They picked berries for a while, eating almost as many as they put in the baskets. They laughed and talked and teased, throwing berries at one another like children. Soon they were stained with berry juice which they discovered wouldn't wash off in the creek. They sat down at noon and consumed their picnic lunch of cold fried chicken, biscuits, corn on the cob and fried apple pies. Clem lay back propped on one elbow while Susannah tried to throw berries to land in his open mouth. More missed than went in but it was fun. They enjoyed each other's company a great deal. Susannah was such a feisty and fun person. Clem was always amazed at what she could come up with to do.

"Susannah, I need to tell you somethin'. This is goin' to be hard." Susannah sobered at his serious tone of voice. "After I was born, my mother saw that I was—well, slow. I didn't walk or talk for a long time, and for most of my life I've had a hard time understandin' things. I used to pass my hand across my forehead like this," he demonstrated, "when I didn't understand. I really had to work at stoppin' that just in the last year or two. G'amps helped me more than anybody. He patiently taught me how to do things on the farm by showin' me over and over. I learned to ride earlier than most children, I guess, and to take care of the animals. I learned to love animals. It was really hard when I lost my mother when I was eight. I just couldn't understand. But my grandparents kept on teachin' me to trust God and keep faith no matter what. I didn't know how I would make it when G'amps died, but God showed me that He is faithful and He's always there. I went through bein' made fun of by boys my age and older, but God helped me there too." He looked up at Susannah and tears were streaking her face.

"Oh, Clem, how my heart goes out to you! You've been through so much. I marvel at how you've done so well. When I see your farm and hear all that you still want to do, I'm ashamed because my life has been so easy. My parents have always given me things. We've never had a hard life. I would never have known that you were slow as a child if you hadn't told me. I think you are the most wonderful person I've ever known. Clem, I—."

"Let me finish, Susannah. I'm not a fancy person and I don't have a fancy house. I'm a simple man with simple thoughts. I've never—well, I've never learned to read or write. I'll probably always be a farmer. But I know that God loves me, takes care of me and is faithful to me. He expects me to be faithful to Him and I try to do that. I have prayed that He would send a wife to me to love and take care of." Big tears began to roll down his cheeks. "I think He has. I love you, Susannah, with all my heart. I don't know how you feel—."

Susannah reached over and put her hand over his mouth. "Let me talk. I wouldn't love a fancy person and I don't care about fancy things. I am attracted to the faith in God that you so strongly have learned in your life. Clem, look at me. The fact that you can't read or write could never change my opinion of you. Clem, I love you too, with all my heart and I always will."

They grasped hands and both had tears softly falling as they looked into each other's eyes. They came together in the most meaningful kiss they had ever shared. They sat simply looking at one another, taking in every detail. "You are the most beautiful woman I've ever seen and God made you that way, Susannah Brady. I want to make you happy and take care of you for the rest of our lives. I promise to always treat you with great respect and tenderness. Susannah, will you marry me?"

With tears streaming down her cheeks, she answered, "Oh, yes, Clem, yes! And I promise to always love and respect you with all tenderness."

They came together in a warm embrace which spoke volumes about how they felt about each other. Clem felt he was home at last. He had a wife to love and take care of! God did provide. And Susannah had never felt so happy and loved! "Let's pray, Susannah, and thank God for each other!" And thus they prayed together the first of many prayers to come over the years.

On the way home, Susannah thoughtfully suggested, "Clem, I could teach you to read and write, if you want. Think about it. That is, if you promise to teach me how to have a strong faith in God like you have."

"Oh, Susannah, I don't have great faith. I just have faith in a faithful God. And I don't know how to teach you how to have faith, but we can pray that God will teach you and me."

❖ ❖ ❖

By the time they arrived at Susannah's house, they had decided on a late fall wedding, maybe October. Clem had decided to ask Joshua Logan to be his best man, and Susannah decided on Miriam Duncan, a friend she had made at church, as her maid-of-honor. They jointly decided they wouldn't have a big wedding and nothing fancy.

Susannah's parents were not surprised when Clem approached Mr. Brady to ask for her hand in marriage. "You certainly do have our approval and best wishes for all the happiness in the world." He vigorously shook Clem's hand and hugged his only child fiercely while he whispered in her ear, "Be happy, pet. I'm going to miss you, but I'm happy for you." Mrs. Brady was a more reserved person, but she embraced her daughter with all the love she had and cried many tears. She also hugged Clem, kissed him on the cheek and wished them well.

"Have you set the date yet?" Mrs. Brady inquired.

"We want it to be in October, maybe late October."

"Oh, Susannah, that doesn't give us but about two months! There's so much to do. A wedding gown, your trousseau, a reception! Oh, my!"

"Mama don't worry about all that. We don't want a big, fancy wedding. We'll have the things we need when we get married. Most importantly we'll have each other."

❖ ❖ ❖

Amazingly by October 28, Susannah had a wedding gown, a trousseau of linens, household items, rugs, pots and pans, quilts and many other items, and a wedding reception provided by the ladies in the church who brought a full meal following the wedding as well as a beautiful wedding cake. By October 28, Clem, with the help of Joshua, Clyde and some other men in the church, almost had his house ready. A few details could be completed later.

The day of the wedding dawned bright and clear with a deep blue autumn sky. The church had been decorated the night before with fall flowers and leaves with candles. The ladies of the church had helped out again. The church was filled to capacity and some folks stood outside the windows to watch. It reflected how much the church and town thought of Clem and Susannah. Susannah was radiant while her mother was tearful and nervous. Clem was nervous while his future father-in-law was radiating pride and joy.

As they waited for the organ music to give them their cue, Mr. Brady whispered to Clem, "Calm down, Clem. There's never been a groom lost yet. You'll live through it. I'm proud for my daughter, Clem, because she's made a good choice in a husband. Look after her, Clem."

"I will and thank you, sir. They'd better hurry though before my cowlick pops up!" Their laughter eased the tension a little.

As George Brady took his daughter on his arm to go down the aisle, he kissed her on the cheek, and with tears in his eyes told her, "You are a beautiful bride, daughter. You've made a good choice. Love him always and make him happy. Learn to trust God in the hard times and praise Him in the good times."

"Oh, Papa, thank you."

Clem's breath was taken away when he saw his bride coming down the aisle in her beautiful white gown, her auburn hair pinned up in curls and her green eyes twinkling. He only had eyes for her. No man could have been happier at that moment than Clem. He never dreamed in his life that this would be happening to him. He was so humbled by this unexpected blessing of the Lord that tears filled his eyes. *How good the Lord is!* he thought. *I really wish my family could be here to see our weddin' today, but somehow I think they see and know and are just as proud as I am. Ma and Pa, see your son who is the happiest man alive today. See his beautiful bride. G'amps and G'amma, see your grandson and be happy!*

George gave his daughter's hand to Clem, but not before he kissed her on the cheek again. He sat down by his wife who had cried all day. Clem and Susannah exchanged the traditional vows, but then Pastor Jennings announced that the couple had something else to say to each other.

Susannah spoke first, "Clem, I will always love you and treat you as my husband with the greatest respect and tenderness."

Clem then spoke his personal vow, "Susannah, I will always love you and treat you as my bride with the greatest respect and tenderness."

There were tears in many eyes after their vows.

"Now I pronounce you husband and wife. You may kiss your bride, Clem."

Everyone was invited to remain for the meal following, and most of the town stayed. The happy couple never had a chance to eat anything, except the beautiful wedding cake, with all the well-wishing and hugging. Someone asked where they were going on their honeymoon, and Susannah quickly answered, "We're going home!"

Finally, they were able to get away from the church and they did go home. As soon as Clem carried Susannah over the threshold at his insistence, she saw her mother's handiwork—rugs on the floor, fall flowers on the table covered with an embroidered tablecloth, a beautiful big clock on the mantle strewn with fall flowers, linens on the bed and cooked food in the pantry. "Oh, Clem, look at all the lovely things Mama has done for us. Oh, we have so many reasons for being happy, don't we?"

"Yes, my love, we do, especially that we have each other."

CHAPTER 25

"This thing sure is heavy, Clem. You sure you didn't put rocks in it before we picked it up!" Joshua and Clem joined in laughter. "Turn it a little yonder way. That's got it. Susannah is sure gonna be surprised when she sees her new wood stove for Christmas."

"I hope so. It oughta make life a little easier for her, I hope. 'Specially since the baby's due so soon."

"When is the baby due?"

"Around the middle of January, the doctor thinks. She's over at Miriam Duncan's house with a lot of womenfolk right now, makin' baby things. She's been knittin' and crochetin' and sewin' for almost nine months now. Did you see the cradle I made for it?"

"A fine job, Clem. Do you hope for a boy?"

"Well, I guess most men want a boy, but whichever the Lord sends is alright with me."

"Got to go, Clem. Your farm is lookin' good. You've done a fine job with things. Jeremiah would be proud."

"Thank you, Mr. Joshua, and thanks for your help movin' the stove."

An hour or so later Mr. Brady brought Susannah home and waited to see her face when she saw the stove. "Clem Brown, what have you done? A new stove! This is wonderful!" She threw her arms around Clem. "Thank you!"

Clem whispered in her ear, "Merry Christmas, Mrs. Brown."

❖ ❖ ❖

"Be patient, Clem. The baby'll come when it's ready and not before. You pacin' like that won't speed it up none."

"But, Mrs. Posey, is Susannah alright?"

"She's doin' fine. I jist came to git some towels. Her ma and Abigail Logan are in thar with her. We're takin' kir of her. Don't worry."

Clem went out to the front porch but didn't really want to be around Joshua, Clyde and Mr. Brady right then. He went back in the front room. The other men got a chuckle out of it.

Then they all heard the sound of a baby crying! Clem ran for the bedroom door, but they wouldn't let him in.

"Susannah is fine, Clem. Just fine. And you've got a beautiful baby boy! We guess he weighs about eight pounds. You can come in soon. Not now." Abigail passed on the news.

The men on the porch came in just as Mrs. Brady brought the baby out to Clem. She was crying and laughing at the same time. "Clem, take your new son." She walked over and hugged George because they were so happy to be grandparents.

Clem took the baby with an incredible sense of awe on his face. "Can I go in and see Susannah?"

"Yes, of course. She's just fine."

Clem creeped around the door, holding their baby as if he would break, "Susannah?" Clem sat on the side of the bed next to Susannah. "He's beautiful. Look at his little fingers and toes. How're you, Susannah?"

"I'm tired, but I'm alright, especially since I saw him. He is beautiful, isn't he, Clem? Can you believe that that little boy came from us, from our union, Clem? It's a miracle from God."

"Oh, yes, Susannah. I loved him as soon as I saw him, little Thomas Griffin Brown. And I love you, my wife." He leaned over and kissed her and she slipped her arms around his neck.

❖ ❖ ❖

In the next three years Clem and Susannah had two more blessed events. Their second child was a girl, Ruth Moriah, who was named for her grandmother and great-grandmother, and the third was another boy, Jefferson George Brown, who was named for both his grandfathers. Clem especially never lost the tremendous awe he experienced with the birth of each child. They were each unique and special and a gift from God.

In those three years Clem and Susannah's farm prospered due to the hard work they both put in. Clem learned from experience how to improve his farming and listened to other men's methods. Susannah learned well how to plant and cultivate a garden as well as to harvest and preserve its fruits. She ran her household well and managed their three children with a loving and firm hand. Love was evident in their home toward each other and visitors. Each night Susannah read from the Bible to all of them by the light of a kerosene lamp. When they had time, she slowly taught Clem to read from the Bible, but he didn't feel confident enough to read aloud in front of anyone but her yet. The children were young and didn't understand most of the words of the scripture, but Clem and Susannah always tried to explain it in a way they could better understand. They wanted to put God's word into their minds starting from their births. This task grew easier as the children grew older.

Life was never dull with three small children. One summer their oldest, Thomas who was five years old, was near the woods playing with Ruth who was almost four and little Jeff who was almost two. Susannah was picking huckleberries and the children were "helping" which meant eating more than saving the berries. As Thomas was zealously eating berries in one hand and chasing a butterfly with the other, he stepped into a yellow jackets' nest which was in a hole in the ground. He hadn't seen it. Soon yellow jackets were swarming around him, and the more he jumped up and down the angrier they became! He screamed, "Mama! Mama! Help me! Help me!"

"Thomas, what is it?"

Little Ruth answered for him, "Bees, Mama. Bees!"

Susannah dropped her basket which sent berries rolling all over the ground. She sized up the problem quickly, jerked him up and carried him away from the nest. She pulled his clothes off him and brushed the yellow jackets off his skin that were stinging him. "Come, Ruthie and Jeff, let's go to the house to see is we can help brother. Ruth, get Mama's basket and take little Jeff by the hand." They got to the house as quickly as they could After laying Thomas on the bed, she went to the front porch, cupped her hands around her mouth and called as loudly as she could, "Clem! Clem! Clem!"

He finally heard her and came running. "What is it? Is it one of the children?"

"Yes, Thomas stepped in a yellow jacket's nest and he's been stung many times. I haven't counted, but I don't know what to do for him. He's swelling pretty bad."

Clem dropped his hoe on the ground and went in to Thomas. "I had this happen to me when I was a little boy. What they did for me was to make a poultice of mud and water, smear it on me and wrap me up in an old sheet." They proceeded to do that, but then Clem remembered, "Somebody also gave me something to drink for fever, I think, but I don't know what it was. If anybody would know, it'd be Mrs. Posey. I'll ride over and ask her. Be back as quick as I can."

"Hurry, Clem! He's really starting to swell. His eyes are almost swollen shut."

Clem returned with a Mason jar of herbs Mrs. Posey had put together. "She said we needed to brew these herbs into a tea and make him drink it. It's supposed to bring down the fever in his skin." Clem looked sheepishly at Susannah. "I'll brew it if you'll make him drink it. She said it didn't taste good and it sure don't smell good. See." He stuck it under her nose. She turned her head away. "Thanks, you coward," Susannah grimaced. Somehow Susannah managed to get the brew down Thomas as only a mother can.

By the next day, the swelling was going down, and in a few days he was back to normal and ready to receive a firm lecture from his Mama to look where he was walking next time!

Another day found the children playing at the creek which was a favorite place to play with the overhanging cypress trees and the pecan grove close by. They had been warned about snakes, places where snakes can hide, fish that bite their feet and anything else Clem could think of, but there was one he missed. The children loved to wade in the cool creek in the summer. Ruthie especially liked to wade in the mud at the bottom of the creek and feel the mud squish between her toes, but this time when she came out of the water she had blobs of brown things on her feet and legs. She tried to wash them off, but they wouldn't come off.

"Thomas, come 'ere. What's these things on me?"

He had no idea, but he tried to pull them off. When he did, they just got longer and wouldn't let go. He looked at Ruth and she started to cry. "I don't know what they are, Ruthie, but let's go home and Mama will know." He took her and little Jeff, who by this time discovered he had them too, by the hands and they ran to the house. As soon as Susannah saw them, she knew they were leeches and wouldn't really hurt the children since they hadn't been on them very long, but it did take some time to convince Ruth and little Jeff to let her pull them off. Once they were off, a little blood trickled out. This scared Ruth, but little Jeff started pulling them off himself just to watch them stretch before they came off. He didn't mind the blood. Susannah applied some salve to all the places on both children and held Ruth for a little while until she was over it.

When Clem came in for supper that evening, Susannah informed him, "Guess what your children did today!"

❖ ❖ ❖

One April evening, Susannah read from the Bible as she did each night to Clem and the children. The children looked forward to this every night because of the exciting stories the Bible had. If they didn't read an exciting story, Clem or

Susannah would make up a story to teach them the principles of the Bible. It was not always an easy task.

On this particular evening, Susannah was reading from the first chapter of the book of Job. The children were spellbound with all the bad things that happened to Job. He lost his livestock, his children and his servants! And then he broke out in sores all over! Thomas had to say something, "If sores are anythin' like bee stings, I know how Job felt." Clem and Susannah exchanged smiles. When Susannah came to the last two verses in chapter one, Clem quoted them:

> "And said, Naked came I out of my mother's womb, and naked shall I return thither: the Lord gave, and the Lord hath taken away; blessed be the name of the Lord. In all this Job sinned not, nor charged God foolishly."

"What does that mean, Pa?" Thomas asked curiously.

"It means that with all the bad things that happened to Job he never got mad at God or blamed Him. He's sayin' he was born without anythin' and he'd die without anythin'. The Lord gives and the Lord takes. It's up to the Lord what we have and don't have. It all belongs to Him. He just lets us borrow from Him whether its things or people. Job had so much faith in God that he trusted Him to do what was right. He had some friends who tried to tell him different, but he knew what's right. God won't let anythin' come to us unless He can use it to help us be more what He wants us to be, which is bein' more like Jesus. There's another verse in Job that my G'amps, your great-grandpa, believed in strongly. Job chapter thirteen verse fifteen: *'Though he slay me, yet will I trust Him.'* And what that means, Thomas, is that even if God killed him, Job was gonna trust God because God knows best. Do you understand what I'm sayin?"

"I think so." Thomas yawned. Ruth and little Jeff had been asleep for a while already. Clem and Susannah looked at one another.

"I guess that's enough for one night. I think it's about bedtime for the young'uns, don't you, Susannah?"

As Susannah started to answer, they heard a very strong wind blowing outside and, more than that, a tremendous noise like nothing they'd ever heard before. "Stay here, Susannah, with the children. I'll go see what it is." Clem stepped out on the front porch, and with just enough light left in the sky he saw it in the distance heading toward them. A twister! Clem ran inside calling, "Susannah, get the children in the root cellar! Now! It's a twister! I'll get little Jeff and you get the other two." He scooped up little Jeff who was still half-asleep, and with one hand he shoved the rocking chair and rug out of the way of the trap door and yanked it open. Susannah was holding Ruth and tugging on Thomas to make him move more quickly. "Move children! Now!" Susannah more or less pushed Thomas in the cellar, and she and Ruth almost slid down the short flight of steps. Clem with little Jeff jumped in after them and pulled the trap door shut.

No sooner had the trap door slammed shut then they heard the most awful noises above them. It sounded and felt like the whole world was coming apart! Every set of eyes in the cellar was large and round and filled with fear as they felt a shaking and tearing above them! Clem and Susannah were praying individually. "Lord, protect us from harm. Watch over us, oh, Lord. Keep the children safe."

Suddenly, it was over. The quiet, in contrast, seemed almost as loud as the noise. "I think it's over, Susannah. Let me see if I can get the trap door open. Here, hold little Jeff." Clem tried to get the trap door open with one hand and then with two, but it wouldn't budge. He put his shoulder against it and it moved a little but still wouldn't open. "Susannah, I'm gonna need your help to get this open. There must be somethin' over it keepin' it from openin'."

"Thomas, here, hold little Jeff and keep holding Ruthie's hand while I help your Pa."

Clem and Susannah put as much force against the overhead trap door as they could, and finally it slowly opened. Clem stepped out first and looked around. The house was gone! Completely gone, leaving only the foundation and most of the chimney! The noise they'd heard was their house being broken apart and swept away! "Susannah, come on up but leave the children for now."

"They won't stay in this dark cellar by themselves, Clem. You may as well help me get them out now." Little Jeff was passed up to Clem and then Ruthie. Thomas came next. When Susannah's head came out of the cellar and she saw the destruction, she cried, "No, Clem! No! No! No!" She looked around and saw nothing but the chimney. She began to dart here and there, crying and covering her face with her hands. "No, this can't be happening! No! No! I won't believe it!"

Clem came to her and tried to put his arms around her, but she wouldn't let him. She was on the verge of becoming hysterical. She finally fell to her knees and covered her face with her hands, moaning and sobbing. Clem went to his knees and pulled her to him, and she finally let him hold her. "We're alright, Susannah, and all of the children are fine." As darkness closed in around them, Clem was holding Susannah to his chest, surrounded by their three sobbing, young children.

CHAPTER 26

Susannah cried for a while with Clem and her family around her. Clem had learned that sometimes when Susannah cried it was best just to hold her until she calmed down. He decided this was one of those times. Reasoning with her now wouldn't get through to her. That would come later.

"Pa, where's our house?" asked the always curious Thomas.

"Let's wait a little while to talk about that, son. Why don't we all move over to the fireplace to try to be more comfortable? Come on, children." He pulled Susannah, holding little Jeff, to her feet and helped her to sit and lean back on the rocks of the fireplace. It wasn't cool like most nights in April, but instead it was warm, sultry and muggy. The stillness before and after the twister was incredible. The sky was cloudy and a little rain was still falling, making the darkness seem even more ominous. It also prevented them from seeing how much damage had been done.

Without even thinking, Susannah took off her shawl and put it around little Jeff and held him close to her. Ruthie snuggled under her mother's arm and sat as close as she could to her. Thomas sat with his Pa. "Pa, what happened?" Thomas whispered.

"I guess this is the first twister you ever saw. It's a very strong wind that gathers into a whirlwind that twists in a circle. It's so powerful it can destroy everythin' in its path, but it's odd how it leaves some things like the chimney and takes others. I've heard a lot of strange stories of what twisters have done."

Susannah interrupted sharply, "I don't think now is the time for that."

"I'm sorry, Susannah. I wasn't thinkin'." He looked at her with love and sympathy in his eyes. "Susannah, it'll be alright. We're all together and that's all that really matters."

"I—I can't talk right now, Clem, please. Later. My children don't even have a place to sleep tonight." Tears spilled over again.

"We'll look around and see what we can find. Come on, Thomas." After they walked off, Clem told Thomas, "Your Mama is really upset and hurt. Be especially nice right now. Okay?"

"Yessir."

Clem looked around their land first to see what had been left. The stable was gone and apparently the horses and the cow. It was hard to see in the darkness what was still there. They found some of their furniture but no beds. They stumbled on two blankets that were still mostly dry and brought them back for the children. Susannah looked up at Clem with such pain in her eyes that his heart almost broke just seeing her like that. He spread one blanket over her, little Jeff and Ruth. He threw the other one over Thomas and himself.

"We may as well try to get some sleep. We'll have a lot to do tomorrow."

They were all in such a state of shock that it was some time before the children dozed off. Susannah and Clem couldn't sleep at all and sat awake all night talking.

"Clem, what'll we do? All the hard work we've—you especially—put into our house! Why? Why does this happen to us?"

"I don't know, Susannah. It hurts me, too, to see it all swept away in a second of time. But what I do know is God's not punishin' us by allowin' this to happen. He's still in control and He loves us as much as ever."

"How can you say that, Clem? How can a loving God allow this to happen to us? Haven't we tried to live right, read the Bible, pray, teach our children what's right? I don't understand. I just don't understand!"

Somehow Clem sensed now was not the time to try to reason with her yet. "It is goin' to be hard to start over,

Susannah. I know that. To rebuild. A lot of hard labor. But I'm young and strong and Thomas can help me some. We'll make it. We'll rebuild. I'm sure some of our neighbors will help."

"Oh, Clem, all of our things are gone! Everything! I just can't take it. This is too much!" Tears spilled over and ran down her cheeks. "Clem, how can you just sit there so calmly and talk like everything is just fine? Don't you even care that we've just lost everything?"

Clem got up, making sure Thomas was still covered, and took little Jeff from Susannah and laid him with Ruthie on the floor. He sat down beside Susannah and put his arms around her. She allowed him to pull her head down to his chest and enfold her in a protective way. She was strung as tight as a fiddle string and wouldn't be able to take much more.

"I love you, Susannah. I always will. I'll always be here for you. You don't have to go it alone. Let's share the burden of the hard times and the joy of the good times." They sat quietly together as Susannah continued to cry softer and softer until she finally stopped. They both sat thinking for a while, but every time Susannah thought of something else she would express dismay over losing it.

"Oh, Clem, my new stove is gone!"

"Oh, Clem, the water pump in the kitchen is gone!"

"All our linens are gone!"

"All our clothes!"

"I know, sweetheart, but some of these things may be around here. We don't know yet. When it's light, we'll look and see what we can find. We may be surprised."

"Clem, I'm sorry I spoke so harshly to you before. I know you care, and it's hard on you too. I'm just so upset! I don't know if I can handle this."

"I know, Susannah, I'm upset too and it hurts to see everythin' we've worked for just gone." Clem's voice cracked with emotion. "But I have to believe that God has a reason for lettin' us go through this. If we don't trust God, we can't make it, Susannah. You remember when we prayed together that God would help us have faith? Well, I believe this is a trial He's allowin' us to go through to grow our faith. It has to be! Don't you see?"

"I'm trying, Clem. Help me."

Clem was quiet for a few minutes before he spoke. "Susannah, the things we lost are just things. All three children are safe and we're both fine. That's a lot to be thankful for. Our crops will be fine because we just planted them. And I'm sure we'll be able to find some of our things scattered around when daylight comes. I've already seen some of the furniture out there. Remember Job?"

"Oh, yes, I remember Job!"

"But how did the book of Job end? He had restored to him his family, his health, his livestock, even more than he had before his trials." He looked at Susannah and saw how tired she was. He pulled her closer and whispered, "Why don't you get some sleep, sweetheart?" Susannah snuggled against Clem and just before daybreak her breathing became deep and regular in sleep.

Clem sat still holding Susannah with his head back against the chimney. Sleep would not come so easily to him. He had said the words to Susannah that he knew to be right and he wanted to comfort her, but in his own heart he had some unbelief to work through also. He managed to lay Susannah down gently and made sure she was covered before he walked the area around the house to see what was there. His interest at that moment was not really in what belongings he could find, but he knew he needed to spend some time alone with his Lord in prayer.

Clem walked a short distance from his family so he wouldn't awaken them when he talked with the Lord. He went down on his knees. "Lord, I can't pretend I really understand why You let this happen. Lord, I want to know why just like Susannah does. Wasn't there an easier way to teach us what we need to learn? It's hard, Lord, to lose all or most of our worldly possessions and our home. It's especially hard to lose the things G'amps and me built together. It's like losin' part of him—." Clem choked up with tears. "It's gonna be hard, Lord, to build it all over again. Be with me and help me have the strength that I'll need to do it. Forgive me, Lord, for not havin' the faith I should have. I feel like the man in the Bible who said, 'I believe, but help my unbelief.' Thank you, Lord, for sparin' our lives and lovin' us so much. I know that all things come from Your hand and they belong to You. You just let us use 'em for a while. Thank you for lettin' us use this house and these things for a while. Help me to keep faith that You will help us rebuild. I think of the scripture that says, 'The Lord giveth and the Lord taketh away. Blessed be the name of the Lord.' Oh, help me have that attitude, God, and live it every day of my life. I also think of G'amps favorite scripture, 'If the Lord slay me, yet will I trust Him.' Help me, Lord, to trust you today and each day for our needs. And, Lord, help Susannah through this trial right now and in the days to come. Help her learn that faith in You. Help Susannah and me live faith in front of our children, so they can know You too and have faith. Protect our children from harm too. Thank you, Jesus, for lovin' us and takin' care of us. In Your Name I pray, Amen."

Clem didn't know at that moment that one of his children was listening to his prayer, and it would have an enormous influence on him. Thomas was awake and watching his Pa when he rose and went off to pray. Thomas was deeply affected by Clem's prayer, though he couldn't have said so at the time, especially the humility and trust he showed. It was one of those memories that Thomas would carry the rest of his life, that of seeing his Pa on his knees before Almighty God in their time of crisis.

❖ ❖ ❖

As the sun rose the next morning Clem's little family began to awaken one by one, stretching and yawning. Clem had been awake all night, partly in thought and partly to watch over his family.

"Well, good mornin', my wonderful family. Glad to see you finally decided to wake up." The children sat up and rubbed their eyes and looked around trying to figure out where the house was. "Well, children, the Lord saw fit to take our house last night, which means He'll probably give us somethin' better. I tell you what. Let's play a game. Let's see who can find the most of our things and bring 'em back here! Okay?" He reached to pull Susannah to her feet, as the children scattered to look for things. She felt very stiff. "And how are you this fine mornin', my princess?"

She looked at him like he had lost his mind and replied, "What's the matter with you?"

"I had a good talk with the Lord last night and I think He wants us to see this as an opportunity not a total disaster. We can be witnesses to other people who don't know Him of what the Lord can do. And I think it would be better to keep things as light as we can for the children, try to make a game of it."

"I suppose that makes sense." Susannah began looking around as she and Clem walked away from what was left of the house.

"Look, Susannah, the stove and it looks like it's alright! The kitchen table and sideboard! Maybe a little worse for wear, but I can fix that."

"Pa, look what I found!" Thomas was leading Blackie toward them.

"Blackie, my faithful horse! You're still here. Look, Susannah, he found Blackie! Maybe Whitey is around and the cow too. We'll keep lookin'."

As the morning crept by, cries could be heard from different ones, "Look what I found!" A few quilts, two sheets, the cow, the rocking chair. Even little Jeff toddling around found spoons and forks in the grass. The children turned it into a game they called "Treasure Hunt" and challenged each other to see what they could find.

In the middle of the morning, Joshua Logan rode up and dismounted. Clem met him with a handshake. "Clem, I just came to see how you faired last night, but I see—."

"We're alright, Mr. Joshua. Our family is safe. That's most important. And we're findin' things all along."

"I'm headin' into town to see if anybody else was hit. I'll spread word about what's happened to you and folks'll be out to help you. You know we'll all pitch in to help you rebuild. I'm really sorry this has happened to you, Clem. I'll help any way I can."

"I know you will, Mr. Joshua. Thank you."

❖ ❖ ❖

By late morning, people from the church began to bring food and clothes, so much so, that by noon there was an abundance of food and many people helping look for things. After the noon meal, people continued to work through the afternoon scavenging the area for any usable items they could find. Clem checked out his beehives and some were lost but not all. His few head of cattle were fine.

Joshua Logan approached Clem in the late afternoon with a question, "Clem, what are you folks gonna do tonight?

You're all welcome to come to our house for the night. No need for the children to sleep in the night air again."

"Let me see what Susannah thinks." Clem found Susannah with the other ladies sorting linens to see if any could be salvaged. He took her aside. "Susannah, Mr. Joshua has asked if we'd like to spend the night at their place, especially the children. What do you think?"

"I think it would be good for all of us. Don't you?"

"Well, I believe I should stay here and keep an eye on our things, but I want you and the children to stay the night with the Logans."

"Alright, Clem, if you think that's best."

❖ ❖ ❖

Clem picked up his family at the Logans the next morning, following a hearty breakfast served up by Abigail. They returned to their farm and continued working. About mid-morning, a group of men from the church and the town arrived with a load of lumber and nails ready to go to work. Clem and Susannah were overwhelmed with gratitude. Clem just kept shaking their hands and Susannah cried.

At the end of two weeks and with direction from Clem and Susannah, the house was basically complete with a large front room and a large kitchen back to back sharing the fireplace, three bedrooms, a pantry and a woodshed off the kitchen. They built on the same site and used the old chimney with some repair. They put on a roof of store-bought shingles, a large front porch for "sittin'" and, to their surprise, an outhouse! In the next couple of weeks, several men helped Clem complete a stable for Blackie and the cow. They never found Whitey, their other horse. Several businessmen in town had donated most of the building materials. George and Martha, Susannah's parents, bought the rest of what they'd need. Clem and Susannah were so overwhelmed with the way people in town had helped who barely knew them. Clem just kept shaking their hands and Susannah cried. During one of those days, Susannah looked to Clem and said, "Now I understand the ending to the book of Job!"

The next Sunday at church at the end of the service Clem stood up to say a word. "I don't make speeches and never have, but I have somethin' to say. Susannah, the children and me—," he choked out. "Well—we just want to thank all of you from the bottoms of our hearts for all you've done and all that you've given us. You and the Lord have been so good to us. We can't really thank you for what you've done, but if any of you ever needs help just call on me. I'll be there. I have to praise the Lord for savin' our lives and givin' us such a good church family and town, since you know I don't have any family left. We want to thank Susannah's parents for doin' so much for us. There are reasons why the Lord allowed this to happen to us. Maybe we've seen some already, the way this church has worked together to rebuild our house has given us unity and love for each other. Let's keep the faith and pass it on to our children. 'The Lord giveth and the Lord taketh. Blessed be the name of the Lord.' 'If the Lord slay me, yet will

I trust Him'." Clem looked up and said to himself, *Thanks, G'amps, for what you taught me.* "For a man who doesn't make speeches, I guess I just did!" A few chuckles were heard in the church which helped lighten the mood. "Pastor, do you mind if I say the closin' prayer?"

"Not at all. In fact, I was going to ask you to. Let's bow for prayer," Pastor Jennings responded.

"Almighty God, we praise You and thank You for givin' us life and bringin' us through calamity. Thank you for savin' my family and me. Thank you for these lovin' people in Your church who gave so much to us. Bless them fourfold, Lord. Help us all keep our faith in You alive and active and never stray from the fold. In Jesus' Name, Amen."

Victory Community Church was filled with sniffles that day when Clem finished his prayer. Susannah had cried through the whole service. When the service ended, people crowded around them to shake hands or pound Clem's back and to hug Susannah.

On their way home from church, Thomas reminded his Pa, "Pa, we never did find Boney." He sounded on the verge of tears.

"Well, son, Boney had a long life. He was about fifteen years old, I guess, a long time for a dog to live. You know he was almost blind and couldn't walk too good."

"Yes, Pa but we never found him!"

"I know, son. The Lord took care of him. Maybe he even 'took' him like Enoch in the Bible." Susannah threw him a glance that said not to put that thought in his son's head. That precipitated a long discussion on the way home about who Enoch was and how God "took" him, as well as if dogs go to heaven.

That night the children were busy playing, Clem had dozed off in his chair, and Susannah was on the front porch looking up at the stars. She pulled her shawl around her as her mind replayed the events of the last few weeks. To go from such loss to such gain was overwhelming to her. She needed some time with her Lord too. "Heavenly Father, forgive me." Hot tears stung her eyes. "Forgive me for not trusting and keeping faith. Clem tried to tell me—." She choked up with the over flow of tears. "I was too stubborn to listen to him. Forgive me. I wasn't trusting You or my husband. He said things would be alright. Thank you for saving my family, Lord! Thank you for restoring our home. Thank you for such good friends and neighbors to help us. Help us to be like that for them. Oh, help my unbelief, Lord! I want to trust You and have faith like Clem does. Don't give up on me, Lord! I have so much to learn. Keep teaching me. Thank You, Jesus, and Amen."

Clem stepped out of the shadows of the doorway and said, "I love you, Susannah." They came together in a loving embrace that expressed so much without words.

❖ ❖ ❖

A few weeks later Clem was in town to pick up supplies, and as he crossed the street Mr. Edwards at the general store commented to Pastor Jennings as they stood talking outside his store, "Pastor, Clem Brown sure is a fine man. I remember when he was fifteen or sixteen there was a group of boys about his age who used to hang around here in town. They laughed at and ridiculed Clem 'til it was pitiful. The worse one called himself Slim Jim. Him and Clem actually had a fight out here in the street one time. I don't know what Clem did after that, but they quit botherin' him all of a sudden-like."

"Maybe the Lord just took care of it for him" Pastor threw in. "Whatever happened to this Slim Jim?"

"Oh, I heard he was arrested for stealin' a horse over in Beaumont and he's still in jail."

They both watched Clem head to the livery stable. "I tell you one thing, Pastor, there goes a man of strong faith."

"Amen."